LETHBRIDGE-STEWART

MIND OF STONE

Based on the BBC television serials by
Mervyn Haisman & Henry Lincoln

Iain McLaughlin

Foreword by Victor Pemberton

CANDY JAR BOOKS · CARDIFF
A Russell & Frankham-Allen Series
2016

Range Editor: Andy Frankham-Allen
Editor: Shaun Russell
Cover: Colin Howard
Editorial: Lauren Thomas
Licensed by Hannah Haisman

Published by
Candy Jar Books
Mackintosh House
136 Newport Road, Cardiff, CF24 1DJ
www.candyjarbooks.co.uk

A catalogue record of this book is available
from the British Library

ISBN: 978-0-9954821-5-9

Printed and bound in the UK by
CPI Anthony Rowe, Chippenham, Wiltshire, UK

For my parents.
Splendid… both of them.

— FOREWORD BY VICTOR PEMBERTON —

Mervyn Haisman was quite a character. He was not only a supremely talented scriptwriter, a fine storyteller, and a wit, but he was also one of my very closest friends. The proof of this lies in the fact that he named one of his *Doctor Who* characters after me. I have to admit that, not being an avid viewer of *Doctor Who* over the years, it was only recently that I was told about Colonel Spencer Pemberton. So typical of Mervyn. It was not only his way of getting his own back on a trick I had played on him in one of my own books many years ago, but it was a mark of the deep affection he had for his close friends. The first name was added by *Lethbridge-Stewart* range editor, Andy Frankham-Allen, who also named Pemberton's wife and son; Joan and David, respectively. Both Colonel Pemberton's name and that of his son was to honour that of my life partner, David Spenser)

Brigadier Lethbridge-Stewart is one of Merv's brilliant creations, and although the actor who played him for so many years is no longer with us, the character lives on and Iain McLaughlin has written a rattling and original good yarn to accommodate him. From the surprise opening, to the intriguing flashbacks, and a Bond-like finale with the villain of the book on board the speeding train, the story takes twists and turns that would have delighted the Brigadier's creator and sent a satisfied smile across his wickedly teasing face. I must say I chuckled at the allusion to the Elgin Marbles, at the same time admiring the wry Shehab, curator of the Cairo Ptolemaic Museum who clearly has a nice line in not-entirely believable Egyptian archaeological know-how. He's one of several good characters, not forgetting the redoubtable Colonel Pemberton, clearly a man of immense stamina and courage (!!), but also wily in the extreme.

Characterisation is so very important in all forms of writing, from television scripts to novels, and whenever I have given talks to my students at creative workshops I have always tried to stress the importance of knowing what a character looks like, how he/she thinks, and what is behind the façade of their personalities. Iain has clearly done his homework.

I remember once sharing a platform at a sci-fi convention with our dear old *Doctor Who* friend Jon Pertwee, and whilst we waited for our own individual turn to talk to the audience, he spent most of the time talking about homework and how there was such a lack of it these days, amongst not only writers but also actors. Iain McLaughlin has avoided this trap. He knows the Brigadier and therefore knows how to use him, to give him the right words to say. Words for a writer are, of course, important. If the dialogue doesn't fit the subject, reality disappears out of the window. I can almost hear Merv saying, 'Oh come now, dear boy. Do you really think brigadier-this or colonel-that would ever say such a thing?' But he would have approved of Iain's dialogue. It rings true, and that's all that matters – well, almost all. There is, of course, the little matter of the story.

Have you ever read a novel and wondered what the hell was going on? Have you ever questioned why various characters have done something that seems quite incomprehensible? In

Mind of Stone there is no such problem. I don't want to give away any of the storyline but it was clear to me that I knew what skulduggery was going on, I knew what heroes and villains were getting up to, were planning in the great feast of things, and dare I say it, had my suspicions about what was coming next.

A novel, whatever the subject, is a game of cat and mouse, of trying to work out what is indeed coming next. Iain McLaughlin has succeeded in creating this quite effortlessly. I liked the mixture of *Doctor Who* characters being caught up in a kind of Rider Haggard type adventure. In fact, the archaeological information, whether true or false, adds a thrilling background to a story that has pace, intrigue, and edge of the seat surprises.

Mind of Stone is well-conceived, well-written, and will keep you guessing.

Yes, I can hear the words of a winged former *Doctor Who* writer, a glass of gin and tonic in one hand and a copy of *Mind of Stone* in the other, telling all his other heavenly inmates what a great yarn he was reading. 'Nothing like a good read to set you up for a long sleep, dear boy.'

Mervyn Haisman would have approved of this *Lethbridge-Stewart* adventure, although I'm not sure I wholly approve of his Colonel Spencer Pemberton creation. I shall have to have words when I next see him!

Victor Pemberton
Spain. September 2016

'Alistair Lethbridge-Stewart, you have offered no plea to the court. Due to the severity of the charges brought against you, and your undeniable abilities as an officer in Her Majesty's Forces, as well as the threat of flight posed by your training, this court feels that there is no option other than to deny you bail. You will be taken from this court and remanded in custody until your trial.'

The tall man in the dock stood stiff-backed, his face expressionless. He offered no reaction, and simply stared impassively ahead. He gave no reaction to anything that had been said.

The judge rapped his gavel sharply. 'Take him away.'

The tall man allowed himself to be led down from the dock by two policemen and paid no attention to the cat-calls and jeers from the public gallery. He also ignored the row of what, had he paid them any heed, would have been very familiar faces. He gave the appearance of a man who was completely and utterly alone.

Sitting in the gallery, Lance Corporal Sally Wright leaned forward and called to the man. 'Alistair. Alistair.'

Anne Travers also called to Lethbridge-Stewart but he was already gone, led through a side door which closed behind him. She put a reassuring hand on Sally's shoulder. 'It'll be all right.'

Sally's voice sounded hollow and brittle. 'The judge didn't even call him by his rank,' she said.

Lieutenant Colonel Walter Douglas sighed wearily. 'This is a civil court. If it had been a court martial he'd have been addressed by rank, but here he's just another prisoner.'

Anne flashed a warning look at Douglas. 'A bit more care in your words would be useful, Walter.'

'It's true, though,' Douglas said.

Anne nodded her head at Sally, who was staring at the door the police had just closed. 'It doesn't help, though, does it?'

'No,' Douglas admitted. 'I suppose not.' He turned to look at the door.

The two policemen guarding Alistair Lethbridge-Stewart had been warned that this prisoner was out of the ordinary. 'A special soldier,' the sarge had told them as he handed out assignments. The policemen had talked about that at some length. What did 'special soldier' actually mean?

Trevor, the older of the two coppers, hadn't liked it at all. 'Does that mean he's one of them SAS types?' he wondered.

'Could be,' Danny, his young partner, answered. 'Or some kind of spy maybe?'

Trevor shrugged. 'Keep an eye on him anyway. He looks like he could be tasty if it gets rough.'

Alistair Lethbridge-Stewart simply sat in his chair, staring at the wall directly ahead.

Mind of Stone

CHAPTER ONE

Anne Travers emerged from the court into pale, watery morning sunlight. It looked like rain was moving in; a typical late November in London. The weather matched her mood. Douglas was a few paces behind her, having failed to reach the door handle before her. His sense of chivalry told him to open the door for a lady. Anne's very modern sensibilities showed little regard for old fashioned gallantry. She reached the bottom of the steps in time to see a white police van with barred windows pull out of a side street and turn into traffic. Without a doubt, that was the vehicle carrying Brigadier Lethbridge-Stewart to prison. She was glad it was gone before Sally or Samson emerged from the court-house.

Douglas also noted the van. 'Yes, he'll be in that one.'

'Where will they take him?' Anne asked.

'Wormwood Scrubs, I think.'

'Can we go to see him there?' asked a shaky voice behind them.

Anne and Douglas turned. They didn't see Sally join them. Regimental Sergeant Major Samson Ware and 2nd Lieutenant William Bishop were at her shoulders. Lethbridge-Stewart's command staff all together. Samson looked as keen as Sally for an answer to her question.

'No, I don't think...' Douglas broke off and took a step

towards a bored looking young man with long hair and a scuffed leather jacket, who was taking photographs of them. 'Get out of here,' he snapped at the photographer. 'And if you print any of those pictures, I'll be down on you like a tonne of bricks.' He turned back to Sally and the rest of his group. 'Come on, we should get out of here, sharpish.'

He opened the door of a waiting taxi and ushered Sally, Anne and the others into the back of the cab. As he pulled the door closed behind them, they were acutely aware of the sound of a photographer's camera clicking noisily behind them.

'Where to, squire?' the driver asked in an annoyingly cheerful voice.

'Is there any point in staying in London?' Anne asked.

'Of course there is,' Sally said quickly.

'Not if we can't see him,' Anne pointed out.

'Driver, take us to Euston Station, please,' Douglas said firmly.

'Wait a minute,' Sally protested.

'Euston Station,' Douglas repeated, cutting across Sally and ignoring the protests from some of the other passengers. 'That's an order.'

The cab pulled away into traffic. Looking back out of the window, Douglas saw the photographer making for a red telephone box.

'Change of plan,' he called to the driver. 'We're all expected in a meeting before we go anywhere.'

'So what was all that about Euston?' Samson demanded.

'Double oh-seven stuff,' Anne said. 'If that photographer followed us, he'd go to Euston instead of...' She looked across at Douglas. 'Where *are* we going?'

'We've got a meeting.'

2

'With whom?'

'I'll tell you when we get there.' Douglas gave the driver an alternative address.

'Make your bleedin' mind up.'

'It'll make sense soon enough,' Douglas promised. It was clear he wasn't going to say anything more on the subject for the time being.

Anne sighed and sank back into her seat, and hoped that the driver wouldn't talk during the journey.

The trip from the court to Wormwood Scrubs was a long and uncomfortable one for Lethbridge-Stewart. Seated on a hard bench, he kept his gaze firmly focused on the metal wall on the other side of the van. The two policemen assigned to him sat on the bench opposite, eyeing him warily. He observed them carefully, without letting them know he was watching. Part of his training had been concerned with how an officer should react when taken prisoner. The first rule was *to observe*. They were a pair of diligent coppers, doing their duty, keeping a wary eye on what they had been told was a very dangerous prisoner. If he chose to, he could deal with them both very quickly, even with his hands cuffed, but what would he do then? The van took a tight right turn and immediately hit a prodigious pot-hole, violently jostling the van's three passengers.

That was the moment he could have taken them. Both hands together in a fist, he would have swung hard at the chin of the one on the left while kicking hard at the one on the right, again aiming for the jaw. Yes, five seconds and he would have finished it.

Instead, Lethbridge-Stewart relaxed his shoulders and continued staring ahead as the van trundled on.

On arrival at the Scrubs, Lethbridge-Stewart was handed over by two very relieved policemen to the care of prison officers, who led him through the usual intake procedures. His own clothes were taken from him and he was issued with his regulation prison uniform. He was carefully examined to ensure he wasn't smuggling contraband or weapons, before being allowed to dress. From there he was taken to the Medical Officer, where Doctor Jenkins, a balding middle-aged man who embraced old age twenty years before his time, gave him only the most cursory of examinations, declaring him to be in peak physical condition before passing him onto a pair of hulking prison officers who led Lethbridge-Stewart to the governor's office.

Governor Clemence, an intelligent looking man in his mid-forties, eyed Lethbridge-Stewart with a cautious mixture of interest and trepidation. He forced himself to suppress a smirk when the new prisoner was brought in. Normally the prison officers, often ex-military men, liked to bark orders at the prisoners, marching them in. It took most of the lags back to their National Service and subliminally enforced a sense of discipline into them. With this prisoner, things were different. He moved with the upright bearing of an officer and marched to stand in front of the governor's desk, forcing the prison officers to hurry to keep up. It seemed that Lethbridge-Stewart forced himself not to salute.

Clemence let him stand for a moment as he perused the prisoner's very Spartan file. 'Brigadier Alistair Lethbridge-Stewart?'

'Yes, sir,' Lethbridge-Stewart replied briskly, depriving the prison officers of their chance to order a new prisoner to call the governor 'sir'.

'Your file doesn't say much.'

'No, sir.'

Clemence set the folder aside. 'It doesn't mention what you're charged with or any of the details of your military career.'

'No, sir.'

'Or why you're here with us instead of in a military stockade,' the governor continued.

'No, sir.'

Clemence pursed his lips. 'And I assume you're not going to furnish me with any of those details while you're here?'

'No, sir.'

'Well, that's honest, at least,' Clemence said with a smirk.

Lethbridge-Stewart's face remained impassive.

'Well.' Clemence cleared his throat. 'Whatever the charge laid against you, the judge clearly had cause to believe you pose a danger of flight or to the public.' He tapped Lethbridge-Stewart's file again. 'And from the little I can see in here that's not redacted or simply missing, I have no doubt that you are a very highly trained and skilled soldier.' He paused and stared intently into Lethbridge-Stewart's eyes. 'You've been sent here because this prison is full of very dangerous men, Lethbridge-Stewart. Oh, I have orders that your rank is not to be afforded you here. I promise you that the men in here will not offer you any respect because of it. Quite the reverse. My rules here are very simple. If you follow them, we should have no trouble at all. Keep your nose clean, follow orders immediately, don't give backchat to the warders and you'll get through this just fine. Understood?'

'Yes, sir.'

Clemence eyed the tall military man for another minute. He had a knack for knowing which of his charges would be trouble and this one might as well have a neon sign over his head. Plenty of them were uncommunicative and surly. Not many were uncommunicative, surly, and with a dozen years training as a killer. No, this one would be trouble, all right. He was correct to assign him to Mr Fulton; one of his... *stricter* officers.

The governor picked up his phone and hit the button for his secretary. She answered at the first ring. 'Send in Mr Fulton would you, Mrs Jamieson? Thank you.'

A moment later, an average height, fastidious man strode through the door. He walked with the stiff back, stiff arms and precise gait of a soldier. He reeked of being a parade ground sergeant. 'Reporting as ordered, sir.' His accent, though refined by years of practice, still carried traces of his Irish mother and Scouse father.

'Thank you, Mr Fulton,' Governor Clemence said. He indicated the new prisoner. 'This is former brigadier... My mistake,' he corrected himself. 'This is Alistair Lethbridge-Stewart.'

Fulton eyed his new charge with interest and a barely concealed distaste. 'Yes, sir.'

'And remember he's here on remand,' Clemence said firmly. 'He hasn't been found guilty of anything.'

'I'm aware of that, sir.'

'Good.' The governor's gaze flitted between prisoner and warder. 'Lethbridge-Stewart, if you stay out of trouble, you'll be fine. Understood?'

'Understood,' Lethbridge-Stewart replied, 'sir.'

If Anne Travers or Sally Wright expected their meeting, which happened to be in Chelsea Barracks, to bring them any satisfaction concerning the sudden arrest of Lethbridge-

Stewart, they were to be disappointed.

Major General Oliver Hamilton was seated behind a desk when Anne and Douglas were shown in. The others were left waiting outside. He returned Douglas' salute briskly.

'I realise this is a difficult time for you all,' he said, 'but you need to be seen getting back to Edinburgh as soon as possible.'

'Really?' Anne said. 'Well, I'm damned if I'm leaving a colleague and a friend in prison while I go back to life as if nothing has happened.'

'Miss Travers,' Hamilton said, meeting her anger head on. 'You will obey orders.'

'I am not a soldier.'

'If you were, I'd have you up for insubordination. But you're a scientist and we need you to get to work. Lives have already been lost, and you're part of a mission to save a lot of others.' He pushed a manila folder across the desk at Douglas. 'Everything's in here. This is to be your immediate priority. Do not discuss it with anyone – and I mean *anyone* – outside the Corps, with the exception of me. This is top secret as well as top priority. That is all.'

'But the brigadier…' Anne began.

'Is in prison,' Hamilton finished for her. 'And with good reason, too.'

'Really?'

'I assure you that nobody goes to prison in this country without good cause.'

'Then you won't mind telling us what he did.'

'Doctor Travers…'

'What did he do?'

Hamilton sighed. 'All right,' he said. 'I'll tell you, but if you repeat a word of this before I give you permission you'll be in there with him, understood? And I promise you I'll throw the key away.'

With another warden bringing up the rear, Fulton led Lethbridge-Stewart through the few winding corridors of the administrative section of the prison to the detention area. None of them spoke until they took a flight of metal stairs to the first floor and walked along the landing to an open door.

'You're in here,' Fulton said. He nodded to the other guard. 'Carry on.' As the other warder moved away, Fulton turned back to Lethbridge-Stewart. 'You're sharing with an old lag. I thought it best to put you in with someone who can show you the ropes.'

'Thank you,' Lethbridge-Stewart replied automatically.

'Thank you, *sir!*' Fulton snapped.

There was a pause before Lethbridge-Stewart said, 'Thank you, sir.'

Fulton glared at the taller man. 'I wore the uniform. I took pride in it.'

'So did I.'

Fulton's head jerked towards the open cell. 'In.'

'Yes, sir,' Lethbridge-Stewart replied mildly, and went into the cell.

The room was small and Spartan. Its brick walls were painted a dull grey and the furniture consisted of a set of bunk beds, a table and chair, and a small cabinet on the wall in the corner. One barred window high on a wall gave the only natural light.

A round faced middle-aged man with a beak of a nose was lying on the top bunk. He put down his copy of *The Sun* and observed the newcomers. 'Room service already? Why don't I pop out to the pub while you get on with it?' He had a thick,

Cockney accent.

Fulton snorted. 'Stanley here thinks he's a comedian.' He sniffed. 'I find it hilarious that he's locked up in here for the next three and a half years.'

'Charming.'

Fulton ignored Stanley's reply. 'Stanley's been a regular in places like this all his days. He knows how things work and he'll show you the ropes; if he knows what's good for him.'

Stanley looked offended. 'No need to be like that, Mr Fulton,' he said. 'My innate human decency and kindness will always lead me to look after any newcomers to our happy little holiday camp.'

'Decency and kindness.' Fulton snorted again. He glanced at Lethbridge-Stewart. 'Give him half a chance and Stanley here will pilfer everything you own.'

'That's slander, that is,' Stanley protested.

'It's true and you know it.' Fulton turned to Lethbridge-Stewart. 'Stay out of trouble.' He spun on his heel and left the cell, pulling the door behind him. It slammed closed with an ominously solid thud and the heavy lock clicked.

Alistair Lethbridge-Stewart looked around the cell quickly, and pulled a deep breath.

Stanley returned his attention to a football report, but glanced at his new cellmate over the top of his paper. 'Your first time inside, is it?'

'Pardon?'

'Pardon?' Stanley repeated. 'That's a change from the usual "what?" we get in here. Posh, are you?'

'I wouldn't say so.'

'The posh never do. So, what's your name, then?'

'Alistair.'

9

'Alistair, eh?' Stanley answered. 'What do you prefer? Al? Ally?'

'Alistair,' Lethbridge-Stewart said.

Stanley nodded. 'Like I said, posh. Bet you got a big, impressive second name an' all.'

Lethbridge-Stewart couldn't keep a smirk from his lips. 'You may have me there. Alistair Lethbridge-Stewart.'

'Blimey, what a mouthful. I'll settle for Alistair.' Stanley tapped the bunk he was lying on. 'You prefer the top bunk, would you?'

'I don't mind one way or the other.'

'Good, because I'm nice and comfy up here and shifting would be a right pain in the Bristols. Talking of which...' Stanley flicked up his paper and stared at delightful Debbie again. 'You can put your toothbrush and comb in the little cupboard,' he said, without looking up from the paper. 'Bottom shelf. I already snagged the top one.'

'Thank you.'

Stanley put his paper aside again. 'Bit of advice, Alistair. You don't want to go thanking people too much in here. Manners is seen as a sign of weakness.'

'Really?'

Stanley reached under his pillow and pulled out half a stick of chewing gum. He unwrapped it and popped the gum in his mouth. 'Definitely. There's a fine line being in the nick. You don't want to get in nobody's face but you don't want them to think you're a soft touch neither. That's a lesson first time prisoners learn quick.'

Alistair put his toothbrush and comb in the cupboard and closed the door. 'I may not have been in jail before,' he answered, 'but don't imagine for a minute this is my first time as a prisoner.'

That certainly caught Stanley's attention. 'And what does that mean?'

Alistair sat on the lower bunk testing the springs. 'What do you think?'

Stanley's head dipped over the side of the bunk, looking at his cell mate curiously. 'What other kind of prisoners are there these days?' he asked. 'You're too young to be a POW.'

'From the Second World War, yes.'

Stanley's legs swung into view and he dropped to the floor. 'You're ex-military?'

Alistair stretched out on the bunk. Disappointingly, his feet pushed against the bottom of the bed. 'Not yet, but I imagine my commission will be revoked as soon as my trial's over.'

'You mean you ain't had your trial yet?'

Alistair glanced at Stanley. 'No, I'm on remand.'

'Then what the hell have they put you in here for?' The convict leaned forward suspiciously. 'Hang about. You said "commission".'

'That's right.'

Stanley sat heavily on the cell's rickety wooden chair. 'So that makes you an officer?'

Alistair nodded in conformation. 'Brigadier.'

'Don't tell nobody.'

'I beg your pardon?'

'I mean it, son. Don't tell nobody. You let on to this lot in here that you're some high and mighty in the army and they'll come after you like you've got a target painted on you.'

'Why would they do that?'

'Because it's us and them in here. We're us; the poor sods who get banged up. And them; they're the officers, the outside, the ones who put us here. Authority. You being an officer makes you authority.'

'Even though I'm in here?'

'*Because* you're in here. We all did National Service and nobody liked the officers. Not as much as we didn't like the NCOs, but all the same... Them and us.'

Alistair smiled ruefully, and chose to not mention that he was an enlisted man during National Service, no more an NCO than Stanley had been, and it was only the things he saw in Korea and the encouragement of an officer that led him to Sandhurst. 'I assume Mr Fulton doesn't get many Christmas cards from the inmates here.'

'Army sergeant,' Stanley said. 'Everybody in here would love to give him a kicking but they can't. You wouldn't be a problem.'

'Because I'm posh and an officer.'

Stanley nodded. 'That's right. So, you keep all that quiet, you got me?'

Alistair cast his eyes around the small room. 'Why this concern for my well being?'

'Beyond that innate common decency I mentioned?'

'Beyond that.'

Stanley leaned forward. 'Because I share this cell with you and whatever happens to you affects me one way or another, and I'm not interested in none of the rubbish that goes on in here.' He sniffed and carried on. 'I do my time, keep out of everybody's way, don't make enemies and don't get too friendly with nobody neither. Here's a thing to remember in here. Enemies pick on you; friends drag you into their fights.'

Alistair's eyebrow rose. 'That sounds rather like how wars start.'

'You get wars in the nick an' all,' Stanley promised. 'You be careful.'

'I try to be.'

'Try harder,' Stanley said firmly. 'If you were any good at it you wouldn't be in here.'

Alistair laughed. 'You may have a point.'

Stanley's gaze returned to his football report. 'So, what are you in for? I know you said you was on remand, but what for?'

'Do you really want to know?'

'I asked, didn't I?'

'But do you really want to know? Really?'

It took Stanley a few moments to reply. 'I don't think I do.'

'Probably for the best,' Alistair said, easing himself onto the lower bunk. 'Been a long day. I think I'll get some sleep.'

— CHAPTER TWO —

Alistair woke early the next morning. He'd slept remarkably well, all things considered. Especially the snoring that came from the top bunk for most of the night. Stanley was definitely anything but a quiet sleeper. Thankfully, Alistair had years of experience in catching sleep between skirmishes and with the sounds of battle in the distance. Compared with a creeping barrage of mortars or the staccato roar of gunfire, a convict's snore was akin to a lullaby.

He lay back on his bunk and closed his eyes. His breathing became deep and regular. He had no intention of falling asleep again. He would rest and begin to study the schedule of the prison, the routine. Eventually he heard noises outside on the landing. Footsteps on the metal floor and those metal hatches in the solid doors sliding open and then closed again as the wardens performed a head-count to make sure that nobody had escaped during the night.

The little shutter in their own door opened and closed, the warden satisfied that they hadn't made a break for it in the cover of darkness.

The noise at the door had, at least, quietened Stanley's snoring. 'Time to wake up, Alistair-boy.' The convict still sounded half asleep.

'I've been awake for an hour,' Alistair said. 'I imagine the whole wing has with your snoring.'

'I do not snore,' came the indignant reply. The mattress above Alistair's head moved and bulged as Stanley moved in his bed. His round face peered over the side. 'I do, however, occasionally purr in my sleep if I'm having a particularly good dream about Diana Dors.' He smiled wistfully. 'Course, she's put on a bit of beef these days. More like double doors than Diana Dors, but in here we make do.'

Alistair threw back his blankets and swung his legs out of bed. The floor was cold and hard under his feet. 'From your purring last night you must have had a splendid time.'

'I hope so,' Stanley sighed. 'In here, dreams is all we've got.'

The overnight sleeper pulled into Edinburgh's Waverly Station just a few minutes late. It was early enough that the station only had the earliest of commuters on its dull grey platforms. Most looked as if they would rather still be at home in bed.

A party of four, consisting of three men and two women, were among the first off the train. Most wore army uniforms.

Private Neil Atkins hurried up and saluted. 'Lieutenant Colonel Douglas.'

The salute was returned briskly and the four weary travellers were quickly led to the two army Land Rovers which irked the taxi rank at platform level by taking the parking spots closest to the platforms. The army drivers ignored the complaints from the cab drivers and soon the Land Rovers were on their way up onto Waverly Bridge, from there they travelled down Market Street before cutting up onto the Royal Mile and along to the Castle.

Ten minutes after setting foot off the sleeper they were

back at Dolerite Base.

Early morning routine in the prison was very basic. After the wardens did a circuit performing the headcount, the inmates had time to wash and dress, and then were taken for breakfast.

Breakfast in prison was simple and unappetising fare. The porridge was thin and watery and the tea could be described in exactly the same way. It was hardly an ordeal for Alistair. In the field he had eaten much worse.

After breakfast, the prisoners returned to their cells for half an hour, after which the men who had jobs went to those and the rest were locked inside their cells. While Stanley went to work in the library, Alistair stretched out on his bunk and gave careful thought to his first morning. He was introduced to several of his fellow inmates. Some were friendly. Others, less so. There were a few who took an instant dislike to him. He heard mutters of 'toff' and 'posh'. Some of them were going to be a problem. One table looked particularly dangerous. It was clear that they were some kind of gang. Nobody sat close to them and when they entered to get their meals, other prisoners stepped aside to let them go first. Alistair knew they hadn't earned their influence through kind deeds and plain popularity. They were vicious and they had set their eyes on him.

'Steer clear of them lot,' Stanley warned him. 'Bad news, they are. They don't bother me cos I don't bother them and that's the way I want to keep it. Understand?'

Alistair understood well enough. He knew he was going to have trouble with that gang and he knew it wasn't going to end well for him.

Lying on his bunk he ran through all the other prisoners he had met, working out who would be a problem and who would give him no concern at all. He had little trouble working out which prisoners fell into which camp. He set about creating a mental map of this wing of the prison, placing the prisoners in their respective cells. In hostile territory it paid to know where the enemy were at all times. He made a note to interrogate Stanley to find out which prisoners had jobs and what they were. His first few days would be a recce, an information gathering exercise. He would learn what he needed to know to get by, and he would prepare so that he was ready for whatever that gang had in mind.

After he created his mind-map, Alistair let his thoughts turn to the prison officers and Governor Clemence. In other circumstances there was a chance he would have quite liked the governor. However, these were far from ordinary circumstances. The man had a job to do, and that made him Alistair's jailer. He was sure that Clemence was a fair man. From everything he heard, Clemence was quite progressive in his thinking. He certainly seemed to be interested in rehabilitating his prisoners. Fulton on the other hand...

No, Alistair thought. *No, I don't like him at all.* The little man reminded him too much of sergeants he'd seen through the years. Good sergeants were imperative in keeping the army ticking over. Bad sergeants got people killed. He'd have bet his money on Fulton having had three stripes. Or maybe it was worse; he could have been one of those who desperately wanted to wear a sergeant's stripes but had been overlooked for the promotions. They were probably the most dangerous of all. They were certainly the most bitter. In a situation like this they would certainly be the deadliest. He would have to keep a wary eye on Fulton.

Alistair stripped down and put himself through as rigorous

a set of exercises as he could manage in the confined space. He did circuits of sit-ups, press-ups, knee bends and squat thrusts. He even used the chair as a dead weight, lifting it over his head by its legs. He repeated the circuit several times, and finished with five minutes of shadow boxing before washing as best he could, and stretching out on his bunk again.

Stanley returned in time for lunch, which was as unappetising as breakfast. A thin, watery vegetable soup with half a bread roll.

'Just as well we're already inside,' Stanley muttered. 'If somebody give us this on the outside we'd all get banged up for attempted murder.' He led Alistair to a table as far as possible from the group who gave them the evil eye at breakfast. 'Blimey, what did you say to them?' Stanley asked. 'They usually wait until somebody's been here a day to take against them.'

'No idea,' Alistair said. 'I must just have that sort of face.'

Stanley's spoon stopped halfway to his mouth. He stared at his cellmate seriously. 'You won't have no sort of face if that lot decide to come after you, Mr Alistair Double-Barrelled name. Sitting in your Officers' Mess sipping G and Ts while sharing stories about Eton don't get you ready for what this lot will do to you.'

Alistair set his spoon down carefully. 'I assure you, Stan, I have done a good deal more than sit in the Mess sipping gin and tonic.'

Stanley met his new cell mate's gaze for a long moment. 'I believe you,' he said finally. 'But these nerks in here won't care about none of that.

'What do they care about?' Alistair asked.

'Best question you asked so far. They care about themselves. They don't give a stuff about nobody else. They

18

care about themselves. They care about getting out of here, but while they're in this place they care about being as far up the food chain as they can get. That means keeping everybody else in their place and standing on anybody who gets ideas.'

Alistair took a spoonful of the soup and forced himself to avoid showing an expression of distaste on his face. 'And what do they do with the new arrivals?'

Stanley paused for a moment. He leaned forward, dropping his voice low. 'You're a smart man. You wouldn't have asked me that unless you have a pretty good idea of the answer. So listen. If they think they can get something by giving you a hiding, they will. If they think they can get money from you, or get whatever little goodies you get hold of – tobacco, chocolate, whatever else they can use as currency in here – they'll do it. If they think you're a threat, they'll put you on the floor. Maybe all they need to do is take a dislike to your face or the way you carry yourself. There's no honour among thieves here. There's not much on the outside, neither. In here you can't trust nobody.'

'Can I trust you, Stanley?' Alistair asked casually.

The older prisoner fed himself a spoonful of soup. 'What did I get told when you was put into my cell?'

'To show me the ropes in here.'

'Exactly,' Stanley said. 'That means I'm stuck with you. The only people in here you can trust are the people who want the same things as you. And I want you to stay healthy and out of trouble because that means less grief for me.'

'I see.'

'And remember, just because people want the same as you at some point, that don't mean they'll want the same as you tomorrow or the day after.'

'Including you?'

Stanley's spoon stopped halfway to his mouth. 'Including me.' He nodded. 'That's the smartest question you asked since you came in here.'

'When can I expect you to turn on me? In my sleep?'

Stanley's smile was natural and genuine. 'Even in your sleep you could give me a hiding. No, I'm the least of your worries in here, but it's just as well that you keep in mind that you can't trust nobody.'

Alistair took another mouthful of soup. 'I'd start with whoever is responsible for this.'

'Well, we *are* in here to be punished.'

'So it would seem,' Alistair said with a grimace.

Stanley pushed his plate away. 'I need to get back to the library. Fancy a book? They're a good way to kill time in here.'

'What do you have?'

'Classics mostly. There's a waiting list for *Lady Chatterly's Lover*. Unless you got Life don't bother asking for that.' He looked as if an idea had just occurred to him. 'A bit of Alistair Maclean might suit a military man like yourself. Tell you what, I just got *Ice Station Zebra* back from the Lord in C wing.'

'The Lord?' Alistair asked. 'Does he run C wing?'

Stanley shook his head. 'No. He's just a bloke with a gammy leg. Fell off a roof nicking lead years ago. Left him with a funny walk, so he gets called the Lord cos he moves in a mysterious way.'

'Very amusing.'

Stanley shrugged. 'It might not be Oscar Wilde, but we have to make our own entertainment in here.'

A shadow fell across the table. Alistair and Stanley both looked up to see three figures looming over them.

Stanley blanched. It was the three men from the table

Alistair was told to avoid.

'Hello, Geggsy.' Stanley tried to sound relaxed. It didn't work, but he carried on anyway. 'Mason, Minty...' He nodded at the other two. 'I don't believe you've met my new flatmate, have you?' He glanced at the clock. 'Anyway, better get back to work.

'He hasn't finished his lunch,' Geggsy said.

'I don't think he's got much appetite.'

Geggsy ignored the little convict. 'Eat it,' he said to Alistair.

'I don't think so,' Alistair said evenly.

Geggsy leaned over Alistair's bowl. He made a harsh sound like he was clearing his throat and carefully spat into the bowl. The thick spit floated in the watery soup. 'Eat it,' he said. His lackeys took half steps closer. 'Eat it,' he repeated. He balled his fist menacingly. 'Or you won't be eating anything again in a hurry.'

Alistair looked into his bowl and flicked a glance at the three men behind him.

'Eat it,' Geggsy repeated again.

Alistair squinted across the table at Stanley, who looked as if he simply wanted to crawl under the table. He slowly switched the spoon to his left hand and moved it towards the bowl. A second later his right hand swept the bowl upwards as he stood suddenly upright. The soup hit Mason square in the face. At the same time, Alistair's left hand shot backwards, ramming the spoon hard into Geggsy's groin. As the thug buckled, Alistair pushed him hard into his two friends and all three went down in a heap. He took a step back, reaching for his chair, ready to turn it into a weapon.

'What's going on here?' Fulton's voice cracked across the room as the warder pushed through the chairs towards the disturbance. 'What's the trouble?'

A chorus came from Geggsy's group.

'Nothing.'

'Sir.'

Alistair added, 'Nothing, sir.'

Fulton looked at the clearly pained Geggsy. 'Doesn't look like nothing to me.'

'These three gentlemen came over to introduce themselves,' Alistair said. 'But they had a slight accident. No harm done.'

'I bet,' Fulton answered sharply. 'What do you three have to say?'

'Exactly the same as him,' Geggsy snarled.

His friends agreed.

'Sir.'

'Exactly the same as him, sir.'

Fulton snapped his head jerkily towards the table Geggsy and his men had left. 'Get back to your lunch. And you, Brigadier,' he said to Alistair, 'it looks like you've finished eating. You probably should get back to your cell.'

Alistair offered no argument. 'Yes, sir.'

As Fulton led Alistair away, the soldier was aware that one word was dominating the low rumbles of conversation in the mess.

'*Brigadier?*'

Anne and Douglas rose early that morning. The rest of their party were still in bed when they met in the kitchen of the London safe house.

'Sleep well?' Douglas asked.

Anne yawned. 'Better than if we'd been on that train back to Edinburgh.'

'Never been able to sleep on those things myself,' Douglas

admitted. 'Coffee?'

Anne nodded and took the mug Douglas offered. 'Our decoys will be back in Edinburgh by now. Silly piece of skulduggery.' She took a sip from the mug and winced. 'Well, *nearly coffee.*' She dropped a couple of sugar lumps into her mug and stirred while Douglas made another coffee for himself.

'There's toast,' he said, pointing at a small plate.

'My, my,' Anne said mildly. 'Aren't you domesticated.'

'Penny wouldn't have it any other way,' Douglas said with a smile. 'And I can't always count on the Naffy being there to do its stuff.'

Anne spread marmalade on a slice of toast. 'Keiller's,' she said appreciatively. 'They must have known we'd become used to the good stuff in Scotland.'

'Actually, I brought it. Breakfast isn't breakfast without it.'

'My stomach thanks you.' Anne glanced at her watch. 'Though the rest of me isn't overly fond of you for getting me out of bed so early.'

'Regular time for a military man,' Douglas chuckled.

'I am neither military nor a man,' Anne said sourly. 'And neither was my grandmother, and she was always up an hour before this, so you can forget claiming army training makes you an early riser.'

'Wouldn't dream of it.' Douglas helped himself to a slice of toast. 'I thought we should get started bright and early. We've got a lot to do, and it's more than an hour's drive to the secure facility.'

'Excellent. That means I can get an hour's sleep on the way.'

*

23

Ten minutes later, a black Daimler with blacked-out windows left the Richmond street that was home to the safe house. It pulled out, slipping into place between a taxi and a bus, and was soon lost among the early morning traffic.

Miss Travers was true to her word and dozed for the majority of the journey out of London. Douglas tried to follow suit but sleep evaded him. Instead he stared out of the window, watching the centre of London give way to suburbs and then the dullness of the A40 and M4.

Just over an hour later, rather than take the turn for Wokingham, the Daimler took a smaller country road and then turned onto a single lane, which led through a wood and stopped at a gate guarded by armed soldiers. A fence ran into the distance from either side of the gate. Douglas and Miss Travers showed their passes and the gates opened for the car to pass through.

After a hundred yards, the road led to a large, sturdy building which looked like a warehouse. Soldiers patrolled the perimeter at regular intervals. A stern-looking RSM met Douglas and Miss Travers as they got out of the car. He saluted smartly as a corporal indicated for the car to follow him to a parking spot.

'We got word you were coming an hour ago, sir,' the RSM said, with a pronounced Scottish accent.

'Sorry to drop in unexpectedly.'

'Not a problem, sir.'

'I'm Lieutenant Colonel Douglas, this is Doctor Anne Travers.'

The RSM nodded a greeting to his guests. 'Warrant Officer Cowie, sir. And don't worry about short notice. More or less everybody who comes here does so at short notice. That's part of our brief. We're always ready.'

'I'm sure you are, Warrant Officer,' Douglas said. 'Shall we go in?'

'I'll need to see your passes first, sir,' Cowie said. His tone was polite but firm.

Douglas nodded, and both he and Miss Travers handed over their passes. Cowie took the passes to the booth by the warehouse's entrance. He and a sergeant scrutinised and compared them to notes on a clipboard. Cowie returned a few minutes later.

'Everything seems to be in order, sir,' he said, returning the passes.

'Thank you,' Miss Travers replied automatically. Douglas only replied with a curt nod.

'This way,' Cowie said, leading them to the building. He looked at the sergeant in the security booth. 'Give them the go ahead to let us in.'

'Sir.'

The sergeant spoke into a desk microphone. A moment later a series of clicks came from the door as all of its locks were released in a careful sequence.

Cowie pushed the door open. 'After you, sir, ma'am.'

Through the outer door was a small room with another door on the far side. It was guarded by two alert looking soldiers, who eyed the newcomers suspiciously.

'Stand easy,' Cowie said and punched in a number on a control pad by the door. 'This is a new addition,' he explained to Douglas and Travers. 'An experimental lock supplied by Electro... ah.' The door clicked open, halting Cowie. He pushed the door open and led the way through.

They found themselves in a corridor leading to what looked like the length of the building. The ceiling was high, around twenty feet or so, suggesting that there was another storey above.

'This way, sir, ma'am,' Cowie said, leading Douglas and Miss Travers along the concrete floored corridor at a brisk march.

'What's in all these rooms?' Miss Travers asked as she passed a door.

'Confidential, ma'am,' Cowie replied. 'I haven't been inside most of the storage facilities, and I'm under the strictest orders not to discuss anything I do see or hear or experience inside the storage facilities with anyone other than those cleared for that specific storage facility.'

'Understood. And out of interest, how much of that little speech was taken directly from your written orders?'

Cowie offered a smile, which lightened his appearance significantly. 'Only about ninety-five percent, ma'am.'

He stopped at a door and punched in a six-digit code. After another series of clicks he pushed the door open and led his visitors inside. 'This is yours. And if you can explain it... I'm not sure I want to know what it is.'

Cowie flipped the light switch and two rows of bright lights flickered into life overhead.

'Well,' Miss Travers said, amazed.

Douglas breathed deeply. 'Good Lord.'

Four statues stood in the middle of the room. They were the size and shape of men. On closer inspection it was clear that they were in military uniforms.

'Army fatigues,' Douglas said. He looked at the stone figures, and noted the wings on the caps; Parachute Regiment. 'Have we been sent here to look at statues?' He peered closely at the statue faces to see if they were supposed to represent the honoured dead.

Cowie shook his head. 'They're much more than that, sir.'

Miss Travers gently ran a finger across the arm of one of the statues. 'Not dissimilar to what we encountered on Santorini,' she said.

Douglas nodded. He'd read the reports about the Corps' mission to that Greek island earlier in the month, and the sentient rock – christened Mutalith – found deep beneath the Aegean Sea. 'Probably why General Hamilton sent us here. You've got a good position to start from.'

Miss Travers nodded.

The soldier statue was standing with his rifle raised in a firing position. She frowned and pressed harder on the arm. The arm wasn't as solid as it first seemed. There was some give as she put pressure on it.

'It's spongey,' she said.

Douglas moved closer. 'What?'

'It's not solid.' Miss Travers pressed on the arm again and felt the surface depress half an inch or so.

'So it's not made of stone,' Douglas murmured.

'Apparently not. First of many differences to the Mutalith, I suspect.' She ran her finger along the arm until she passed the hand and examined the rifle. She stopped and peered at a section. 'What on earth?'

'What is it?' Douglas asked.

Miss Travers pulled her hand away. 'See for yourself. Exactly where my hand was.'

Douglas peered closer at the rifle. The 'stone' ran along the stock of the weapon until it reached the magazine underneath. Where the clip was inserted, a small section of the rifle was metal. It lasted two inches at most before becoming stone again, but it was definitely metal for those few inches.

'How did they get the metal in there?' Douglas asked. 'I

can't see a join of any sort.'

'Nobody can,' Cowie said. 'Plenty have tried since they were brought in.'

Miss Travers moved to the next statue. This soldier was frozen in the act of raising his rifle. 'Part of this gun is metal, too.' She moved around the back of the stone figure. 'Some of his fatigues feel like they're made of material.'

Douglas joined her and inspected the patch of dark green material. 'They are,' he said. 'I know the feel of that material well. I've worn it for long enough.' He inspected the edges of the patch of cloth. 'But there's no join here either.'

Miss Travers moved on to the next statue. 'Oh my God.'

'What is it?' Douglas demanded, hurrying to her side.

'His eyes.'

'What about them?' Douglas followed Miss Travers' gaze and peered intently at the stone face. It was frozen in a silent scream, his mouth wide open, his eyes tightly shut. 'God almighty,' Douglas whispered.

The stone eyelids were struggling to open.

The right eye opened just a fraction but the left opened fully. A living, human eye stared at Douglas and Miss Travers. There was no doubting the terror in that eye.

'It's alive,' Miss Travers said.

'Hang on,' Douglas said. 'That Mutalith stuff; didn't it transform people into rock?'

'Yes, made them part of a gestalt, but this is different. It's not rock for a start, and the Mutalith didn't leave elements unchanged. Every bit of a person, clothes and all, were altered at a molecular level.' Miss Travers peered at the blue eyes. 'Are you alive?'

The statue didn't answer, but Warrant Officer Cowie did. 'None of them can talk, ma'am.'

'Has anybody tried a different kind of communication?'

'Not that I know of,' Cowie replied, 'but most of the people who have been in here didn't want a parade ground sergeant major around while they were doing their research. However, from what I've seen, three of them can open their eyes to some extent. This one,' he indicated the previous statue, 'is the most aware of them.'

'*Aware?*' Miss Travers turned her attention back to the stone soldier. 'Can you hear me?'

The eyes flickered again.

'Can you hear me?' Miss Travers repeated. 'If you can hear and understand me, try to blink twice. Do you understand?'

The soldier was still for a moment until the eyes moved again. It was painfully slow but the eye did blink twice.

'Definitely not Mutalith then. When people were transformed by that, there was no individual awareness. They were all driven by the sentience of the rock itself.'

'Are you alive?' Douglas blurted.

'Oh, really, Walter,' Miss Travers snapped. 'Of course he is.' She turned back to the statue. 'Are you all soldiers?' she asked. 'Is that why parts of your guns and clothes are real?'

Two more painful blinks answered her.

'Did this happen to you on a mission?' Douglas asked. Realisation that he was talking with another soldier softened his tone.

Again, two blinks came as the reply.

'Do you remember what happened?' Douglas continued.

Two more painful blinks.

'What was it?'

'He can't answer that,' Miss Travers said irritably. 'We only have "yes" and "no", remember?' She managed a

29

sympathetic half-smile towards the stone soldier. 'Are you in pain?'

Two more blinks.

'Does it hurt to blink?'

The same laboured pair of blinks came back in reply.

'Do you want me to stop?'

No blinks came in reply.

'All right,' Miss Travers said. 'I'll be as quick as I can. Did this happen to you suddenly on your last mission? Or was it slow from a previous mission? Blink twice if it was your last mission.'

Two blinks answered.

'Was it a weapon of some kind?'

There was no reply.

'Did someone do this to you?'

There was a long pause, then only one blink followed.

'One blink?' Douglas murmured. 'What does that mean?

'It means I have to be more precise in my questions,' Miss Travers said, more to herself than to Douglas. She tried again. 'Was this done to you deliberately?'

Two blinks.

Yes.

Douglas looked at the soldier closely. Its cap, although mostly grey like the rest of him, showed just a hint of purple. The colour of 1 Para. What kind of weapon could do something like this to troops of the Special Forces Support Group? They underwent some of the most advanced training in the British Army...

Douglas turned to Miss Travers. 'What the hell is going on?'

Anne didn't answer. She didn't *have* an answer.

Warrant Officer Cowie swore quietly. Anne understood the soldier's outrage but ignored his reaction. She needed to focus on the pitiful figure in front of her. 'Was it a man who did this to you?'

One blink.

'A woman?'

No blinks came in response.

'Not a woman,' Douglas said.

'But not a man, either,' Anne finished for him. 'We know there are more things in the universe than humans,' she said quietly, 'but let's exhaust our human options first.' She spoke to the statue. 'Was it more than one man? Was it several men?'

Two blinks came in reply.

'Now we're making headway,' Douglas said.

A third blink stopped him short.

'More than several men?' Douglas asked.

'Or more than just men?' Anne suggested. 'When you answer, please answer my question rather than the colonel's.'

Two blinks.

'More than men,' Anne said softly. 'Was it an alien creature of some kind?'

No answer.

'Was it a weapon?' Douglas asked.

Again, there was no answer.

Anne ran a hand through her hair. 'Several men, not a weapon, but done deliberately and something more than human.'

Two blinks.

Douglas sucked a deep breath. 'Oh, hell,' he said.

'Do you have a family?' Anne asked.

The statue blinked twice.

'Have they seen you since this happened?'

No blinks came.

Behind Anne, Cowie coughed. 'That wouldn't be allowed ma'am.'

'Don't you think he has a right to see them?'

Cowie moved closer and spoke very quietly and gently. 'They've already been told he's dead, ma'am. It was considered kinder than putting them – and him,' the RSM flicked his eyes towards the statue, 'through a meeting.'

'We understand,' Douglas said.

'Do we?' Anne demanded.

She was about to argue her point when a slight movement from the statue stopped her. He blinked twice. Anne fell quiet. She didn't agree with the decision to keep this soldier from his family but that didn't matter. This man did. She felt her anger fading, replaced by an enormous respect for the soldier.

'I don't know if we can help you,' she said. 'But I swear to you we'll try.'

— CHAPTER THREE —

A listair's first afternoon in prison passed with little incident. He was locked in his cell so nothing was liable to happen, though he was aware that several of the prisoners were allowed out to roam the communal area. He heard them moving and talking, and there was no doubt that he would be a topic of conversation. He also had no doubt that the three thugs he had crossed would also be talking about him. The question was whether they would make another move against him. The answer was, of course they would. This was their territory, their patch. He was the newcomer and when they tried to bring him to heel he had embarrassed them. As far as they knew he was just a remand prisoner who would be gone in a few weeks or months. He was a nobody and they couldn't let a nobody challenge their authority in the prison. He would have to be slapped down.

So they would be coming for him. The question was *when*.

Alistair thought he would have at least a few days' grace before the attack came. After the incident at lunch, the wardens would be keeping an eye on the situation between him and those three idiots for a couple of days. It might even be a week, but sooner or later they would come for him. They wouldn't do it publicly. They daren't take the risk of another embarrassment. No, they would get him when he was alone. Nobody would see what happened but they would all see the results, and that would be what kept everyone in the wing under the control of that little gang.

So where was he most vulnerable? The cliché was that he would be attacked in the showers. It may have been a cliché, but clichés only became such because they happened so often. So, that was a possibility. The shower, or if he used the bathroom when the prisoners were all together. Exercise times would be dangerous, too. The wardens wouldn't be able to keep an eye on everyone.

Sooner or later, Geggsy and his friends would have the opportunity to attack without being seen. The movement in that kind of area was fluid. There was nowhere he could position himself to be really safe from them. Besides, he didn't want to be completely safe from them. Another confrontation was inevitable.

The best thing would be for that clash to happen on his terms at a time of his choosing. Alistair would have no back-up, so he would have to plan it very carefully.

The trip from Berkshire back to Richmond took half an hour longer than the outward journey. Rush hour was long past, but the roads were still much busier with the regular daytime traffic.

Miss Travers was quiet for most of the journey back to the safe house. Douglas didn't try to instigate a conversation. Seeing the calcified soldiers had clearly affected her deeply. Douglas had to admit that it affected him too. Soldiers took risks. That was part of the job. They faced their enemies on the battlefields, they took risks against gunfire, artillery and whatever the other side's army could throw at them. They were trained to face the worst that humanity could throw at each other. They had heard the atrocities of the Nazis in

World War II. Not just the Germans. The Japanese and the Russians had committed appallingly depraved acts of their own. Soldiers knew all of that.

But nothing prepared them for whatever turned those brave men into statues, clinging to whatever vestige of their humanity they still possessed. Since joining the Fifth, Douglas had seen a lot that he would never have believed. It occurred to him that it had only been four months since his first actual alien encounter outside *The Auld Hundred* in Edinburgh – not long at all, so it was unsurprising that sometimes it still had the ability to shake him. In truth, he hoped it would never stop being a shock. If he ever became blasé about the extraordinary, he would be putting himself and everyone around him in danger.

The car finally arrived back at the Richmond safe house just as a light snow started to fall, melting as it hit the ground, turning the light grey cobbles a darker hue and giving them a slick sheen.

Inside, the rest of the party were waiting impatiently. Samson was making lunch in the kitchen, while Bishop sat there doing the only thing a soldier did when at a loose end; he was polishing his equipment. He looked relieved and pleased when Douglas, and particularly Miss Travers, returned. Corporal Wright, who had been asleep in one of the bedrooms, emerged as soon as she heard the front door close.

'Where have you been?' she asked. 'Did you go to see him?'

'No,' Douglas replied quickly. He held back on a rebuke, allowing her current emotional state to account for her lack of respect towards her commanding officer. 'You know that's not permitted. We can see him on visiting day if he chooses to see us.'

'And that's if we're not still sneaking about under all this cloak and dagger nonsense,' Miss Travers added.

'Orders,' Douglas reminded her.

She snorted.

Douglas ignored Miss Travers' interruption. 'Did we get a delivery today?' he asked Bishop.

'This way, sir.' Bishop led the group into the hallway. 'Through here.'

He moved past the stairs. At the end of the hall, an open door led into a study which had been set out as a working space somewhere between a study and a home laboratory. A desk sat on one side of the room, with a couch just off centre towards the window. A long work-bench ran down one of the walls. It looked like a room in which Sherlock Holmes would have been perfectly at home.

'It's not exactly what we have in Edinburgh, sir,' Bishop said, 'but it's the best we can manage here.' He indicated four large cardboard boxes. 'Those were delivered earlier this morning.'

Miss Travers inspected the bright red stencilling on each of the boxes. 'These are all marked for incineration.'

'Well spotted,' Bishop said with a grin. Miss Travers play-slapped his arm, an act Douglas chose not to see. 'I think somebody might get into trouble for mislaying them.'

'As long as it's not us.' Miss Travers lifted the lid off the first box and looked at the piled of papers inside. 'It looks like we have a lot of reading ahead of us.'

Douglas glanced at Samson. 'You better get a good supply of coffee ready to go with lunch.'

Late in the afternoon, Stanley returned from his job at the

prison library. Alistair opened his eyes just in time to see a paperback book land on his chest.

'You don't deserve it,' Stanley said, 'but I brought you *Ice Station Zebra.*' He held up another paperback. 'And I got *Where Eagles Dare* for myself. I'll swap you after we're both done.'

Alistair peered at the book's cover. Rock Hudson and Patrick McGoohan stared back at him from an icy plain with the conning tower of an American submarine behind them. He was sure that it wouldn't be particularly accurate on the military side of things, but a good yarn might pass the time.

'Thank you, Stan,' he said.

'So, what have you been up to in here all afternoon?'

'Sleeping and thinking.'

'You don't want to do too much of that in here. Thinking, I mean. You'll do yourself a mischief with too much thinking.'

Alistair put the book aside on his bunk. 'Very funny.'

Stanley's face was deadly serious. 'I'm not joking,' he said. 'Worst thing you can do in here is too much thinking, especially if you start thinking about what you've left on the outside. You got a wife, have you?'

Alistair answered carefully. 'Not a wife, no.'

'But you do have a girl,' Stanley stated. 'You gave that away, you did.'

'Yes, there is someone.'

'A looker is she? I mean, you're a good-looking important feller. She's bound to be a bit of all right.'

'She's beautiful,' Alistair agreed.

'Don't think about her,' Stanley said earnestly. 'Don't think about the things on the outside that you like. Don't think about your girl, don't think about a pint with your mates or a nice Sunday roast. Just think about getting through each day. One day at a time is the way to go.'

'Are you always so cheerful?'

'You can be as sarky as you like, Mr General,' Stanley said, 'but I'm just trying to help you out here.'

'I thought you said we shouldn't worry about anyone but ourselves.'

'Oh, you're a smart one. But will you be smart when you've been in here for a year?'

'I don't intend to be here that long.'

'Got a good brief, have you?'

'Something like that.'

'Well, don't get your hopes up. Hope doesn't kill you in here. Disappointment does.'

'I have no intention of being disappointed,' Alistair pointed out.

'You'll see.'

That ominous warning brought the conversation to a halt.

Alistair picked up the paperback he had been given and let himself become immersed in the story's opening beats. He had seen the film years before but the novel still captured his attention, and for once when reading an action thriller about the military, he didn't snort at the inaccuracies. Snoring from the bunk above told him that Stanley was passing the time in an even more relaxed manner.

Just before six, the door opened and Fulton entered. There were no pleasantries. 'Lethbridge-Stewart, with me.'

Alistair swung his long legs off the bed and followed Fulton outside. The warden put an arm across Alistair's chest to stop him in his tracks.

'You know why you're out here?' Fulton asked.

'No,' Alistair replied. 'No, *sir*.'

'The governor asked me to keep an eye on you for the first few days. You've already been in one fight with the biggest thugs in this place.'

'They did come looking for trouble,' Alistair said.

'Sir!' Fulton snapped back.

'Yes,' Alistair said. 'They did come looking for trouble, *sir.*'

'And you gave it to them.'

'I defended myself. Sir.'

'And now I have to defend you in here,' Fulton snapped. The warder stared at his prisoner for a moment. 'You're trouble. I can feel it.'

Alistair didn't reply.

Fulton leaned closer. 'What are you in here for?' he asked. 'What did you do?'

'I haven't been convicted of anything.'

'That's not what I asked.' Fulton took a step closer. It was obviously a threat. 'What are you in for?'

Alistair refused to back down. 'I haven't been convicted of anything,' he repeated.

Fulton bristled at the response. 'We hear things,' he said. 'We hear that you were in a nearly closed court, that the government didn't think you could be held in a military prison safely, that the Prime Minister has decided not to cover up what you did.' He took another step closer. Alistair could smell coffee on the man's breath and could see the spit fly from Fulton's mouth as he spoke aggressively at him. 'They say you committed mass murder. Killed a village, maybe some soldiers, too. One of the rumours is that you're like the Cambridge mob. Philby, Burgess and McLean. You're a posh boy like them. Are you a traitor like them as well?'

'I haven't been convicted of anything,' Alistair replied

carefully.

'I wore the uniform,' Fulton hissed. 'I was in France and in Burma. If I thought for one minute you betrayed this country...'

'Yes?' Alistair asked mildly. 'What would you do?'

The smaller man controlled himself. 'Come with me. You're eating on your own tonight.'

Fulton led Alistair to collect his meal, which he then took back to his cell while Stanley and the others ate together. He remained in his cell alone until Stanley returned, at which point one of the prison officers took his tray away after carefully making sure that all the cutlery was still present.

As soon as the door closed, Alistair could see that Stanley was agitated. 'Indigestion?' he asked.

'This is nothing to laugh about,' Stanley said. His voice was harder than Alistair had heard it before. 'Those three you embarrassed. They're on the warpath. The whole wing's on edge.'

'I hadn't noticed,' Alistair said mildly.

Stanley shook his head. 'You're going to wake up one day and find out that being smug and arrogant don't work in here. You're going to get hurt, Alistair. I don't want that. Nobody does except those three idiots out there. But we're all scared of them because we know what they can do. Even the wardens avoid them if they can.' He sighed. 'Listen, you say you won't be here long. That's not the word out in the wing, but we can ignore that. If you're here for a long stretch, we don't need you starting a war with Geggsy and his mates. *If* you're right and you get out, we don't need you coming in, giving Geggsy a black eye and then disappearing, because we've got to live with what happens next. What you do affects the whole wing. Do you understand that?'

Alistair was quiet for a moment before answering. 'Yes,' he said finally. 'I see what you mean.'

'Good. I told you already. The best way to get by in here is to keep your head down and keep your nose clean.' Stanley paused to put half a stick of chewing gum in his mouth. 'Just stay out of trouble.'

Alistair didn't answer. Staying out of trouble was one thing he'd never quite got the hang of.

For once, Leslie Johnston's spy network had drawn a near total blank. They were still digging but so far they had come up with nothing on the charges against Lethbridge-Stewart.

The charges were read in front of the judge, the solicitors, the defendant, and a few court officers before the crowd were let in to hear the judge decide whether or not bail would be granted. Johnston's people were looking into the background of everyone who had been there for the reading of the charges. If any of them would talk, or could be coerced into talking, he would be listening. He also had feelers out in Westminster and at the Ministry of Defence. Sooner or later somebody would talk. They always did. Someone would always spill the beans after one whisky and soda too many, or if they thought being in the know would benefit their careers even slightly.

As for Lethbridge-Stewart's comrades, they had returned to Edinburgh on the sleeper. Johnston's people observed their group from a distance and watched them being picked up from Waverley Station. What they were up to now he had no idea. Probably licking their wounds for a while until they got a new commanding officer. Dougie, for all his training, was far too junior to take over from Lethbridge-Stewart – a point Johnston took a little satisfaction over. Either way,

Dougie and his people were less of a threat without Alistair Lethbridge-Stewart.

Johnston rubbed his chin thoughtfully. The General had sent him to find out what was going on, and as ever the General would not be happy unless he got results. So yes, Johnston wanted to know what was going on, and he definitely wanted to know sooner rather than later.

'Any news?' Douglas asked again.

Anne looked at him irritably over a sheaf of papers. 'Walter, I can no more answer that now that I could the last time you asked. Five minutes ago.'

'I'm sorry, but it's frustrating just having to wait.'

'And your frustration will only become more pronounced if you keep asking me a question and I can't give you an answer.'

'Can you at least give me a clue what's so urgent?' Douglas indicated the papers in her hands.

'I thought you were leaving me to read these papers in peace because they're science-based?' Anne sighed loudly and immediately felt guilty for such a petulant action. 'All right,' she said, forcing herself to sound reasonable. 'Some time ago, a rock which was in the possession of the British Government was stolen.'

'A rock? What in the devil are we doing with a rock?'

Anne carried on as if he hadn't spoken. 'Of course, given that we don't actually have the rock, it's rather difficult for us to examine it and come to any conclusions about it.'

'But they want us to anyway?'

'Give that officer a coconut,' Anne replied. 'They want us to go through the reports they have, find out what we can about it, what it's made of, where it comes from, what its properties are.'

'Properties? I don't like the sound of that one bit.'

'And then we have to find a way to make it completely safe. Oh, and if we could find a way to find out who stole it they'd appreciate that too.'

Douglas' eyebrows rose. 'Is that all?'

'Well, they did ask if we could stop the Cold War and end poverty but I told them we were short staffed and they could blow it out of their... ears.'

'Right, which documents have you read?'

Anne indicated a small pile. 'These'

'Right,' Douglas said, reaching for the pile. 'I'd better play catch-up.'

'Good plan.' Anne picked up a hefty report. 'Oh,' she said, after reading a bit. 'Oh dear.'

'What is it?' Douglas asked.

'Nothing,' Anne lied. She grimaced slightly. 'Well, nothing we can do anything about. Just a name from the past. Captain Ben Knight.'

'Knight? What's he got to do with it? He served under Pemberton, didn't he? Died in the Underground.'

'Yes, him,' Anne confirmed sadly. 'And I don't know, but...' She waved the paper in her hand. 'His name is here.'

'1 Para,' Douglas said. 'Those statues... *Men*. They were part of 1 Para. And so was Knight.'

Anne was silent for a moment. 'That's no coincidence.' She shook her head. 'I wasn't always kind to Captain Knight. He was a decent sort of fellow. I should have been... Better with him. Not so damn superior.'

'Every soldier who has ever lost a comrade in battle feels exactly the same way, you know,' Douglas offered sympathetically.

'Do you?'

'Yes. You serve with a chap for nine months, have one barney with him and the next day...' Douglas shrugged, brushing off an unwelcome memory. 'Well, it's his turn to buy it. You never have the chance to put things right.'

'How do you deal with it?'

'Remember the better times with them.'

'Captain Knight and I didn't have any better times.'

'You survived, didn't you? If he gave his life so that you could live and do good work after the Underground, those are your better times.'

Anne didn't look convinced. She picked up the heavy document.

Leslie Johnston sat at his desk in the Vault, and stared hard at the report in front of him. It made very little sense. It was a jumble of half facts. The largest of those facts was that Lethbridge-Stewart was now residing at Her Majesty's pleasure in HMP Wormwood Scrubs. The confusion was still over why the damn man was in prison. Equally pressing, why was he put in front of a civil court rather than a military one?

Johnston reached out through his web of contacts. Normally, his contacts never let him down. On this occasion they were able to provide very little. What came back was that the government was trying to keep a lid on the story until there was absolutely no alternative other than to go public.

That meant it was bad.

Among the few facts Johnston had gleaned was that it had something to do with a village, Durnham, which was now very suddenly completely abandoned. A gas leak from old mine workings was being blamed but nobody was able to track down any of the inhabitants of the village. Nearby farmers reported hearing gunfire and one claimed to have seen a tall army officer firing his pistol randomly. At least, he claimed that in his first statement. In his second statement he recanted the testimony and claimed to have seen nothing. The only other solid piece of information Johnston had was that a number of ambulances were seen going into and leaving the village.

Johnston had not got as far in life as he had by jumping to conclusions. He could piece together a story that looked very bad for Lethbridge-Stewart, but Johnston knew better than to try to pull together a narrative from too few facts. He picked up the next folder.

It showed Lethbridge-Stewart's friends and colleagues coming out of the trial. The pictures were taken by the photographer Dougie had taken offence with. *How like Dougie to be chivalrous*, Johnston sneered. Perhaps the man might show some gumption and actually lead the Fifth with Lethbridge-Stewart out of the way.

Johnston looked through the photographs. Dougie and his team were unaware of Johnston's photographer taking their pictures as they went into the court. Even if they had spotted him, they couldn't have known that the camera also had a directed microphone built into it, which recorded snatches of their conversations.

Johnston flicked through the transcripts. They were mostly dull and mundane. For the most part, none of them said anything interesting. A good deal of it had been platitudes consoling the girl, Sally. However, he did find a snippet of conversation which interested him.

> ANNE TRAVERS: Why is he being put in a Civil Court?

LT COL DOUGLAS: Apparently the same reason he's likely to be remanded to a civil prison.

ANNE TRAVERS: Which is?

LT COL DOUGLAS: The way it was put to me was – and I quote – it would be too dangerous to let the army have him when word got out.

ANNE TRAVERS: But they didn't say what he's accused of doing?

LT COL DOUGLAS: They didn't tell me a damn thing except that I was in command until further notice. And one other thing.

ANNE TRAVERS: Yes?

LT COL DOUGLAS: The old general I saw said they couldn't cover this up. What would be so bad that they'd worry about covering it up?

ANNE TRAVERS: I don't like the sound of this. Not one bit.

Johnston rubbed his chin thoughtfully. Had Lethbridge-Stewart gone rogue and killed someone in a village? Had he gone on a killing spree ? That didn't seem likely. He was the most straight-laced and by the book soldier Johnston knew. However, in the war Johnston had seen superb soldiers driven to madness by the stresses of the job. Could the same have happened to Lethbridge-Stewart? He thought it unlikely, but not impossible.

A memory nagged at the back of Johnston's mind. *Durnham?*

The village where everything had apparently happened... That definitely rang a bell with him. Why did he remember that village's name?

He reached for the phone.

A few hours later Johnston looked at the brief report in front of him with satisfaction. His memory hadn't played him false. There had indeed been a good reason to remember the village of Durnham.

The names of the officers involved caught his attention. They were linked to Lethbridge-Stewart, and that linked the man to the village.

However, it all left a lot of questions with damn few answers. Whatever happened there, Johnston wanted to know the details. He had the feeling that whatever brought Lethbridge-Stewart to his knees was major. That meant Johnston *needed* to know about it. In his experience, knowledge was currency and currency meant the power to influence. The General had his own reasons for pursuing Lethbridge-Stewart, and Johnston had his. Sometimes they didn't mesh, and Johnston had a feeling this was one of those occasions.

He really needed to know *everything* about this situation.

The Convoy, Part One

Lowbridge Army Barracks in Derbyshire was not a normal army barracks. On the surface it was a regular Ministry of Defence army camp, acting as a temporary home to various regiments as they came and went to any one of a number of postings overseas.

What was less known about Lowbridge concerned the troops who were stationed on site permanently. A platoon of highly trained elite troops was on round-the-clock alert at a nondescript two storey brick building at the heart of the compound. Officially titled the Long Store, it was part of the camp that none of the temporary troops had any reason to ever visit. Those soldiers billeted on a temporary basis at Lowbridge had no idea that they were the first line of defence at one of Great Britain's most secret and secure facilities. Behind the dull metal doors of the Long Store was another set of doors. These were made from reinforced steel. Beyond those doors were computer controlled lifts which led deep underground to storage rooms made from reinforced concrete and steel. Those storage rooms served a number of purposes, holding unexplained objects including the possible remains of extra-terrestrial craft and the bodies of unexplained creatures. It also acted as a prison for the country's most dangerous and extraordinary criminals.

When Colonel Spencer Pemberton's convoy arrived at

Lowbridge, they were shown immediately to the Long Store. Under normal circumstances, Pemberton and his second-in-command, Captain Knight, would have paid a courtesy visit to the camp's commanding officer. It was simply the done thing. However, Lowbridge was not an average army camp. If Pemberton had visited the CO, he might have been seen and questions might have been asked. Visitors to the Long Store never answered questions.

Pemberton's convoy consisted of one Bedford lorry, two Land Rovers and four motorcycle outriders. The back of the Bedford contained a safe welded to the floor and a steel mesh cage surrounding the safe. Four soldiers sat in the back of the Bedford with another in the passenger seat in the cab. Each of the Land Rovers had four armed men in the back. The rear Land Rover also had a soldier in the passenger seat. There was no doubt that security on this convoy was of prime importance.

Colonel Pemberton climbed out of the passenger seat of the front Land Rover and walked over to the Bedford. Knight jumped out of the back of the truck.

'Comfortable trip?' Pemberton asked.

'Not too bad, sir.'

'Really?'

Knight chuckled. 'Well, you know what the benches in the back of that thing are like.'

'Of course I do,' Pemberton said. 'Why do you think I'm in the Land Rover?'

'RHIP.'

'Come on, Little Spence,' Pemberton said, using the nickname the squaddies of 1 Para had given his 2-in-C, and led the way to the Long Store.

Fifteen minutes later, after going through rigorous security checks and scrutiny of their passes and orders, a small Welsh scientist named Professor Thomas directed Pemberton and Knight through one of the lowest levels of the storage facility.

'We've got it out of the way down here, you see,' he said, absent-mindedly pushing his round spectacles back up his nose. 'Haven't seen it in action myself and damn sure I don't want to, neither. Rather see Barry John and Gareth Edwards turning out for England, I would.'

'What does it do?' Pemberton asked.

Thomas' eyes widened in surprise. 'Don't you know?'

Pemberton smiled charmingly. 'I always ask questions when I already know the answer.'

Thomas snorted. 'You're a sarky one, en't you, boyo.' He led them around a corner to a door secured by a keypad. 'In here.' He punched in a six-digit code and pushed the door open. 'Follow me.'

Thomas led Pemberton and Knight into the plain concrete room beyond. 'There you go.'

A single wooden table was the only furniture in the room. On it sat an open metal briefcase. The case was packed with foam padding to protect the case's contents. Inside a plain glass jar with a hinged glass lid rested a single rock. It was smaller than a fist. One face of the rock's surface was curved and ridged, with spidery bulges on it. The other sides were rough and sharp, showing that it had been broken from a much larger object.

'That's it, sir?' Knight asked. He sounded thoroughly disappointed.

'Doesn't look much, does it?' said Thomas.

'Not really.'

The little scientist pointed at the stone, particularly focusing on the curved face. 'Does that remind you of anything?' he asked. 'That curved side. Does it look like something?'

Knight examined the shape. There was something vaguely familiar but he couldn't quite place it. 'It does, but I'm dashed if I can think what.'

'And it's not our place to work it out,' Pemberton said, interrupting the conversation. 'Our job's just to get it where it's going and then forget we ever saw it.'

Knight nodded firmly. 'Yes, sir.'

Thomas looked aghast. 'Aren't you curious?' he asked. 'Don't you want to know?'

'Sorry, Prof,' Knight said with a shrug. 'Orders trump curiosity.'

'Flaming military.' Thomas closed the case and scrambled the barrels on the lock. 'That's it shut. Only the boys in London know the combination to open it.'

'Thank you,' Knight said, taking the case from Thomas.

'All right,' Pemberton said to Thomas. 'It's time for us to get moving. We have a schedule to stick to.'

'Right you are,' Thomas agreed. He led them out of the room and locked the door behind them. He indicated the case. 'I'm glad that thing's out of here, to be honest with you. Makes me feel a bit safer if that's not here.'

'That's cheering,' Pemberton said sourly.

'Given that we're taking it on a journey,' Knight added.

Thomas shrugged. 'That's why you get paid the big money, isn't it?'

Both officers snorted.

A few minutes later the three men emerged from the Long Store. Thomas stopped just outside the building and squinted at the pale sun. He clearly didn't get out of doors often.

Pemberton saluted the scientist. 'Thank you for your help, Professor Thomas.'

'I told you,' Thomas replied. 'My pleasure.' He turned and headed back indoors.

Pemberton nodded at the case in Knight's hand. 'Let's get that under lock and key,' he said. 'Quick as you can.'

'Yes, sir.'

Knight hurried to the Bedford and clambered into the back, with Pemberton close behind him. The three keys that secured the cage released the mesh door, and then the safe's treble locks were also opened. It required two keys and a combination. The case was quickly put inside and all of the locks on the safe and cage were secured again. The case was as safe as it could possibly be for its journey.

'Right,' Pemberton said, 'let's get a wiggle on. We've got a schedule to keep.'

Leaving Knight in the back of the Bedford, Pemberton returned to his Land Rover. With two motor cycle outriders ahead of him, Pemberton's Land Rover left Lowbridge Army Barracks, followed by the Bedford, the second Land Rover and the final two outriders.

Colonel Pemberton was never a man to be complacent about his job. He brought more armed men than recommended and he took every precaution with security that he could. There was always the chance that a convoy like this would be spotted, but they had the firepower to defend themselves and in the journey of under two hours there were few places where they would be vulnerable to attack. He was confident but not complacent.

He remained on edge as the convoy passed through narrow country roads, many of which had trees lining at least

52

one side of them. Woodland like that was always good cover from which to launch an attack. Pemberton only relaxed when the convoy finally turned onto an A-road and started moving along a more major artery.

Travelling faster, they would reach their destination sooner. These roads also had less potential for ambush. The motorway ten miles ahead would have less scope still.

Pemberton eased himself back into his seat but his eyes never stopped searching for potential trouble.

Unfortunately, Colonel Pemberton, his outriders and the soldiers peering out through slits in the canvas covering of the Land Rovers, had no way of knowing that four cars positioned about a quarter of a mile behind them on the road were filled with men, all armed with a mixture of sawn-off shotguns and Russian automatic rifles. One of the men in each of the cars carried a walkie-talkie and they communicated with each other and with colleagues elsewhere.

These men were professional. They chose four different cars, all of diverse colours and manufacturers. They kept a distance apart, and allowed other cars to overtake and sit between them. There was no way to tell that these cars were travelling together, and no way to tell that they had targeted Colonel Pemberton's convoy.

They were going to test his confidence to the full.

— CHAPTER FOUR —

Alistair's third day in prison looked as if it would continue as his second had ended, with him segregated from the rest of the inmates. He was taken for breakfast alone and returned to his cell. He used the time to exercise, and to go over the information he had gleaned on the running of the prison. Just before lunchtime, he was returned to the general population of the wing.

The bulk of his contact was through Stanley. In spite of himself, Alistair found that he was warming to the tubby thief. Stanley did seem to have Alistair's best interests at heart and continually dished out advice on surviving in the prison system, most of it delivered in a caustic and sarcastic manner, though usually with good humour underpinning it.

Just after lunch, Alistair heard an agonised scream from the far end of the central communal area. He recognised it immediately as the sound of a man suffering a sudden brutal pain. It usually accompanied a broken bone. Sure enough, when Stanley hurried across a few minutes later with an ashen face, Alistair's fears were confirmed.

'That scream was Pontoon,' Stanley said.

Alistair swung his legs from his bunk. 'Pontoon?' he asked.

Stanley nodded. 'Bloke with no neck. We call him Pontoon because if he gets one more twist he'll burst.' There was no humour in Stanley's voice as he explained the nickname.

The conversation was curtailed for a moment by a prison officer hurrying the inmates back to their cells.

As soon as the door closed behind them Alistair asked, 'What happened to him?'

'No idea,' Stanley answered automatically. 'None of my business, neither.'

'That's your official answer. Now what about the answer you tell me?'

Stanley shook his head sourly. 'When do you think we got to be best mates, eh? Why am I going to tell you anything?'

'Because we're stuck in this room together and whatever impacts one of us impacts both of us.' Alistair's eyebrow arched upwards. 'You see; I do pay attention.'

Stanley sank down onto a chair, which scraped on the harsh floor for a second. 'I wish you'd paid attention to me when I warned you to watch out for Geggsy.'

Alistair nodded thoughtfully. 'I assume whatever happened to this chap, Pontoon, was the responsibility of Geggsy?'

Stanley shook his head. 'I heard his two muckers gave him an alibi. Said they was no place near Pontoon when it happened.'

'And the truth?' Alistair demanded quietly.

Stanley put another half stick of chewing gum into his mouth. 'It was them all right,' he said quietly. 'They grabbed Pontoon when the screws were crossing over. It gave them about a minute. They didn't need that long. They grabbed Pontoon, forced his leg between a couple of stairs and snapped it.' He shuddered. 'We all heard it. Sounded like a gun going off.' Stanley looked up. 'Most of us done our time in National Service. We know what a gun sounds like.' He nodded again. 'Yeah, we all heard it all right, and we all saw who done it, but you can be bloody sure none of us is talking about it.'

Alistair chewed his lip thoughtfully. 'That's the idea, I imagine? To make sure everybody knows they're still in charge of this wing.'

'You imagine right, and so do they. Yeah, we know they did it but not one of us will say a word about it. And neither will you,' Stanley added. 'Cos you was in here when it happened and if you blab they'll know it was me what told you and it'll be my leg next. Or my neck.'

Alistair nodded his understanding. 'I think I've done enough damage already, don't you?'

'At last you're getting it. This ain't like the outside.'

'Have they threatened you yet?'

'No,' Stanley answered quickly. 'And I could do without the "yet" you had in there.'

Alistair slapped the older man's shoulder in a friendly manner. 'Don't worry, old chap. I'll make sure nobody hurts you on my account.'

'And just how do you plan to do that cooped up in here?'

Rubbing his chin thoughtfully, Alistair was forced to admit that he didn't actually have an answer to Stanley's question.

Anne looked out of the window of the Super Vickers VC-10 as it dipped through the clouds towards Cairo International Airport. Her stomach dipped with it, and she wondered if she'd ever really get used to flying. If she hoped Egypt would offer warmer weather than London, she was to be disappointed. Outside the window she saw heavy, dull cloud cover.

She glanced at Sally, who was seated next to her. Sally

said very little all through the flight, preferring to read a magazine. Anne knew that Sally didn't want to come on this mission. She wanted to stay in London, close to Lethbridge-Stewart. However, as Douglas had flatly stated, this was an order and as long as she was in the Corps, Sally would follow orders.

Sally was far from happy but she obeyed.

Anne knew why Douglas had been so harsh. The poor girl was beside herself with worry about Lethbridge-Stewart. Getting her working was the best way to distract her.

Among the documents that were delivered to the safe house was a folder full of references to statues in Egypt, which showed some of the same properties as the stone soldiers in the Berkshire facility. The statues, dated at being at least two thousand years old, were part of Egyptian myths and legends for millennia. A number of statues, along with historical documentation on them, were held at Cairo's Ptolemaic Museum. Anne and Sally were travelling as two sisters from Birmingham. Ten rows behind, Bishop was travelling as a salesman from Crewe, on his way to discuss mechanical parts. Each of them carried a counterfeit passport and travel documents. Initially the plan was for Bill to travel a day before Anne and Sally, to avoid them all being seen together. However, flights to Egypt were heavily booked in advance and, in truth, they needed to find answers quickly. Wasting a full day was not an option.

The VC-10 landed smoothly at Cairo International, which was located in Heliopolis, just over nine miles northeast of Cairo. The airport had begun as a wartime American airstrip, transforming into a modern facility over the following years to become Egypt's primary airport in 1963.

Anne and Sally disembarked and made their way to

reclaim their baggage without seeing Bill. They arrived in the middle of the afternoon and the airport was mobbed. It seemed to be far busier than was safe or in any way efficient.

After collecting their luggage Anne and Sally took a taxi to the outskirts of Cairo and the house they had rented. They were in the house for half an hour before Bill arrived.

'What kept you?' Anne asked. 'Taxi driver get lost?'

'Not a chance,' Bill replied, taking off his jacket and dropping it onto the back of a chair. 'I had the best taxi driver in Egypt.'

'Ah.' Anne nodded. 'I was forgetting that you were going to hire a car at the airport.'

'I'm glad I did. Some of the taxi drivers I saw on the roads as I drove in were... Well, let's say I thought I was driving with Jackie Stewart and Graham Hill.'

'Our driver was the same,' Sally agreed.

Anne nodded her agreement. 'If I find any grey in my hair he'll be hearing from my solicitors.'

Bill chuckled and checked his watch. 'It's too late to visit the museum today. We'll go first thing in the morning.'

'Fair enough,' Anne agreed. 'A good night's sleep won't go amiss.'

'Do you think our cover's solid?' Bill asked.

Anne nodded again. 'As long as you leave any discussion of science or history to me.'

'You think I'm not up to blustering my way through it?'

'I know you're not,' Anne answered with a smile. 'Unless you have a secret fascination with the chemical composition of various rocks.'

'Not as such, no,' Bill admitted.

'I didn't think so. If I'm honest it's not my area of expertise either, but I'll get by.'

'I've no doubt. I suggest we get some provisions in and get an early night.'

'Sally and I will go,' Anne said. 'You report back that we've arrived here safely.' She smiled slightly. 'If that's the proper jargon.'

The attack on Pontoon was written off as an accident; the prisoner had slipped and caught his leg between metal stairs. As he fell, his weight had broken the leg. Nobody believed it, but that was the story.

Stanley returned to his duties in the library, leaving Alistair alone in his cell. He had almost finished reading *Ice Station Zebra*, and had to admit he preferred the book to the film. The book delved into the characters' psyches with the greater depth one expected from a novel. He made a mental note to read *The Guns of Navarone* at some point.

Stanley had been gone for approximately half an hour when the cell door opened and a prison officer entered. 'Exercise,' the man said gruffly. He was another new face to Alistair.

He mentally logged the man's face and which day he was working.

Alistair swung his legs from the bunk and nodded. 'Yes, sir.'

He followed the warder along the quiet landing. Inmates were either doing their jobs or were locked up in their cells. He followed the warder down the steps to a metal door, leading to a corridor which, in turn, led into a small yard.

The warden nodded at a door. 'You'll be outside for an hour and a half. Better use the bathroom now before you go out.'

Alarm bells rang in Alistair's head as soon as he entered

the bathroom. He couldn't see anything amiss but he *knew* something was wrong.

This was it; a warden he didn't recognise, an enclosed space.

Alistair turned to the door, but it was closed and he couldn't open it.

Yes, this was where it was going to happen.

He turned back to the room. It had urinals, stalls, and an area to shower in. Plenty of places for someone to hide.

He heard the footsteps. Multiple sets of them. Three. And then there they were. Geggsy and his two friends, Mason and Minty. Alistair tried the door again. It wouldn't move.

'No use trying that,' Geggsy said. The three men continued to approach. 'It's locked till we say otherwise.'

'So you have wardens in your back pocket,' Alistair said.

He squared himself, carefully eyeing his three opponents. Mason was the biggest of the three, but Geggsy was the most dangerous. He would be the one to take down first, if there was to be any chance of winning the fight. Even as he thought it, Alistair knew he had no chance. The space was too enclosed. There was no room to manoeuvre. He had no weapons to defend himself with. The only plus was that these three goons weren't armed either. They didn't have to be. Three against one in a fight like this... They didn't need anything but their fists and their feet.

Geggsy shrugged. 'This is our wing,' he said. 'We run it. Nobody shows us up.'

'Really?' Alistair said calmly. 'And you broke Pontoon's leg to prove that?'

'Pretty much.'

'And I assume you've got worse in mind for me?'

A vicious smile spread across Geggsy's face. 'Of course.

You posh boys are used to special treatment.'

The pause seemed to last an eternity. Alistair was as ready as he could be. He knew they were playing mind games, making him wait for the attack. The longer they waited, the more terrified he would become, that was their thinking. He had seen worse than this lot.

Minty made the first move. He lunged forward. A straight right hand broke Minty's nose and sent him stumbling backwards. Alistair spun to the others, but they were already on him. Geggsy went low, driving a knee hard into Alistair's groin. As he buckled, Mason slammed a fist into his cheek. Alistair tried to fight back. He was dazed but instinct made him swing his fists. He felt a left hand connect with a jaw but he couldn't see what was happening. Fists reigned in on his face and arms. Another huge punch dropped him to his knees.

Now they were kicking, driving their boots into his face and body. He felt a rib crack and he tried to fend them off. They just kept kicking. He slumped to the floor. They kept kicking. He tried to force himself upright again but his body wouldn't obey. Blackness was seeping in. He didn't want to fall unconscious. He might never wake if it did. He couldn't stop it coming.

The last thing he was aware of was seeing the door open and a man in uniform speaking briskly.

'That's enough. Back to your cells, the three of you.'

The kicking stopped instantly and his three attackers hurried out.

He was almost unconscious now but he recognised the face of the man in uniform. It wasn't the guard who had taken him into the trap. It was Fulton.

'Should have stayed out of trouble,' the warden was saying, but the voice was very far away and disappearing into a tunnel.

A moment later, Alistair slipped into the relief of unconsciousness.

Twenty minutes after leaving the rented property, with the clouds beginning to break, Anne and Sally headed towards a shop they'd spotted when they arrived.

'I should have kept my mouth shut about not wanting to be here,' Sally said gloomily.

'Probably.' Anne had to agree.

'It wasn't very professional.'

Anne grimaced. 'Stuff professionalism. If it had been my father you could have set the entire army, Navy and Air Force in front of me and I wouldn't have left London.'

'Or if it was Bill,' Sally added.

'Bill?' Anne gave the younger woman a sidelong look. 'I have absolutely no idea what you mean, Corporal Wright.'

'Of course you don't, dear,' Sally replied easily.

'And neither do you.'

'I didn't say a word.'

Anne glanced at the younger woman. She was relieved that Sally's mood had lightened slightly. 'Nobody blames you for reacting the way you did,' she said kindly. 'We all understand. We all like Briga—' Anne caught herself and looked around. 'What am I doing?' she muttered. 'Bill has me thinking like James Bond now.' She started again. 'We understand how you feel about Alistair. We're all fond of him, we all respect him. He's our leader and our friend.'

'He's a lot more than that to me.'

'I know,' Anne said gently. 'And I know he would rather you were on a mission, doing your job, instead of sitting in a flat worrying about him.'

'I know.'

They reached the shop and gratefully went inside out of the rain. They bought enough food and provisions for three days. They anticipated being on a plane back to London within two days, but picked up a little extra in case the job took longer than they expected.

After a very quick meal of scrambled eggs cooked by Bill, all three retreated to their beds for an early night. They had a long day ahead of them when they woke.

Alistair tried to open his eyes. They seemed swollen and even the dull light seemed to glare and burn his eyes.

Pain hit him hard. It seemed that as soon as he reached a level of consciousness the pain arrived. He groaned. It was a reflex, ripped out of him. Doctor Jenkins was by his side a moment later.

'You're awake again, eh?' Jenkins said, peering down at his patient. 'You seem more aware this time.'

Alistair had no memory of waking before. He tried to answer but his mouth was swollen and refused to form the words he wanted.

'Don't try to speak.' Jenkins prepared a hypodermic. 'Rest is the best thing for you just now. I'm going to put you out again till morning.

Alistair tried to move, tried to tell the MO not to inject him, but everything hurt too much. He could barely move. He felt a pressure on his arm and the sharp prick of the needle breaking the skin. Within twenty seconds the pain stopped and the world went black as he fell unconscious.

'He's what?' Bill asked. He looked quickly around the living room of the rented house.

'What is it?' Anne asked. She wasn't sure she actually wanted to know.

Bill waved his hand to quieten her, which elicited an indignant look from Anne, and he listened to the phone for a long moment.'

'Understood, sir,' he said finally. 'You'll keep me informed of his condition? Thanks, Colonel.' There was another pause for a reply. 'Right. I'll call tonight at twenty hundred our time.' He hung up and turned worriedly to face Anne.

'What is it?' Anne asked. 'Has something happened to the brigadier?'

Bill thought for a moment before answering. He indicated for Anne to sit. She ignored his suggestion. 'Yep, but... orders are that Sally's not to hear any of this until we get back to London, okay?'

'What happened?' Anne demanded, considerably more worried now.

'Anne, you need to promise. We can't tell her until we're back in London.'

'Okay, Bill.' Anne wasn't too keen on the shadow crossing Bill's face. 'What happened?'

Bill sighed. 'The Brig is in the infirmary at the Scrubs.'

'What?'

'He was attacked. A warden found him beaten very badly in one of the toilets. They don't know how he got there or who did it. He's still out cold so they haven't spoken to him about it.'

Anne forced herself to ask pragmatic questions. Using the logical part of her brain forced just a small part of the worry aside. 'How bad is it?'

Bill repeated what he had been told. 'Broken ribs, lots of

bruising. They won't know the exact damage till that's had time to develop. Colonel Douglas didn't have time to go into detail but it sounded like he got a hiding. What they'll be worried about is...'

'Internal injuries,' Anne finished for him. 'You can't see them and you can't tell what damage they're doing.'

Bill nodded miserably. 'Exactly. They're trying to find out exactly what happened. On the QT, of course.'

Anne slumped into a chair. 'It must have been an awful beating.'

'You could say that. That's why we're not telling Sally.'

'I understand,' Anne said after a moment. 'It's the right thing to do.'

'She's not going to think so,' Bill said ruefully. 'Still, at least Colonel Douglas and Samson are in London. They've known the Brig the longest. Friends and all.'

'They'll get to the bottom of it,' Anne agreed. 'But you're right, not telling Sally is the right decision for now.' Instinctively she gave Bill's arm a squeeze.

Bill offered a tight smile. 'Thanks.'

They both heard movement from the stairs. Sally was on her way to join them.

'Change subject,' Anne said softly, before continuing at a more normal tone. 'Well, I'm definitely not facing a trip to the museum without at least a decent cup of coffee.' She turned as Sally came into the room. 'What about you, Sally?'

Sally's smile seemed just a little forced. 'I never turn down a coffee... Unless that's a subtle hint that you want me to make it? God knows Colonel Douglas has me making it for him often enough.'

Anne laughed. 'It wasn't, but having tasted Bill's coffee, I wouldn't advise that we let him anywhere near it.'

'You didn't object to my scrambled eggs, though,' Bill grumbled in a good-natured way.

'Come on,' Anne said, ushering Sally to the door. 'You do some toast, I'll make the coffee.'

Sally headed off to the kitchen. Anne and Bill exchanged a quick glance, punctuated by a sympathetic smile. She followed Sally to the kitchen.

An hour after finishing their coffee, Bishop, Anne, and Sally were shown into the office of Ayman Shehab, the curator of the Ptolemaic Museum. He was a tall man, tanned and athletic, and he looked fifteen years younger than his actual age of fifty-five. Despite his formidable reputation as an academic, Shehab spent a good chunk of the years since the war out in the field, uncovering Egypt's heritage. It was rumoured that during the war he had also been out in the field, taking part in the resistance against the invasion of Axis forces. Whenever asked about the subject, Shehab would never confirm any of the stories regarding the actions he undertook. Tellingly, he would never deny them either. The curator would always simply say that it was a different time, long ago and his sole interest now was in protecting his country's heritage. Those who knew the truth of Ayman Shehab's war-time exploits knew that over a hundred Italian and German soldiers died at his hands as he protected his country.

Douglas obtained a copy of Shehab's war-time file and passed it on to the three members of the party, and they all read it on the flight from London. When looking at the man superficially, it was hard to see him as the individual who had detonated explosives on a cliff-side road, causing forty men in troop lorries to fall hundreds of metres to their deaths.

Then again, under the smile and the charm, there was a definite edge of steel to Shehab.

The curator met each of his guests with a firm handshake. 'It is a pleasure to meet you all. Please take a seat.' He indicated the three chairs that were placed facing his desk, before returning to his leather swivel chair. 'May I get you anything? Coffee? Or should we have tea? I studied at Oxford. I am aware of how much the English love their tea.'

'We're fine,' Bill replied, smiling. 'Though you're right, Britain runs on tea. We don't worry about oil running out, only tea.'

Shehab chuckled. 'That sounds very like the Britain I knew. Now, what can I do for you? Especially you...' He glanced at Anne before making a show of checking the paper on his desk. 'Miss... *Carter?*'

Bishop squirmed.

Anne just smiled. 'I wasn't aware I was quite so recognisable.'

Shehab grimaced apologetically. 'If I am honest, it is your father's work that I really know. However, you are in several photographs with him, particularly following the evacuation of London early this year.'

Anne glanced at Bill. 'I told Walter the double-oh-seven stuff wouldn't work.'

'Did you?' Bill asked, remembering with some amusement Douglas' reaction to Anne's comments during the briefing at the safe house in London.

Anne turned back to Shehab. 'I'm sorry about this, Curator.'

Shehab waved a hand dismissing the offence. 'I am more interested in why a famed scientist is so interested in seeing some old statues. And why she is desperate to keep it secret.'

67

He smiled a most charming smile. 'Why else would you hide behind a false identity? Did you travel under this false name also?'

'Well…' Anne's guilty expression was enough to answer that question.

'And now,' Shehab leaned forward intently, 'now I am very interested indeed.'

Anne looked at Bill, who thought for a moment, carefully considering the situation. How would Douglas react to this, or Lethbridge-Stewart himself? Both would probably let it slide and adapt. He nodded his consent. 'All right, Anne. Tell him.' He turned to Shehab. 'But I must request, in the strongest terms, sir, that you keep the details of this discussion secret.'

Shehab's eyebrow rose in surprise. 'I will do my best.'

'We're going to trust you, Mr Shehab,' Anne said. 'We'd like to see a particular set of statues you have stored within your museum. The Armete Statues.'

'Armete?' Shehab seemed surprised. 'They don't get much attention these days. May I ask why you are interested?'

'Because,' Anne said, 'we saw four more of them a few days ago.'

The curator's handsome face instantly lost its playfully bemused edge. He was suddenly very serious. 'Too many of my country's treasures have been taken over the centuries,' he said in a quiet but surprisingly rigid tone.

'It's nothing like that,' Anne assured him. 'The statues we saw in Britain were new. Less than a year old.'

Shehab chuckled. 'I think you must be confused. The Armete Statues are thousands of years old.' He reached for his pipe. 'But I think you must have a very interesting tale to tell me.'

And so, Anne told him.

'There are many legends about the Armete soldiers,' Shehab said, after Anne finished explaining the reason for their visit.

'And you are your country's greatest expert on the statues,' Anne added. 'That is why we have come to you.'

Shehab nodded thoughtfully. 'With an extraordinary story.'

'Which you don't believe a word of,' Bill said wearily.

'I would not believe a word of it,' Shehab said slowly, 'if I had not seen the eye of one of the statues move myself.'

'You believe us?'

'I believe my own eyes,' Shehab replied. 'I am an educated man, but I have seen things I do not understand with those statues. Things I have never told another soul for fear of ridicule.' He paused and smiled. 'And I do not believe the famous Anne Travers would tell me so tall a tale. These are my countrymen and they are fellow soldiers. I will help you in any way possible.'

'Excellent,' Bill said. He was as surprised as Anne but delighted. 'Anne, what do we need?'

Anne ran through a mental check-list. 'Tissue samples, soil samples from the location, copies of any written records you may have.'

'Is that all?' Shehab asked mildly.

'No,' Anne answered with a smile. 'We'd like to X-ray one of your statues.'

'You ask a great deal.'

'Is it too much if we can find answers to what happened to your countrymen?'

'No,' Shehab replied. 'You will have everything you ask for, on the condition that you share with me everything you learn.' His voice hardened. 'Everything.'

Anne exchanged a glance with Bill, who gave a slight nod. 'Agreed,' she said.

Alistair forced his eyes open, and ignored the pain which hit him hard. He just kept telling himself that he had been through worse. He was awoken by Doctor Jenkins moving around the ward. Alistair tried to talk, but the swelling around his mouth and the cuts to his lips made the attempt painful.

'Welcome back to the land of the living,' Jenkins said.

Alistair made a sound halfway between a mumble and a groan.

'No, don't try to speak. I'm going to give you some water.'

Alistair felt the solid pressure of a glass against his lips. It turned cold for a second before he felt the cool relief of water trickling into his mouth. It stung and tasted metallic but it soothed the dry area at the back of his throat. He coughed hard as he tried to swallow. The cough sent waves of agony through his face and body.

'Steady,' Jenkins said softly. 'Don't rush it. Just sip it down.'

The water slowly slid down Alistair's throat. It was warmer than he'd expected. He didn't care. The water was soothing. 'Thank you,' he croaked.

Jenkins pressed the glass into Alistair's hands. 'Drink it slowly,' he said. 'There's a jug on the cabinet by your bed if you want more.'

The MO moved the bedclothes and opened Alistair's pyjama jacket. 'Well?' Alistair asked. 'What's the diagnosis?' He barely recognised his own voice.

'I can't be precise until the swelling goes down, but I'd say broken ribs for sure. I don't think anything is broken in your skull. I was worried about the orbital area, but I think you got lucky.'

'Do I look lucky?'

Jenkins snorted. 'Not a bit. But you're alive and more or less in one piece, and that's a start.'

'Try to keep me that way, would you, there's a good chap.' Alistair was unsurprised at how exhausted he sounded.

Jenkins chuckled. 'I'll do my best. I'm an old quack, but I'll do what I can. Listen,' he said, 'the best thing for you is more sleep.'

'No. I don't want to be unconscious for any further length of time.'

'It would be for the best,' Jenkins argued. 'You'll heal quicker and it won't do you any good to be awake and brooding over what happened.'

'It won't do me any good to be unconscious when there are people out there who put me in here.'

Jenkins patted his arm reassuringly. 'You're safe in here. You're the only guest in this wing. My other patients are in another ward. It's locked and so is this one, so you're safe enough, I assure you.'

'There's no such thing as safety,' Alistair said.

'Well, there's a bleak view.' Jenkins chuckled. 'Well, I'm your doctor, so this is my decision.'

'No,' Alistair protested as he felt pressure on his arm.

A few seconds later there was another sharp prick and he simply waited for sleep to overtake him again.

The Convoy, Part Two

Colonel Pemberton's convoy emerged from a slip-road onto the motorway, heading into London precisely on schedule. The motorcycle outriders held position to the front and rear, with the Land Rovers immediately in front and behind the Bedford. Once on the motorway, the convoy accelerated. It moved at exactly seventy miles per hour, just as planned. Nothing was left to chance.

With the convoy sticking rigidly to the speed limit, they had to overtake slower vehicles, and on occasion, were overtaken by drivers exceeding the maximum speed limit. A number of drivers looked in surprise at the sight of motorcycles on the motorway. A few slowed to look at the convoy curiously, but accelerated again when waved on by one of the outriders or a soldier inside the Land Rovers.

None of the soldiers noticed anything unusual in the sky-blue Cortina, which passed them at a touch over eighty, or the Morris Oxford that followed a minute or so later. They were perfectly ordinary cars, apparently driven by perfectly ordinary men going about their perfectly ordinary days. What was not perfectly ordinary was that as soon as the cars were a quarter of a mile ahead they dropped their speed to seventy and held station just ahead of the convoy. A quarter of a mile behind the convoy two more cars, a green Jaguar and a cream Vauxhall Viva, began to close in on the rear motorcyclists.

The Cortina and Oxford passed an off ramp, leading to a bridge across the motorway two hundred yards ahead. As they passed it, both cars flashed their headlights once. The moment the cars passed under it, four men appeared on the bridge. They waited until the motorcycles were less than a hundred yards from the bridge before hurling suitcase sized packages over the side.

Inside his Land Rover, Colonel Pemberton saw the packages being thrown and reacted immediately. 'Brakes now!' he shouted.

Huge explosions erupted from each of the packages. The motorcycles in the lead had no chance to stop and were engulfed in the explosions. Pemberton's Land Rover slewed into a wild skid as the driver tried to stop before going through the flames. Neither Pemberton nor the driver were wearing seatbelts and both were thrown forward as they braked hard. Pemberton threw out an arm to brace himself against the dashboard. It jarred his shoulder and elbow but saved him from being thrown through the windscreen. He turned to the driver.

'Reverse–'

He was cut off as the Bedford slammed into the back of the Land Rover. The impact threw him forward, crashing his arm against the dashboard and cracking his head viciously on the windshield. He forced himself to remain conscious, refusing to give in to the waves of blackness threatening to envelope him. He forced himself to push the door open and staggered out onto the road.

Broken glass scrunched underfoot and he struggled to clear his head. The back of his Land Rover had buckled. The Bedford took a good deal less damage, but the soldiers inside its cab had been thrown around as their driver tried to avoid hitting Pemberton's vehicle. Pemberton ran around to the back of the Bedford. Knight dropped to the road. He looked shaken but unhurt.

'What happened, sir?'

Pemberton pointed at the flames on the road ahead. 'Somebody on the bridge; three explosives dropped onto the road.'

'An ambush,' Knight said automatically.

Pemberton nodded urgently. 'Eyes sharp. They'll be coming at us from somewhere.'

He barely finished the sentence when he saw two cars screech to a halt on the road behind the convoy. They stopped at angles, blocking the route back. From inside two men quickly emerged and threw canisters which belched smoke as soon as they hit the road. A rattle from near Pemberton's Land Rover told him that the attack was coming from both ahead and behind.

'Smoke bombs,' Knight said. 'Everybody stay sharp!'

The smoke quickly reached Pemberton. The sharp smell caught his nose and throat. 'Tear gas,' he said.

'Cover your mouths and noses!' Knight shouted.

'They'll be coming soon,' Pemberton said. He could feel his eyes beginning to burn and sting. Tears started to pour down his face. He could hear boots hurrying towards them on the road, but he couldn't see a thing. Something hard slammed into the side of his head and he went down. As he fell he heard Knight also come under attack.

Pemberton closed his eyes, trying to ignore the pain. He needed to get to his feet, rally his troops, but his eyes....

He couldn't let his cargo get stolen.

Utrinque Paratus...

CHAPTER FIVE

A day after their meeting with Curator Shehab, Anne, Bill and Sally were aboard a plane returning to London. The curator was as good as his word. They had tissue and soil samples, X-rays, and copies of every document Shehab had on the statues. He also showed them the Armete statues, and when she looked into the yellow, rheumy eye of one of the soldiers and it moved agonisingly slowly, Anne understood why Shehab was willing to take the risk of helping her party. These statues were probably the saddest thing she had ever seen.

The plane was half empty for the return flight and while Sally dozed, Anne read through the history of the statues. After she finished reading she slipped back along the aisle and slid into an empty seat next to Bill.

'We're not supposed to know each other,' he said tersely.

Anne wrinkled her nose and then smiled. 'If anyone asks just say I'm a loose floozy trying to chat you up.' She nudged him. 'Anyway, I've got the potted history of the statues.

'Cheerful reading?'

'Not particularly.'

'All right,' Bill said. 'Tell me.' He settled back in his chair and listened as Anne told the sorry tale.

Thousands of years before, a very old woman of almost eighty related her memories to a young student. The old woman was nine years old when it happened.

During an unusually violent and wild storm, she and her two older brothers saw strange lights and, being children, ignored their parents' warnings to stay away. Green lightning floated in the middle of heavy mist. Twelve soldiers arrived. They looked confident and assured.

The gods saw their confidence as arrogance. A great roar came from the skies and the gods made the lightning explode. The mist faded and the lightning was gone. The soldiers had gone with the lightning and in their place, in a circle of burned ground, stood the stone statues.

In the centre of the stone soldiers and scorched earth, a single stone sat in a hollow. When one of the local men went close to the stone, his skin blistered and burned as the rock gave off a great heat for a day. Nobody wanted to touch the stone, which was smaller than a fist, or to take it back to the village. Until the girl's brother, keen to prove he was as brave as any of the men present, picked it up.

His courage earned cheers from the men and a beating from his mother for being foolish. The statues were left in place so as not to offend the gods, but the small stone was taken to the nearest village. It was largely forgotten for a time until a madness began to sweep through the village.

It was a hysteria which caused those who had been in contact with the stone to become obsessed with it. The girl's brother was among those infected. By the time he was taken by the mania he had grown and was a young man. He was almost killed in his desperation to get to the stone. Others were killed. The village's leaders, in an effort to save their people, sent the stone to Cairo where the wisest minds in the world could study it. Some believed that sending the stone away would offend the gods, and they were proven correct when one of the wise men in Cairo disappeared and was replaced by a statue. That statue was quickly destroyed and the rock placed inside a lead jar and hidden away.

That was where the old woman's memories ended and other documents picked up the story.

The stone remained in a lead jar for over a century and was largely forgotten. It was hidden away, not to be disturbed until the Roman troops of Octavian, fresh from the defeat and death of Marc Antony and the Egyptian Queen Cleopatra, chose to loot several of Egypt's treasures. Among those treasures was a lead jar containing an apparently worthless rock.

From there the stone began a long journey, taking it across the known world. Throughout its travels the rock left a strange trail of madness, separated by decades or even hundreds of years. The records collected by the museum came to an end just after the end of Constantine the Great's reign as Roman Emperor.

From there onwards, Anne and her team would have to rely on the records supplied to them by Hamilton. They also had a number of documents which were only in Egyptian, none of which seemed to be from a point further forward in time.

Bill puffed his cheeks out and blew. 'A cursed stone,' he muttered. 'I'm sure I saw Peter Cushing in a film about that.'

'Quite possibly. So,' Anne said. 'What do you think?'

Bill laughed, but without any humour. 'You're really asking that? I think we don't know nearly enough about this, and I think I'm glad we're heading home.'

'I can't argue with you there. Talking of heading home, I probably should get back to my own seat.'

'Probably,' Bill said. 'On the other hand, you could just let Sally sleep. It'd be a shame to wake her.'

'True,' said Anne, and she settled back into the chair.

Alistair opened his eyes. Actually opened them without the light feeling like it was burning. The swelling had gone down a little in the night. It was remarkable how much better he felt after a night of induced sleep.

He shifted uncomfortably in his bed. Everything still hurt, especially his ribs. On the other hand, he was moving more freely. He looked at his hand. The swelling on the knuckles had all but gone down and the discolouration of the bruising started to show a greenish tinge. That meant it was on the mend.

For the first time he really looked around the ward. Pale, uninspired daylight was coming in through the windows. The sky seemed to be as grey as the walls of the ward. He thought he was alone in the ward until he heard a sound from the bed immediately to his right.

Stretched out on it and completely immersed in a paperback novel was Stanley.

'Did they get you as well?' Alistair croaked.

Stanley gave a small shriek and looked startled. 'You're awake.'

'I hope so. I'd hate to think I was dreaming about you.'

The lag swung his legs over the edge of the bed and stood up, looking down at Alistair with concern. 'You're a mess, son.'

Alistair knew the words weren't meant unkindly. 'I know. At least I don't have to look at it.'

Stanley smiled, but without any humour. 'You know who done it, don't you?'

'I know exactly who did it.'

'So does everybody else in the wing,' Stanley said quietly.

'And that means those three are in charge again. Anybody crosses them they get what you got. Or worse.'

'Have they attacked anyone since me?'

Stanley shook his head. 'Haven't needed to. You've been enough of an example to everybody.'

'It's good to know this has been useful for someone.'

'Listen,' Stanley said. He looked serious, scared and angry. 'That's the sort of smart attitude that landed you in here. This hospital wing, I mean. I don't know what you done to get yourself banged up, but it's your attitude and your mouth since you got in that put you in this bed.' His expression softened. 'You've got to quiet that down, son, or it won't be a hospital bed you're in next time. It'll be a wooden box.'

Alistair didn't answer. He knew Stanley's words were well-intentioned. They did, no doubt, have a good deal of self-interest in them. If his cell mate was beaten or worse, Stanley could get pulled into the whole affair, and Stanley was clear on what he wanted. He was only interested in doing his time before going home to his family. There was little to be gained by arguing with the man.

'How long have I been in here?' Alistair asked instead. He wanted to be certain of his timing, just in case the MO kept him out longer than he thought.

'It's Friday,' Stanley answered. 'You got your hiding on Wednesday. You've been here since.' Alistair nodded in relief. He hadn't lost track of time. Stanley continued, oblivious, 'I'm not surprised you lost track of days. The doc said he'd kept you doped to stop you trying to get out of bed.' He sniffed. 'Why you'd want to get out is beyond me. Best place you could be if you ask me.'

'What were you doing in that bed?' Alistair asked.

Stanley glanced back at the bed he had been resting on. 'Privilege of working at the library,' he said. 'I get to bring books to you poor sods in here, and if there's nobody about, I put my feet up for a few minutes.'

'I won't tell anyone.'

'Good lad.' Stanley turned as he heard the door open.

Mr Fulton was in the doorway. 'What are you doing here?'

'Just bringing the lad a few books to pass the time, Mr Fulton, sir,' Stanley answered.

Fulton entered the ward and flicked his head back at the door. 'You've delivered them now. On your way.'

'Right, sir.' Stanley gave Alistair an encouraging look. 'Look after yourself.'

Fulton crossed to Alistair's bedside and watched Stanley leave. 'Close the door behind you.' He waited until the door was closed before talking to Alistair. 'I heard you were recovering.' He looked at his charge at length. 'Dangerous places, prisons.'

'So I've noticed,' Alistair said warily.

'I imagine you did.' Fulton sniffed. 'Whoever did this to you has probably made their point now. If you stay out of trouble, I imagine you'll stay out of here.'

'Whoever did it?' Alistair choked on the words.

Fulton cut him off. 'Yes, we have suspicions of who it was but there's no proof at all. Nobody saw anything.' He paused before continuing. 'Nobody saw anything at all.'

Alistair clamped his mouth shut. He was in no position to say anything to the contrary and he was in no physical condition for any kind of confrontation. He said nothing.

Fulton nodded his approval at Alistair's silence. 'You're learning.' He spun smartly on his heel and headed for the door. 'Your cell mate is right,' he said, looking back at the hospital bed. 'In this place you have to look after yourself. The MO reckons you're well enough to be back with us this afternoon. I'm not anticipating any more trouble from you.' With that, he left the ward.

Alistair watched him leave. 'Anticipate what you like,' he muttered. 'We'll see.'

'I'm terribly sorry you've had a wasted visit,' Governor Clemence said, 'but I'm afraid regulations are quite clear. The prisoners are only to have visitors on designated visiting days. That applies to prisoners on remand as well as to those who have been convicted.'

Samson didn't back down. 'And what do your regulations say about prisoners your men were too amateur to keep safe?'

The governor's normally calm manner disappeared and he snapped upright in his seat. 'Lethbridge-Stewart was the cause of his own misfortune. Since arriving here he has alienated himself from the other prisoners and has been involved in physical altercations with three convicts.'

'And your officers weren't able to stop him?' Samson asked.

'Steady.' A precise voice came from the back of the room. Samson turned to look at the prison warden who was standing quietly there. He reeked of being ex-military. 'Your officer's the one who got into fights.'

'That's enough, Fulton,' Clemence said to the warder. He turned to Samson. 'Mr Fulton is one of the warders detailed to the wing housing Brig... *Mr* Lethbridge-Stewart. He was one of the warders who found him after the... incident.'

'After he was assaulted,' Samson corrected quickly.

'We're still working out exactly what happened,' Clemence said, equally as quick. 'We will be talking with the prisoner once he regains consciousness and he feels up to talking.'

'That may take a while,' Fulton added. 'The MO doesn't think he'll be up to talking for a few days at least, possibly longer.'

Samson was far from impressed by Fulton's statement. 'Though I assume you'll be starting your investigation before then.'

'We know how to run an investigation,' Fulton replied, obviously irritated by Samson's attitude.

'But not how to protect the men you're supposed to be looking after!' Samson snapped back. He cursed himself for not controlling his temper. He should have known better. There was no doubt that Fulton had real disdain for the Brig, but Samson had seen something else in the prison officer's eye, something he saw too often in too many eyes. But still, he should have his temper under check better than he had.

Governor Clemence spoke, cutting across Fulton. 'We will find out which of the prisoners did this to your officer,' he promised Samson. 'And given that he hasn't been convicted of any crime, we may be able to arrange a visit once he is recovered.'

'*May* be able to?' Samson asked mildly. 'Is that the same way I *may* be able to ensure that my report doesn't leak to the press about how bad your security here is?'

'We don't put up with talk like that in here,' Fulton growled.

Samson resisted the urge to rise to his feet. 'And I'm not one of your prisoners, so I'd advise you watch your tone with me.'

Clemence tried to calm the situation. 'No one is trying to disrespect you, Sergeant Major Ware,' he assured his guest.

'We are all deeply concerned by what has happened to Mr Lethbridge-Stewart, and it is definitely putting us all under strain. I promise you that I will arrange for you to see him as soon as he is able for visitors. It is simply not safe for you to be taken into the prison wing. It currently houses a number of prisoners who have been convicted of violent crimes.'

'Don't worry about me, Governor. I can handle myself.'

Clemence glanced at Fulton. 'Yes, I'm sure. However, we are bound by procedures, and we can't have you on the prison wing. I hope you can understand that.'

Samson thought for a long moment then nodded. 'I understand,' he said. 'But I will hold you to your promise. We'll send someone to see Brigadier Lethbridge-Stewart soon.'

The Super Vickers VC-10, which left a warm, sunny Cairo afternoon a few hours before, arrived in a cold, damp and darkening London precisely on time.

Anne and Sally came through customs and baggage reclaim without acknowledging Bill. They observed security protocols to ensure that they hadn't been spotted or followed before heading back to the Richmond safe house, where Bill arrived an hour later.

'You took your time,' Anne said, opening the biscuit tin. 'We're never leaving the boys alone again. I think they must have lived on biscuits for the last three days.'

Sally held up greasy newspapers. 'And visits to the chippy.'

Anne turned her eyes back to Bill. 'Which doesn't explain why you took so long.'

'Just making sure I wasn't followed.'

Anne scowled at him half-heartedly. 'I think you enjoy this James Bond stuff.'

'More like Harry Palmer,' Bill said. 'But it got the job done. I wasn't sure about one fella at the airport so I took a circuitous route. I stopped off for a quick half, and doubled back. He was gone, probably just a civvie going home, but I wanted to play it safe, so I trebled back and took an exit through a side door.'

'I didn't realise Mons taught spy classes,' Anne said, an amused glint in her eye.

Bill didn't smile in reply. 'Orders said we were to stay incognito. I was just following instructions. And, lest you forget, my skills came in very useful when you and Patricia needed my help.'

'All right,' Anne conceded. 'I'll let you off this time.'

'Anyway,' Bill said, looking around, 'where are the others? I'd have at least expected Samson to be here when we got back.'

'We don't know,' Sally said. 'There was no sign of them when we arrived here.'

Bill grinned. 'Probably skived off to the pictures.'

Sally smiled in return, and set off out of the room. 'I'll let Colonel Douglas know we're back.'

Leslie Johnston read the sheet of paper in his hand a second time. Somehow he wasn't surprised to hear that Lethbridge-Stewart was unable to stay out of trouble in prison. The man couldn't steer clear of trouble if he tried. Johnston expected to hear of some disturbance from Wormwood Scrubs, but he hadn't expected it to come quite so quickly.

The governor's report to the Home Secretary was easy for Johnston to obtain. The report was a thorough job of work from a man who was gifted in being able to make it seem that he was telling a good deal of information without actually saying anything. It was a talent most of the more skilled civil servants learned. Johnston considered himself an expert at it, not that he was a civil servant. Far from it.

One thing in the report caught Johnston's eye. Samson Ware had asked for permission to visit the prison, which was given.

Johnston tapped the edge of the sheet of paper against his chin thoughtfully. He'd never met Ware, but he recognised the name. Shortly after Johnston, Lethbridge-Stewart and Dougie had graduated Sandhurst, Lethbridge-Stewart met Ware on the Kent coast during manoeuvres. They kept in touch for a while, as Johnston understood, until Ware was shipped off to Cyprus. And then the man resurfaced back in August as a stuntman working for LWT.

So, if Ware had visited Lethbridge-Stewart, then the question was why? Concern for an old friend, or something more? Johnston supposed it could have been the former, after all Lethbridge-Stewart had a habit of engendering loyalty in those he met, but Johnston suspected the latter.

Which meant there was another reason for his old friend being inside the Scrubs.

'You went *where?*' Douglas thundered.

Samson blanched under his CO's outburst, but didn't back down. 'I went to the prison.'

'What the devil did you do that for?'

'You told me to find out what his condition was,' Samson answered. He was every bit as angry as Douglas but kept his tone calm.

'Not by just going to the prison and asking!'

'They beat him half to death. You can't expect me to sit here and do nothing about it. We've both known him—'

85

'That's exactly what I expect you to do, Sergeant Major,' Douglas stated firmly. 'And you twisted the meaning of my orders to go there.'

'Wait,' Sally said. Her eyes were wide with surprise and a growing horror. 'What do you mean, *they beat him half to death?*'

Samson turned to her. 'What? He didn't tell you?'

Sally looked at Douglas, who shifted uncomfortably under her gaze for a moment before a stoical mask slid back onto his face.

'You knew he was hurt and didn't tell me,' Sally breathed. She turned to Miss Travers, who looked sheepishly at the floor. 'You knew, too?'

Miss Travers stepped forward. 'Yes, Bill found out when he reported in.'

Sally shook. 'You've known since before we left Egypt?'

'Steady on, Corporal,' Douglas said. 'Miss Travers and Lieutenant Bishop were right to keep it from you. You were on a mission, not a social call.'

'But, it's…' Sally shook her head, and Samson let out a sigh. It was difficult enough for him, after all the years he'd known Alistair, but Sally was his fiancée, it had to be harder for her. As for Douglas…

'He needs to be out of jail,' Samson said. 'It's that simple.'

'No, Sergeant Major!' Douglas snapped. 'It isn't. We have jobs to do, and we will do them.'

Anne could see the situation was deteriorating very quickly, which could mean punches being thrown, judging by the murderous looks on the men's faces. Or Samson ending up on report, either way…

'What Lethbridge-Stewart doesn't need is for us to start

tearing each other apart,' she said crisply. 'He would certainly want us to work together as the team he built to get our jobs done.' Her tone softened as she looked at both Sally and Samson. 'We're all worried about him,' she said, 'but he's in there and we're out here. So we need to do our duty and stick to our plan.'

Samson and Sally looked ready to continue their insubordination, but Samson finally nodded and stood back. 'Yes, ma'am.'

'Fine,' Anne said. And looked at Douglas.

He shook his head. 'Consider yourself on report, Ware,' he said, and turned to Anne. 'What do you need, Miss Travers?'

'I need to requisition some equipment on the QT. I'll need your help for that. And I'm going to need to call in some favours from friends to get a complete analysis of the samples we took.'

Douglas nodded his assent, though Anne would have continued whether he approved or not. 'As long as it's all under the radar and on the hush-hush,' he said.

'Understood.'

Douglas gave each of his group a look in turn, lingering a bit longer on Samson, who refused to look away. 'Right,' Douglas said tightly, 'let's get on with work.'

Doctor Jenkins gave Alistair a final examination before declaring him fit enough to be returned to his cell. He gave his patient a piece of advice before Fulton arrived at the door of the ward.

'Don't let anybody in your block see how badly you still hurt,' Jenkins whispered. 'If you show any weakness, they'll prey on it.'

'I understand, thank you.'

'You really shouldn't be going back to your cell yet,' Jenkins continued, and Alistair wondered if there was pressure from above to return everything to the status quo as soon as possible. That would certainly make the incident easier to sweep under the carpet.

'I could get you an extra couple of days here,' Jenkins offered.

Alistair shook his head. 'Thank you, but I'll be fine.'

Jenkins brought his voice up to a normal level as Fulton approached. 'Now, I want to see you back here every day for a week. Just to keep an eye on how you're mending.'

'Don't coddle the man,' Fulton said sourly. 'This is a prison, not a hotel. Besides, he's a soldier.'

'He's my patient,' Jenkins corrected the warder. He glanced at Alistair. 'I'll see you for a once-over tomorrow.'

'Thank you, Doctor,' Alistair said with a tight smile.

'Hurry along now,' said Fulton.

They entered the wing just as the other prisoners were being gathered together. Alistair didn't doubt it was deliberate. He was being shown off. But whether as an example or a target he did not know. Probably both.

The inmates fell silent as Alistair was led through them to the stairs leading up to his landing. Fulton stopped at Alistair's cell.

'Get settled,' he said. 'You're back among the other inmates from tonight's evening meal.'

'Understood,' Alistair said. 'Sir,' he added a second later.

'Doesn't come easy to you, does it?' Fulton rocked back and forth on his heels as he scrutinised Alistair. 'You've spent years being called "sir". You're not used to saying it to somebody else... Or maybe you just don't like saying it to an

NCO.'

'The army doesn't work without good NCOs,' Alistair replied instantly. 'That was one of the first lessons I ever learned. One of the most important as well.'

'Well, on that we agree.'

'And we all have superiors, even at my rank.'

'Yes, and don't forget that.' Fulton slammed the door shut, locking Alistair back in his cell.

Aware that he had a few hours to kill, Alistair settled onto his bed. It was a lot less comfortable than the one he had left in the hospital and the mattress was a good deal lumpier than he remembered. That was, no doubt, down to the aches he still felt on his back and sides. They went to town on him with their boots. Still, he was on the mend.

Before long, he would, no doubt, be summoned to see Governor Clemence. He was sure that the governor was the one who pushed for him to be returned to the wing early. No one else inside the prison would have that authority.

He was convinced that Clemence wasn't the kind of man who would risk his career by being involved in a beating like this, but it was happening under his command. Damn it, ignorance was never an excuse for any commander. If Clemence didn't know what was going on inside his prison, he damn well ought to. In his time, Alistair had been responsible for prisoners taken in battle. He knew it wasn't an easy job, and prisoners never made the task any simpler, but everything that happened to the prisoners in his charge was a commander's responsibility.

He closed his eyes and drifted off into a light doze.

Alistair's first evening meal back among the general prison population passed without any real incident. Stanley returned to the cell at his usual time and looked pleased to see his cell mate well enough to be back.

The meal was surprisingly palatable. Alistair sat with Stanley. None of the other prisoners chose to sit near them. There was a definite sense of tension in the air, but there was no hint that there would be any trouble at the meal.

After they finished their food, the prisoners had two hours before being locked into their cells. Alistair played a game of dominoes against Stanley before returning early to the cell, protesting that his ribs were still causing him difficulty. On his way back up the stairs to the landing, Alistair was aware that Geggsy and his two cohorts were watching him. His eyes locked with Geggsy. There was a vicious gleam in the thug's eyes.

Lying on his bunk, Alistair knew that more trouble was coming with Geggsy and his friends. Well, that suited him fine. This time it would be on his terms.

When Stanley arrived back at the cell, he was chatty and keen to talk. Alistair let his cell mate carry the conversation. His own mind was focused on the three other prisoners and the best way to deal with them.

A surly looking man in a tan leather coat and a flat cap nonchalantly wandered towards the front of the Richmond safe house and pressed the buzzer. He was carrying a large box which seemed to be filled with fresh fruit. He was buzzed in a few seconds later. He whistled an out-of-tune rendition of The Rolling Stones' *(I Can't Get No) Satisfaction* as he trotted up the pathway. He knocked at the door. There was no one about, but had anyone been paying attention might have noticed how precisely he rapped out the knocks – two, three, one. Ten seconds later the door opened and he entered. The door closed quickly behind him.

Beyond the front door, the delivery man set the box on the floor and snapped smartly to attention, saluting Douglas. 'Sir!'

'At ease, Sergeant,' Douglas said easily. The delivery man relaxed a little – but only a little. 'Any trouble?'

'None, sir,' said Sergeant Pearson.

'Good man.' Douglas nodded at the kitchen. 'Pop the box in there.'

'Yes, sir.' Pearson hefted the box through to the kitchen and set it on the table. It made a substantial thudding sound as he put it down.

'Sounds like a lot,' Douglas said.

'Yes, sir.'

Douglas called Miss Travers through to the kitchen. She arrived a moment later. 'What is it?' she asked.

'Your results are coming in,' Douglas explained. 'In bulk by the way it shook the table.'

'At last.' Miss Travers sounded relieved. She lifted the layers of fruit from the box. Bishop arrived at the door just in time to catch an apple lobbed at him by Miss Travers. 'You'll need your strength to carry this box of papers through to the study,' she said.

'Anything for us, other than these?' Douglas asked the sergeant.

'Yes, sir,' Pearson replied. 'I was ordered to tell you that Brigadier Lethbridge-Stewart has been sent back to his cell.'

Miss Travers looked up from the box, genuinely startled. 'I thought he'd be in hospital for another three or four days at least.'

'Sorry, ma'am. That's the message I was ordered to

deliver.'

'Understood, Sergeant,' Douglas said gruffly. 'Nothing for you to take back.'

Miss Travers prodded the box. With all of the fruit now removed, all that was left was an-almost full box of papers and folders. 'Hopefully we'll know more after trawling through this lot.'

'All right, Sergeant,' Douglas said briskly. 'On your way.'

'Yes, sir.'

Sergeant Pearson carefully adjusted his posture to again resemble the round-shouldered delivery man he appeared to be when he arrived. Back in character, he opened the door and slipped out onto the landing.

Douglas quickly closed the door behind him.

'Would you mind taking the box through?' Miss Travers asked Bishop.

'Right you are.' Bishop picked up the box and disappeared along the hall with it.

Douglas cleared his throat. 'Right then...'

'This isn't good, Walter,' Miss Travers said.

'No, it isn't. But I've known Lethbridge-Stewart a long time; he'll be fine. Besides, they wouldn't let him out of hospital if he wasn't well enough.'

Miss Travers just raised an eyebrow. 'Is that to convince me or you?'

Douglas didn't answer.

'As I thought.' Checking to make sure Bishop was out of earshot, Miss Travers crossed the room. 'I know you're worried about him, just as much as we are. He's your friend, Walter; Samson's friend, too. We've got a long night ahead of us. Perhaps you should go and have a word with Samson? Pop to the local pub, maybe? Unless you want to read all these reports with me?'

For a moment Douglas wasn't sure what to say. Miss Travers was well aware of the need for discipline among the troops, and that Douglas had to maintain that no matter the personal angle. But she was right, too. Samson had known Lethbridge-Stewart almost as long as Douglas had. There was a time and place for pulling rank... He smiled. 'Very well, Anne. I'll leave you and Bishop to your studies. See you in the morning.'

And with that Douglas went off to find Samson.

CHAPTER SIX

Johnston once again looked at the photocopies of Lethbridge-Stewart's injuries. They were bad, but not life threatening. While Johnston had no love for Lethbridge-Stewart, he still considered him an old friend, and disliked the idea of a serving member of the British Army being beaten by a bunch of thugs in jail. Of course, that did make him wonder again exactly why Lethbridge-Stewart was in prison.

His enquiries brought him nothing. Lethbridge-Stewart's solicitors remained quiet over his remand. That was to be expected. Less normal was the silence from the British Government. They were attempting to keep it as quiet as possible for as long as possible. The only mention Johnston heard of Lethbridge-Stewart came a few days earlier when one of his agents had been eavesdropping on old Hamilton.

Some junior on his staff mentioned that Lethbridge-Stewart's injuries weren't life-threatening and that he was recovering. Hamilton's only response was 'pity'. That probably explained why Lethbridge-Stewart's mob up in Edinburgh were so quiet. Hamilton must have told them to keep their heads down and their mouths closed. It would all come out at the trial obviously, though Johnston was damn sure he would find out long before then.

Another titbit of information Johnston gleaned was that a name had been put forward as replacement for Lethbridge-

Stewart as commander of the Corps; one Colonel Maxwell-Lennon. It was a name Johnston had never heard before, and so he put feelers out to discover all he could about the man who would be the new king.

Things changed in the prison on Sunday when Lethbridge-Stewart saw Minty, one of Geggsy's gang moving across an open area and disappearing through a door into a toilet.

Alistair waited, making sure that no one paid any attention to Minty's movements. He slipped backwards into the darkest shadows he could find and moved quietly to the door Minty passed through.

The convict was alone in the bathroom. His back was to the door and there was the harsh sound of a zip being done up. Alistair crossed the small room quickly. Minty didn't have time to turn before a forearm smashed into the back of his neck. His face hit the tiled wall hard and his knees buckled. Alistair pushed forcefully at the back of Minty's head. The convict's head cracked against the wall and he slumped unconscious to the wet floor.

Wiping his hands on his trousers, Alistair quietly slipped out of the toilet and returned to his seat. Nobody noticed his absence and a few minutes later Grimwade came across to join him. They talked about Grimwade's experiences in the army. The ex-soldier had a fondness for reminiscing. Stanley sat with them a few minutes later. Stanley's recollections of National Service were less happy. All three shared memories and laughed until a yell came from the toilet. The warders ran to the toilet. A minute later, Geggsy was pushed out of the toilet and the warders hurried all of the prisoners back to their cells. There was a rumble of interested conversation as the prisoners were herded away.

'What happened?' Stanley asked, craning his neck to get a better look back at the doorway, giving up only when there was no chance of seeing the level below.

For a quarter of an hour, Stanley offered his theory that Geggsy had been caught up to no good in the toilet, either beating somebody up, taking drugs or stealing from other prisoners.

The cell door opened and Fulton entered. He ignored Stanley and focused his attention on Alistair.

'According to Grimwade, you were with him when Mason was beaten up.'

'Mason, eh?' Stanley said. 'Never thought one of Geggsy's mob would get a beating.'

'Quite a thrashing, too.' Fulton's attention didn't shift from Alistair. 'So, you were with Grimwade when it happened?'

Alistair kept his voice calm and even. He was aware that the warder wouldn't believe a word he said. 'I was sitting with Grimwade when someone started causing a commotion.'

'A commotion is one word for it.' Fulton looked down at the bed. 'Mason's quite a size. Whoever worked him over knew what he was doing.'

'Really?' Alistair put as much disinterest into his voice as possible.

'Let's see your hands,' Fulton demanded.

'As you wish.' Alistair sat up and extended his hands for inspection.

'Turn them over,' Fulton instructed.

Alistair did so. The only marking on his hands were the ageing bruises from the attack that landed him in the hospital. 'Are you expecting to see something?'

'Just checking.'

'Did you think I gave... Who was it? Mason? Did you think I gave him a thrashing with my fists?' Alistair flinched his hands into fists. 'I'm afraid my knuckles aren't up to that.'

'No fresh markings,' Fulton said sourly.

'Sorry to let you down.'

Fulton leaned closer. 'I don't know how you did it, but I know you did.'

'In my condition?' Alistair feigned surprise. 'Who did you say it was? Mason? He'd have to be a weak sort to be thrashed without me getting a mark on my hands.'

'Or you're just very well trained.' Fulton straightened. 'Whoever did it had better watch out. I imagine Geggsy will be on the warpath.'

Alistair didn't answer.

'By the way, I made a mistake,' Fulton said, moving towards the cell door. 'It was Minty, not Mason.'

The door closed behind Fulton.

A moment later, Stanley dropped to the floor. He looked at his cell mate, horrified. 'It was you that done him over, weren't it?'

'Probably for the best if I don't answer that.'

Stanley shook his head, looking appalled. 'You ain't listened to a word I said, have you? You bleedin' idiot. You don't give a stuff, do you? You don't give a monkey's what happens.'

Alistair snapped upright and Stanley took a nervous step backwards. 'On the contrary, I care very much what happens. I know exactly what I'm doing.'

Stanley eyed him carefully. 'I believe you do, and you know what? That bloody terrifies me more than anything. Fulton's right. You're trouble.'

'That's hardly the most original observation anyone has

ever made about me,' Alistair said. 'However, I do assure you that I won't put you in any danger.' He smiled. 'In fact, I'll be out of your hair shortly.'

Stanley nervously rubbed the top of his head. 'I'll be lucky if I've still got any hair left after sharing with you.' He paused as Alistair's words sank in. 'You reckon you'll be getting out soon, do you? Fresh evidence?'

Alistair relaxed back onto his bed. 'I imagine you'll be living alone again quite soon.'

Whatever Stanley expected to happen, what *did* happen was considerably more sudden and violent. After lunch, Alistair positioned himself by the stairs, chatting in a relaxed way with both Stanley and Grimwade.

There was an edge in the air after the attack on Minty. Most of the inmates were sure Alistair was the culprit, though none of them knew exactly how he had done it. Some were nervous about the repercussions of the attack on Minty. Others looked on with approval at seeing the wing's thugs taken down a peg.

An hour or so after lunch, Mason and Geggsy came down the metal stairs. Alistair slowly moved away from his friends and stood under the stairs. As Mason's foot landed on the step by his head, Alistair's hand flashed out. He caught the man's ankle and pulled hard. Mason toppled forward, striking his head on the metal railing. Alistair pulled Mason's foot through the gap between the steps and twisted hard. There was a horrific sound of bone against bone, ended only by Mason's horrific high-pitched scream.

Geggsy's head spun as he searched for the cause of his friend's suffering. He saw Alistair and roared with fury. Ignoring his screaming friend, he leaped to the bottom of the stairs and turned to face Alistair. He charged, fist raised. Alistair side-stepped quickly and drove his right hand hard into Geggsy's jaw. The crook staggered. The seconds he needed to regain his balance gave Alistair the opportunity to land a straight left and another hard right.

The convicts gathered around in a tight circle, enjoying the sudden spectacle, chanting and baying as the two prisoners fought.

Geggsy dipped his shoulder and charged. He rammed his shoulder into Alistair's stomach. The pain in his ribs caused his knees to buckle for a moment. He pulled himself together and hooked his arm under Geggsy's chin. Samson called it a front face lock. He locked the muscles in his arms, tightening his grip on Geggsy's neck and he pushed his weight forward, forcing the convict's head down and forward, cutting off the flow of both blood and air. Almost immediately Geggsy began to weaken. The convict threw blind punches into Alistair's legs and body but it was impossible for him to get any weight behind the blows. Geggsy's arms began to slump heavily. Alistair could hear the voices of warders over the baying of the other prisoners. They were trying to get through the tight ranks of the convicts. He was almost out of time. He released his grip on Geggsy and drove his knee upwards, catching the convict on the chin, straightening Geggsy up enough to be defenceless against the brutal right hand that sent the thug sprawling backwards, unconscious before he hit the floor.

The warders finally managed to force their way through the cheering mass of prisoners. Fulton was at the front.

'What's going on?' He saw Alistair. 'You? I might have known.'

Alistair raised his hands out wide to the sides of his body

in submission. 'All right. You'll get no resistance from me.'

'You're damned right we won't!' Fulton shouted. 'Take him to the governor.' He pointed at Geggsy and Mason. 'And get those two to the MO. Quickly now.'

A warder took each of Alistair's arms and marched him away. As he went he offered Stanley a slight smile.

'What on earth made you attack those three men?' Governor Clemence demanded.

Alistair stood stiffly to attention in front of the governor's desk while the desk's occupant seemed uncertain as to whether he wanted to sit or stand, regularly leaping from his chair like a jack-in-the-box.

Alistair indicated the bruises on his face. 'I'd have thought my reasons were rather obvious.'

'Sir!' Fulton bellowed. 'Call the governor "sir".'

'Sir,' Alistair added affably.

'You...' Fulton took a threatening step towards Alistair but was halted by Clemence.

'Stop, Fulton.'

The warder forced himself to take a step backwards. 'Yes, sir.'

'All right,' Clemence said. He sighed and sat heavily. 'While I understand your reasons for taking the action you did, I can't condone them. Neither can I in any way allow them to sway any decision I make here.'

Alistair nodded. 'I quite understand, Governor.'

Clemence flicked through a few A4 pages on his desk. 'Very well,' he said. 'We have a high security area set aside for prisoners who have caused us more difficulty than the rest. You will be transferred there immediately.'

'Sir, he should be punished with a stretch in solitary

confinement at least,' Fulton protested. 'He's put three men in the hospital wing.'

'We only have evidence for one of those,' the governor replied quickly. 'There are no witnesses for him being involved in the attacks on Mason and Mintern. And,' he added, 'I am told that Geggs charged at him, so he could argue self-defence.'

'With all due respect, Governor...'

'With all due respect, Mr Fulton, *I* am the governor of this prison and that is my decision. We cannot make these accusations stick against this man without gathering a good deal of publicity, and I have been ordered to avoid that at all costs.' Clemence closed the folder and pushed it to the side of his desk. 'That's an end of the matter.'

'Thank you, Governor,' Alistair said.

'Oh, no,' Clemence said severely. 'Don't thank me, Lethbridge-Stewart. You're being sent into a much harsher environment. If you behave in Maximum Security the way you have behaved in your current wing, I assure you that your fellow inmates will treat you a good deal worse than Geggs and his friends ever did.'

'Understood, sir.'

'I hope so,' Clemence snapped. 'There's a reason these men are in Maximum Security and small-fry like Geggs aren't. I strongly advise you not to pick a fight in there, Mr Lethbridge-Stewart.'

With that warning, Alistair's interview with Clemence was over. He was returned to his cell to collect his few belongings before being escorted away from the wing.

On his way out he saw appreciative nods from some of the prisoners. Grimwade snapped out a salute. He also saw Stanley shaking his head sadly.

'You was right,' his cell mate said as he passed. 'You did leave pretty quick.'

Alistair offered a wry smile and a shrug in response.

Word soon reached the safe house about Lethbridge-Stewart's transfer to Maximum Security. Immediately Douglas was summoned to a meeting with General Hamilton. He returned a couple of hours later to a tense house.

He called his team together in the sitting room, and once they were all comfortable he said, 'Now that Lethbridge-Stewart has been put in Maximum Security, I've been authorised to tell you exactly what is going on. There's a lot you need to know.'

— CHAPTER SEVEN —

This was not how she expected to start December. Anne reached for the calendar on the table and ripped away the top sheet. Monday 1st. She should have been planning Christmas with her father in Edinburgh, not be stuck in London worried about what was really going on with Lethbridge-Stewart in Wormwood Scrubs.

She was ready to scream.

She sent samples to everyone she could think of for every test she could think of, and every report that came back was telling her the same thing. This was good, rich soil, excellent for farming, solid enough for building on. She knew its chemical makeup, knew the plants that grew there, knew almost everything about the Egyptian location in which the first soldiers had changed to stone. She just didn't know anything useful, and she was starting to wonder if she ever would. She found one report which gave the composition of the stone layer. It had a high percentage of silicon, and there was nothing in its construction she couldn't explain. Until she spotted that a slight trace of radiation had been picked up.

That in itself wasn't a surprise. Space was a radioactive environment. The entire universe had traces of radiation. But the measurement in the report...

She looked at it again, and checked that it wasn't a

misprint. Just to be sure, she phoned an old friend at Cambridge, who confirmed her thoughts on the readings.

'Well,' Anne said once she put the phone down. 'Now *that's* a real mystery.'

Douglas was confused. A look at Samson and Sally told him he wasn't the only one. He found that both reassuring and worrying.

'In English?' he requested, looking at Miss Travers.

'That *was* English.'

Douglas grimaced. 'I recognised most of the words,' he said sourly. 'It's the sentences you put them in that I had trouble with.'

'So did I,' Sally admitted.

'We all did,' Samson added. He nodded at Bishop. 'Except him, of course.'

'It pays to study, Sam,' Bishop said with a grin.

'All right.' Miss Travers sighed. 'Translated for non-scientists. The whole universe is drenched with radiation. It's part of the nature of the universe.'

'Us too?' Samson asked. He sounded concerned.

'Yes. It's at a low level and it's just something that exists and doesn't hurt us.' Miss Travers held up a hand to halt any questions. 'There are lots of different kinds of radiation. This isn't like the radiation from the Hiroshima bomb. It's just there in the background and doesn't cause any trouble.' Her face screwed up slightly. 'Well, most of the time. Just don't worry about it.'

'Okay,' Samson said dubiously. 'We'll forget the radiation.'

Miss Travers laughed. 'The best way to think of this background radiation is like it's a piece of music just bubbling away in the background. You can't hear it unless you really try to.'

'All right, like white noise,' Douglas said.

'Exactly like that.' Miss Travers picked up a folder. 'A friend of mine up at Cambridge did a set of tests on the samples we brought back. The background radiation detected in that soil is wrong.' She paused to find a simpler way to explain it. 'The white noise in that sample is being played at a slightly different frequency than everything else in the world.' She looked around, no doubt waiting to see if they all understood.

'Is that possible?' Douglas asked.

'According to Liz, it should be utterly impossible. Then again, many of the things we've experienced would fall into that category.'

'That's true,' Sally muttered.

'What does it actually mean?' Douglas asked. 'Why is it different?'

Miss Travers shrugged. 'I have absolutely no idea. Lizzie is doing some research into that for me.' She glanced at Douglas. 'Don't worry, she has no idea what this is all about or where we are. However, it does prove that this rock, or whatever it was, definitely didn't originate on Earth.' She paused thoughtfully. 'Neither did it come from anywhere even remotely close.'

'Any idea where it's from?' Douglas asked.

'I haven't the first clue.' Unexpectedly, Miss Travers smiled broadly. 'As a scientist, that's a wonderful challenge for research.'

'And as a soldier, it's a damn inconvenience.'

'Don't worry, Walter,' Miss Travers said. 'I have lots of very interesting ideas.'

'Well, that is good to know,' Douglas said dryly.

*

Superficially, Maximum Security looked to be a more comfortable option than the regular wing of the prison. Alistair was put into a cell on his own. He had to admit that he rather missed Stanley's chatty company, but the move to Maximum Security was imperative.

As with his previous wing there was a communal area, and a small open yard for exercise. The most obvious difference was in the level of security, with warders far more clearly in evidence. There seemed to be at least twice as many as on the regular wing. Every prisoner had his own cell, presumably to avoid them planning any mischief. When he was brought out into the communal area for breakfast on his first morning Alistair recognised many of the convicts.

He had seen a number of them in newspapers, and others he was able to find out about before his incarceration. There was no doubt that he was in the company of the most hardened and unpleasant criminals within the prison. The atmosphere within Maximum Security was also different. In the previous wing, most of the prisoners simply wanted to keep their heads down and avoid trouble. Here, it was clear that many of the convicts were keen to cause as much trouble as they could. The tension all through Maximum Security was a constant. He could feel it. He could almost *taste* it.

Whereas Geggsy and his cronies ran their wing, no single group ran Maximum Security. There were powerful personalities there but there were too many of those strong individuals to allow anyone to dominate. It added to the sense of tension pervading the place.

Alistair took a few moments on that first morning to remind himself of names and faces.

The King Brothers were a pair of East End heavies who

were contemporaries of the Krays, and who tried to fill the void when Ronnie and Reggie were arrested. They lacked the guile to be successful, which was why they were now in prison. They did, however, have the greed, ambition and brutality to be exceptionally dangerous. Several of their heavies were locked up with them in Maximum Security, which made them considerably more dangerous.

On the more intellectual side of crime was Hugh Godfrey, a middle-aged, balding man with the look of a bank manager, but who was recently convicted of racketeering, running brothels, black marketing, and smuggling. His genial exterior hid a venomous nature. He was responsible for countless gangland murders over the years, though only ever through orders. He had always been careful to keep himself clear of doing the dirty work himself. He was a rival to the King Brothers and the Krays but studiously avoided the limelight the brothers sought. He was obvious about his criminal behaviour and he never flaunted his wealth or socialised with showbusiness celebrities. It was a job to him. It was business. However, his arrest made the front page of most of the newspapers. Alistair recognised the man immediately.

There were others Alistair recognised, and he would be wise to be wary of most of them. There was only one man in Maximum Security he didn't recognise at all, and he was another newcomer to the wing. This man looked solidly built and hard enough to look after himself. There was something in the man's eyes that said he didn't belong in that company. He had bruised knuckles, and came off worst in a fight with a warder, which landed him in Maximum Security. His name was Nolan, and there was no doubt that if any of the inmates ever wanted to make an example of someone, Nolan would be their choice.

As it transpired, at lunch, Nolan sat near Alistair.

'Mind if I sit here? Looks like I'm not welcome anywhere else.'

'Neither am I. I only arrived in here last night.'

'They never like the new boys.'

'I noticed. I'm Alistair.'

'Nolan.' The convict introduced himself, although Alistair already knew his name, and pushed a spoonful of porridge into his mouth. 'Why did they put you in here?'

Alistair indicated Nolan's bruised knuckles. 'Probably the same reason as you. I didn't get on with some of the people I was sharing a wing with.'

Nolan chuckled. 'Looks like there's a lot of people it's hard to get along with inside this place.'

'I'd say so.' Alistair cast a quick glance around the room.

'You don't fit in here,' Nolan said cautiously. 'There are a lot of different types in here but you're different. You've got more education, more class.'

'Is that a compliment?'

'It's a fact. You don't fit. You're the only posh one in here.'

Alistair snorted. 'I'm hardly posh.'

'You seem posh enough, like the bunch you see in the paper or on telly with the double-barrelled names...' He paused as Alistair raised an amused eyebrow. 'Wait, you're not double-barrelled, are you?'

'Lethbridge-Stewart.'

'Well, there you go.'

'But I assure you I'm not posh. Far from it.'

Nolan laughed. 'That makes two of us. Where you from?'

'Originally a small Cornish village, would you believe?'

Nolan laughed. 'Going by your accent, no.'

'Well, like you said, I've got education,' Alistair said,

doing his best to sound self-depreciating.

Nolan nodded. 'Fair enough. Mind if I ask what you're in for?'

'Nothing yet. I'm on remand.'

'For?'

'For about a week so far.'

Nolan raised his hands in defeat. 'All right. You don't want to say. That's fine.'

'I was advised not to discuss the matter.'

'By your brief?' Nolan nodded. 'Sounds like what they'd say. You never know who's listening in here, that's what my dad said.'

'He had experience?'

'You could say I'm following a family tradition being in here. Or you could say I was stupid enough to let him talk me into something because he was my dad, and then he legged it and left me to get nabbed. He was a rotten dad when he was inside. Who'd have guessed he'd be a worse one when he was on the outside?'

Before lunch they spent an hour in the open exercise yard. It was an enclosed area with walls of old stone and newer brick, and too high for anyone to consider climbing. A small corridor that opened out into the yard had the same rough stone walls. The yard was angular, with a few areas recessed by a foot or so. The protruding sections seemed to be made of larger stones, so Alistair took the odd design to be structural rather than aesthetic.

A football was produced, resulting in a boisterous game that didn't seem to have any set sides. Alistair excused himself, protesting that his ribs were still bruised, besides he was more of a rugger man, he told them. Nolan, on the other hand, threw himself into the game. Most of those who didn't play watched the game with interest, shouting and cheering. Alistair took the chance to drift away from the crowd.

He leaned against the wall at the far end of the yard, ostensibly watching the football from a distance. He spent the rest of the exercise period staying out of the way of the game, slowly wandering around the perimeter of the yard, sticking close to the wall. He was relaxed, and looked like he was simply avoiding the hurly burly of the game. When the warders called an end to the game, Alistair simply rejoined Nolan as the men were led back inside to be returned to their cells.

'Enjoy the game?' he asked, as they passed through the little stone corridor.

'Loved it. Bit rough but pretty good fun.'

'And a good chance to meet our fellow inmates?'

'Nothing like kicking lumps out of each other for getting to know folk,' Nolan said with a chuckle. 'Though I think it'll take a lot more than a kick-about to make me everybody's best mate.'

'Quite probably,' Alistair agreed.

He felt Nolan nudge his arm. 'You should join in. Wouldn't do you any harm to be one of the lads.'

Alistair nodded. 'I understand.' He tapped his ribs. 'Just give me a few days to let the ribs mend a bit.'

'All right,' Nolan agreed.

Once they were back in their cells, Alistair relaxed on his bunk. He ran through the way events were progressing and took a deep, contented breath. Everything was going exactly as he needed it to.

The North Pasture Graveyard in London had been full since

the earliest days of the twentieth century. Any children of those laid to rest in the cemetery were, for the most part, dead themselves. The graveyard received few visitors and acted mostly as a shortcut from a housing estate to local shops and a school. During the day it was also a favourite spot for locals in search of a quiet place to drink in the open. At night it was a popular place for couples who were unable to find peace and quiet to go in search of privacy to kiss and cuddle. Despite the occasionally wayward antics of those who frequented it, the council's gardening department impeccably tended the graveyard.

Standing in the heart of the cemetery, Anne found it a beautifully serene place. The cobbled paths wound through the tidily mown grass and rows of gravestones. A winter breeze whistled softly in the branches of the trees. All in all, she thought it wasn't a bad spot to spend eternity.

'Which way?' Bill asked. He was dressed in jeans and polar-neck, around which was wrapped a thick scarf, with a leather jacket done up against the lunchtime chill, but his eyes were on the constant lookout for trouble. Anne smiled. Anyone with even half a brain would have him twigged as army or police as soon as they clapped eyes on him.

'This way,' she said after quickly reading the hand-written notes in a small black notebook that she's found in one of the boxes. Following the directions she had written, she led Bill along a path, under a tree which tenaciously clung to its thick canopy of leaves despite winter's icy fingers pulling at it. The path took a tight turn to the left, stopping at a secluded mausoleum. Standing on either side were two stone figures dressed in Victorian clothes.

She inspected the statues. The first had no hints of its human origins, but the second was more forthcoming. The lace pattern on the dress on the underside of her left arm had some give in it. Anne took a sample of the lace. Beneath it she could make out a hint of soft tissue. She took a sample of that, too. The tissue was grey but after she took her sample the tissue seeped a dark, unhealthy blood. A stab of guilt hit Anne.

'I'm sorry,' she said to the statue. 'I'm not sure if you can hear me, or if you understand what I'm saying, but what I did was to try to help. I really don't know what we can do for you but we'll do everything we can, I promise.' She saw Bill watching her with a strange expression on his face. 'Don't look at me like that,' she scolded him. 'These people have suffered enough. If we're going to experiment we should at least do it with sympathy and respect.'

'I know,' Bill answered. 'I was just remembering what happened on Santorini.' He shuddered. 'Really going off statues, I have to admit.'

'I know what you mean. Makes me think, though,' Anne said. 'I should have taken samples from the soldiers in Egypt.'

Bill was examining the nearest statue. 'Why?' he asked.

'To see how they alter over time, maybe even work out how they can still be alive.' She sighed and peered at the impassive stone face in front of her. 'If you can call this any kind of living.'

'It's not something I'd like to go through,' Bill admitted. 'I know this is different to the Mutalith, but I spoke to Owain before he left Santorini. To think something similar happened to lads I might have served with...'

'Be grateful it wasn't you,' Anne said, touching his arm briefly. She spoke to the statue quietly for a few moments before turning back to Bill. 'All right. We're finished here.'

The Convoy, Part Three

Ready for anything, that was the moto of 1 Para, and Pemberton was damned if he'd let this ambush make a mockery of that!

Both he and Knight clamped cloth over their mouths, but it did little good. They were still blinded for a few seconds by the tear gas, which was heavier than the air and clung to the ground, rising no more than twelve or fifteen feet from the road. After what seemed like forever, the gas was caught up by a breeze and dissipated slightly.

They started to recover, pouring water from their canteens into their eyes to cleanse them. Their eyes still hurt like hell and watered heavily, but at least they could see.

'Get the men,' Pemberton cried, with a choked sound.

They grabbed their troops and hauled them onto a grass verge unaffected by the gas. Up ahead, the road was still in flames.

'They didn't go that way,' Pemberton said. He splashed water in his eyes again and swilled a mouthful before spitting it out.

Knight looked back along the road. A tailback of cars had formed a hundred yards or more behind them. In the distance they could hear the wail of a siren. In the far distance, the flashing of a police car's light. 'They didn't go east, and they didn't go west.'

Pemberton pointed at an off ramp they passed a little way back. 'They must have taken that.'

'Did they get the cargo?' Knight asked. 'That has to be what they came for.'

'Stay here,' Pemberton instructed.

He ran to the Bedford and made to climb into the back. He pulled open the flap, and a waft of tear gas hit him in the face. He dropped back down and waved it out of his face. The covering over the back of the Bedford kept the gas out initially, but it eventually seeped through the gaps. Certain that the gas had dispersed, Pemberton climbed onto the back of the truck once more and threw the canvas flaps wide open. When he did, he saw the buckled wreckage of the cage surrounding the safe, and the door of the safe open.

As he feared, their cargo was gone.

Knight was seeing to the troops, instructing them to sluice their eyes and mouths from their canteens.

'Get to the vehicles!' Pemberton bellowed, running towards them. 'They can't have gone too far.'

'Some of the men aren't up to it, sir,' Knight reported. 'Carlisle and Lyndon went at them and were worst affected. Brave, but it's left them out of commission. I'd say seven are down.'

'Damn it. Can't be helped. We'll have to leave them for the police to look after. Get them moving, Captain.'

Knight reacted immediately. 'Come on you lot. You heard the colonel. Move sharp. Land Rovers only.'

'Lyndon,' Pemberton called to the tall, blond corporal, who was hurriedly washing out his eyes.

'Nearly ready, sir.'

'No,' Pemberton said firmly. 'I'm leaving you in charge

here. Explain to the police what happened and get yourself and the men to hospital. Got it?'

'Yes, sir.'

Pemberton ran to his Land Rover. It lived up to its reputation for toughness. Despite having been shunted by the Bedford, the Land Rover was still fully operational. Knight took over behind the wheel. He pulled away before Pemberton had the door closed.

Knight pushed the car up through the gears, dropping briefly to second to take the near one-hundred-and-eighty-degree turn onto the off ramp. The road led up a steep hill to a roundabout. The Land Rover's new four-wheel drive easily dealt with the incline.

'There,' Pemberton called and pointed at a black streak from the tyres of a car moving too quickly.

'It's a guess, sir,' Knight warned, swinging the wheel hard.

'It's all we have. Do you know this road?'

'Not well. Wrong side of the city for me.'

'Never mind.' Pemberton yanked an Ordinance Survey Map from the dashboard. He pored over the weaving lines. 'This is a straight road,' he said. 'No way off it for fifteen miles.'

'They have at least a five-minute head start on us, sir. They'll have covered half of that distance by now.'

Pemberton sucked his lip thoughtfully. 'They'll know that we will have made contact with the authorities, blocking their way into London. They've got to be expecting roadblocks.'

'They'll have to cut off somewhere.'

Pemberton was already scouring the map for potential escape routes. He found two likely options. 'It'll be one of these two,' he said. 'One is a bit of a winding road that eventually leads to the motorway. The other goes to a village.'

'It's a lot easier to hide a car in a village than on a motorway, sir.'

'My thoughts as well,' Pemberton said quickly. 'Second off ramp.'

'Yes, sir.'

Pemberton flicked a glance at the speedometer. The Land Rover was running at just under seventy. 'Can this thing go any faster, Knight? I don't give a damn about the speed limit.'

Knight shook his head. 'They're not built for speed, sir. We're only at seventy because the chaps in the garage soup the engines up for us.'

'Damn. Just give it everything you've got.'

— CHAPTER EIGHT —

A n unruly game of football again dominated the exercise period. Alistair remained on the outside, watching as he leaned against the wall. Hugh Godfrey was another who watched the game rather than participated. Unusually, neither Brian Kearney nor Jan Pieters played in the game. Brian Kearney was an Irish Republican who had moved to London to make money after his actions made life in Ireland too hot for him. Jan Pieters was a South African who came to London on business early in the '60s and found the work to his liking, the work in question being debt collecting. They were both brutal and known to be regular hands for the King Brothers. Alistair watched them with interest. They were studiously observing the match for the most part, but both constantly glanced at Godfrey, keeping close to him. That Godfrey was paying them no attention, and that they were being so clandestine about their surveillance, told Alistair everything he needed to know.

Slowly, they made their way towards him, one from either side. Their progress was slow and could only have been noticed by someone distanced from the proceedings.

Alistair moved around the wall, keeping a careful watch on them. He saw Pieters' hand slip into his pocket, and something metallic glinted in the sunlight when he withdrew it again. A knife of some sort. Pieters caught Kearney's eye

117

and nodded. They made their move.

Kearney caught Godfrey's arms and pinned them behind his back. Pieters drove his blade towards Godfrey's gut.

It didn't reach there.

The South African screamed in pain as Alistair slammed his fist down on Pieters' arm. His grip on the blade loosened and Alistair saw the bowl of a spoon in the man's hand. He barely recognised the sharpened point of the spoon before it was rammed towards his stomach. Training took over and Alistair moved to the side, catching Pieters' wrist. He brought his knee up and drove Pieters' wrist down onto it. The thug's hand opened and he dropped the spoon. He roared with anger and pushed Alistair away. Kearney released Godfrey and charged towards Alistair.

The fight was evened as Nolan slammed into Kearney's side. Before Kearney could stand, Nolan was on him, punching him hard, slamming his fists into the man's face. Alistair took advantage of the distraction to strike Pieters' solar plexus before punching the man hard on the point of the chin, putting him down to one knee. A knee to the side of the head sent the South African sprawling.

Warders were already separating Nolan and Kearney. Alistair took a step away from Pieters and held his arms out wide to the side. One of the warders scooped up the spoon, just ahead of one of the prisoners. The five prisoners involved in the skirmish were quickly marched out of the yard while the others were herded against the furthest wall.

Warders came to collect Alistair. He was marched down the steps to the communal area where Nolan and Godfrey were waiting under guard. The warder in charge, a huge man by the name of Richards, rapped out instructions.

'No talking, you three. Keep it quiet and show respect when you're being questioned.'

They were marched through the corridors to the governor's office, where a thoroughly annoyed Governor Clemence sat waiting.

'Well,' he said, immediately turning his attention to Alistair. 'You seem to be a magnet for trouble, don't you?'

'It would seem so, sir.'

Clemence sniffed uncomfortably. 'Well, in this case, I have to say I'm rather pleased it does.' He nodded at Godfrey. 'I've taken reports from all of my officers. They tell me this man would likely be dead if you hadn't intervened.'

'That was how I read the situation, sir.'

'And what is Godfrey to you?'

Alistair answered quickly. 'He was one man about to be murdered by two. It didn't seem right to me.'

Clemence's gaze shifted to Nolan. 'And you became involved how?'

'Alistair was down two to one. *That* didn't seem right to *me*.'

'I appreciate it,' Alistair said quickly. 'Thank you.'

'Quiet, you,' Richards barked. 'Speak when you're spoken to.'

Clemence ignored the interruptions. 'Godfrey,' he said, struggling to keep the disdain from his voice. 'Why were you targeted by these men?'

'I'm afraid I have no idea, Governor,' Godfrey replied coolly.

The governor's expression left no doubt that he didn't believe Godfrey. 'I'm sure you don't,' he said sourly. 'However, I would advise you strongly to try to remember. This was a serious attempt on your life.'

Godfrey spread his hands wide and smiled benignly. 'And I am completely unharmed. As a businessman, I'm aware that there are risks in this world, Governor, but I have complete faith in you and your warders, and in your ability to keep me safe. After all, none of us want the legal trouble, not to mention the paperwork that would be needed if you did allow something to happen to me.'

Even Clemence, normally a man well able to keep his anger in check, looked incensed by Godfrey's tone. He forced himself to remain calm.

'We do our utmost to keep every inmate of this prison safe,' he said icily. 'Of course, there will be a full inquiry and you will all be questioned at length. However, having heard the reports of my warders, I'm content to return you to your cells now and put you back into the population of your wing, though everyone in Maximum Security will be under constant scrutiny from the warders, just to keep an eye on things. You won't have to worry about the other two involved. I spoke to them a few minutes ago and they have been moved to solitary confinement until this matter is resolved.' He indicated to Richards that the meeting was over. 'Take them back please, Mr Richards.'

'Yes, sir.'

Richards led the three prisoners back to their wing, keeping the three men quiet and ensuring there was no conversation. Which suited Alistair just fine.

Life in the wing returned to normal the next morning. Alistair ate breakfast with his fellow inmates. He chose to sit alone but was soon joined by Nolan and Godfrey.

'Mind if we join you?' Nolan asked.

Alistair frowned slightly. 'You don't usually ask, Nolan.'

'I'm usually alone,' Nolan answered quickly. 'Mr Godfrey would like to talk to you.'

Alistair's eyebrow raised quizzically. '*Mr* Godfrey?'

'Yeah,' Nolan confirmed. '*Mr* Godfrey.'

Alistair sat back in his chair and stared at Godfrey. 'All right,' he said after a moment. 'Feel free to sit.'

'Thank you.' Godfrey sat opposite Alistair, with Nolan at his side. 'Alistair – may I call you Alistair?' Alistair nodded and Godfrey continued. 'I wanted to thank you for what you did yesterday. I wouldn't be here if you hadn't stopped Pieters.'

Alistair held up his spoon. 'It would hardly have been a dignified obituary. Murdered by a spoon.'

Godfrey chuckled. 'It wasn't my dignity I was worried about.'

Alistair spooned more porridge into his mouth. It was the worst he had ever tasted. 'I quite understand,' he said. 'They were certainly keen to kill you.'

'I noticed that, as well.'

'Why now, though? How long have you and they been in here together?'

'Months,' Godfrey answered. 'Probably six months at least.'

'So why did they attack now? What changed?'

'Apart from your arrival?'

'Apart from that,' Alistair confirmed.

Godfrey pulled himself upright. 'I'm a businessman.'

Alistair looked him in the eye. 'And I'm aware of what kind of business you're in. I read the newspapers.'

'Good,' Godfrey said easily. 'That means there's no need for beating about the bush.' He leaned forward. 'The King Brothers and I are rivals outside this place. We all want to take what Ronnie and Reggie had and add it to our own territory. With good behaviour I'll be paroled in eighteen months.'

'What about the King Brothers?'

Godfrey shook his head with a malign grin. 'Five years at least. However, that doesn't mean they don't have their hands on what their firm is up to.'

'Just as you have control over your... business interests?'

'Absolutely. We're moving against each other even now as we speak.' Godfrey leaned even closer. 'They know I have something I can use against them and they want me out of the way before I make my move.'

'What do you mean, something you can use against them?' Alistair asked. 'Information? Evidence of some kind of crimes?'

'That's none of your concern,' Godfrey said quickly.

Alistair shrugged. 'I'm happy to keep it that way.'

Godfrey scrutinised Alistair for a moment. 'What are you in for?' he asked. 'What did they send you down for?'

'Nothing.'

Godfrey snorted again. 'Everybody says the same when they get here. Come on. What are you in for?'

Alistair carefully supped another spoon of porridge before answering. 'I'm on remand,' he answered. 'There's no date for my trial yet.'

'Interesting. You must have been a bad lad to land in here on remand. They normally prefer to take it easy on you lot.'

A half-smile tugged at the corners of Alistair's mouth. 'They won't be taking it easy on me, I assure you.'

'That suits me,' Godfrey said bluntly. 'You saved my neck yesterday. That made me realise that I need some protection in here. More than the governor and the warders will give. You're handy in a fight, and you were able to see it coming.

You're obviously ex-military. I could use a man like you to make sure nothing happens to me while I'm here.'

Alistair made a point of appearing surprised by the idea. 'You're offering me a job?'

Godfrey leaned closer. 'And I'll make it worth your while, too.' He nodded sideways at Nolan. 'Your friend here has already taken my shilling.'

Alistair flicked his gaze to Nolan. 'Is that true?'

Nolan nodded. 'It makes sense, Alistair. Mr Godfrey's a powerful man. If we keep him safe, we get paid and when we get out we get looked after.'

'Looked after?'

'You know, work.' The idea clearly appealed to Nolan. 'You can make good money as part of one of the big firms. They look after you. It's safer being part of one of the big outfits.'

Alistair remained impassive and let the moment stretch as though he was seriously weighing the notion. 'Thank you for the offer,' he said finally, 'but I'm not interested. I'm not for hire and I'm definitely not for sale. I haven't been found guilty of anything.' He paused for a moment before adding, 'And I don't expect to be either.'

'Think you're getting out of here, do you?' Godfrey asked. 'Everybody feels that way for a while. You'll get it knocked out of you.'

Alistair sat back and eyed Godfrey warily. 'Perhaps. Perhaps not. Look,' he said, carefully measuring his words to hit their target. 'I have no personal grudge against either of you. In fact, I'm grateful to Nolan for sparing me another beating, but I'm not interested in being anyone's hired muscle. The answer is no.'

Godfrey was clearly a man who was not used to being

refused, but he made no attempt to change Alistair's mind. 'If that's your choice it's your choice,' he said, taking his breakfast over to another table. Nolan followed, pausing only for a moment to look back at Alistair and shake his head sadly.

After having had the company of Nolan for a day, Alistair was back to being alone. He remained wary and watchful of everything happening in the wing. Nolan now went everywhere with Godfrey, and he could see the King Brothers smarting after losing two of their favourite lieutenants. However, nobody bothered him and he bided his time, relishing those hours when he was allowed out into the yard for exercise.

When the football match went ahead, now without Nolan, Alistair remained detached, watching the game while leaning on the wall.

Anne's contacts worked quickly and their results made for interesting reading.

The tissue samples from the British soldiers, and the statues from the cemetery, had been tested by Anne's friend in Cambridge. All exhibited the same form of radiation as the soil samples from Egypt. The soft tissue samples were similarly irradiated. Quite how the radiation affected the cellular decay and slowed degeneration, Anne wasn't sure. In fact, as test results came back to her she began to wonder if there was only one way to actually begin to understand what happened.

It was possible that she could only find the truth by dissecting one of the statues.

Douglas visibly paled when she raised the prospect of cutting into one of the statues. 'Aren't they still alive?'

Anne puffed her cheeks out and blew hard. 'And that's the problem. One of them anyway, along with how on earth I'd go about actually doing any examination or post mortem.'

'Particularly while keeping it quiet,' Douglas agreed. 'I'm assuming you have a few answers to go with your questions.'

'Not a one,' Anne admitted sadly. 'Although the unusual radiation is equally as strong in all of the samples, so it's not like a half-life where radiation fades over time. This is constant. The effects seem to be as potent now as they were two thousand years ago.'

Douglas leaned back in his chair, pushing his spine against the back of the seat and stretching. 'I read the reports. The Victorian one was useless. Nobody saw anything at all.'

'No. They were all distracted by the storm.'

Douglas snorted. 'Well, they didn't have telly, or even radio.'

'Though there was a storm back in the Egyptian reports, too,' Anne said thoughtfully. 'I wonder if that's a coincidence?'

'But there wasn't a storm at the most recent event,' Douglas pointed out. 'It was warm and sunny.'

Anne started rifling through papers. 'I wonder,' she muttered. 'I wonder.'

Leslie Johnston was going through papers and like Anne Travers he had a breakthrough. It was quite a minor event in the great scheme of things. He wasn't surprised that he hadn't noticed it before. Logs from a High Security storage facility just outside London showed that Douglas' mob had been signed in twice within the space of a week or so... The week or so when they were supposed to be laying low in Edinburgh waiting for the dust around Lethbridge-Stewart to settle. One visit could be easily dismissed. Two? That suggested a pattern. It also suggested they had an interest in something there.

Johnston glanced at his watch. It was too late to make the trip that day, but he could spare a few hours the next morning to ease his curiosity.

He also received information on Colonel Maxwell-Lennon. Or rather, no information. No such officer existed in the British Army. Which, for Johnston's money, meant a lot of powerful people were involved in the subterfuge surrounding Lethbridge-Stewart's life inside. Why else create a fictional officer and put out word that he was taking command of an outfit like the Fifth Operational Corps? Lethbridge-Stewart's cover story was deep, and very well thought out.

It was too late to visit that storage facility, but it wasn't too late to make a few more calls. All he needed was some names, something to help him put together the puzzle of Lethbridge-Stewart's incarceration.

The Convoy, Part Four

K night had his Land Rover flat out at seventy with the second vehicle keeping pace close behind. They were both well over the speed limit for a country road but Pemberton demanded that Knight keep the speed up. Eventually the captain had to slow as they reached the outskirts of a village. The sign said they were half a mile from Durnham.

Pemberton checked his map. 'Small village. Pick the speed up when we're through.'

'Yes, sir.'

Durnham was a quintessentially English village with a small green, a few rows of houses and even less shops to serve the community. They passed the village's only garage as they entered. From the look of the locals, the village also served a number of farms in the area.

Knight took his speed down to twenty-five. As the road turned to exit the village, Pemberton spoke quickly.

'Park on the verge,' he said.

'Sir?' Knight was confused, but did as he was told.

'Why would a garage be closed in a village like this in the middle of the day?' Pemberton asked. 'It's the only one in the village, so this would be one of its busiest times.'

'I suppose it is a bit odd, now you mention it.'

Pemberton climbed out and walked over to the second

Land Rover. 'We're taking a look in that garage,' he told the corporal at the wheel.

'You think they've hidden out in there, sir?'

'We'll soon find out.' Pemberton walked back to the Land Rover and lifted the canvas flap at the back. 'Come on, you lot,' he ordered, while Knight did the same with their Land Rover.

While the men disembarked from the vehicles, Knight joined Pemberton.

'How many lads have we got, Ben?'

'Around ten, sir.'

Pemberton nodded firmly. 'It'll have to do. Let's get moving. No talking.'

They ran through the village at a quick trot. Before coming into sight of the garage, Pemberton split their forces in two. Half of the men were put under Knight and he kept the other half with himself.

'Take your lads around the back,' he ordered Knight. 'Make sure they don't escape that way. If they're in there,' he added.

'Right, sir.'

Pemberton caught Knight's arm. 'I'll make the first move from here. If they're inside, we'll have them trapped between us. No risks, Captain.'

Knight smiled. 'As if I would.'

For a moment Pemberton watched Knight take command of the section. *Good soldier, that one, will go far. Be giving me orders before long*, he thought, with a little bit of pride.

Knight and his troops quickly moved off, slipping between two buildings. Out past the small gardens they turned right, using garden hedges and fences to cover their progress.

Once he and his own section were under cover, Pemberton

checked his watch. Knight had enough time to reach his agreed position by now.

'Right,' Pemberton said briskly. 'Keep to the left, in the shadows. Stay under cover as long as you can. Take no chances. If they're in here, they're organised and undoubtedly armed.'

They moved with the precision and speed Pemberton expected from his troops. Quiet, flitting from shadow to shadow, staying out of sight of the garage as long as they possibly could. Between the last house and the side of the garage was a gap of around ten yards. Crossing that forecourt, he and his men would be visible to anyone watching from inside the garage, Pemberton knew, but there was no alternative. At Sandhurst, instructors drilled into young cadets' heads that they should never ask their men to do anything they wouldn't do themselves, and so Pemberton took the lead, running from the cover of the building to the side of the garage. One by one, his four troops ran to join him. Their luck held until the last of the men was making his run.

A gunshot cracked in the air and the soldier dropped to the asphalt, clutching a wound in his leg.

Pemberton didn't hesitate. 'Return fire.' He loosed two shots from his Browning pistol at the window from where the gunshot came. He ran and threw open the small door set into the garage's sliding doors, and dived through. He heard bullets ping off the concrete wall behind him, and he dived behind a workbench. He loosed another couple of blind shots around the side of the bench and was relieved to hear the roar from a Colt M16 rifle at the door. The first of his men were through.

He risked a glance around the bench and saw the enemy

panicking. There were four of them, shouting at each other and trying to take cover behind their cars.

Pemberton's men spilled in and took what cover they could. Gunfire fizzed back and forth for a few seconds before the windows and door at the back of the garage disintegrated under a hail of fire from Knight's men.

Pemberton heard a cry of 'More of them!', and another of 'Get out of here!', through the gunfire. The thieves threw themselves into their cars and drove straight at the old wooden doors on their side of the garage. The first of the cars smashed the doors open.

'Shoot the tyres!' Pemberton bellowed to the soldier nearest the door.

The trooper let loose a burst and Pemberton heard a screech and a thump as the car hit something and came to a sudden stop.

Pemberton ran out onto the forecourt. The lead car had smashed into the petrol pumps. The nearside door was wide open and he could see the stolen cargo had spilled out onto the ground. The metal case was open, and a dull black rock, smaller than his fist, fell onto the ground. Pemberton looked around and noticed that petrol had spilled from the ruptured petrol pumps and was flooding the forecourt.

His men ran for the item. Immediately the thieves from the front car opened fire from behind their car.

'Stop!' Pemberton bellowed. 'Cease fire. The petrol...'

A stray bullet hit one of the pumps.

A huge explosion tore through the air, blasting Pemberton backwards off his feet. He landed painfully, expecting the petrol station to erupt into a ball of flame. But the explosion simply stopped. It was as if the explosion had been switched off half way through. Pemberton's ears were ringing and the blast knocked the wind from him. He tried to rise to his feet, tried to make his legs work but they wouldn't obey him. He dropped back to the ground hard.

He was vaguely aware of his men standing still ahead of him as a figure ran out and collected the stolen cargo. A car came out of the garage. It must have been the second car. It pulled away and screeched along the road out of the village.

Pemberton tried again to rise and forced his legs to obey him. It was only after a moment he realised that hands were under his arms helping him to rise. He turned to find Knight holding him.

Pemberton tried to speak but he was still struggling for breath. His knees felt like jelly and his head pounded. *Concentrate. Focus on the job.* He sucked deep breaths in and made himself talk.

'Situation report, Captain.'

Knight opened his mouth to speak. He seemed to be having trouble forming words as well.

'Get a grip, Knight,' Pemberton choked out.

The rebuke stung Knight into action. 'Best you see for yourself, sir.'

Knight helped Pemberton take a few steps towards his men.

'Why are they standing there?' Pemberton demanded. 'Get after that car.' The men didn't move. 'You heard me. Get after them.'

'They can't hear you, sir,' Knight said in a hollow, shocked voice.

'What are you talking about?' Pemberton reached the nearest of his men, and then he saw it.

They were just standing there, frozen. He recognised their faces, recognised the fear in their expressions, but impossibly, each of the men was turned completely to stone in the blast.

Pemberton's knees buckled and he toppled to the ground, despite Knight's efforts to catch him. His stomach heaved and he threw up on the asphalt. There was a small amount of blood mixed in with the vomit.

The surviving soldiers looked at their frozen comrades, and Pemberton knew that he had failed them all.

— CHAPTER NINE —

R SM Sandy Cowie had a long career behind him. One of the reasons he prospered in that career was that he was an excellent judge of character, and he knew that about himself. He trusted his instincts when it came to people. It helped him read situations and saved the lives of men under his command on numerous occasions. When he met Leslie Johnston he took an instant dislike to the man. Every instinct told him that this man was not to be trusted. Of course, he remained cordial and pleasant to his visitor.

Johnston arrived early Wednesday morning with papers showing his authority, given to him by the Ministry of Technology, signed by Prime Minister Harold Wilson himself. They also showed he was once a lieutenant in the 5th Infantry Brigade. Thus, Johnston outranked Cowie considerably, and this was an occasion when Cowie followed the old army adage that you should respect the rank not the man. He took Johnston to the room with the statues.

He answered Johnston's questions honestly up to a point, but gave no details regarding the activities of the room's previous visitors. He had no doubt that Johnston's agenda was not the same as Colonel Douglas and Doctor Travers, even though Johnston insisted this was a follow up inspection. Doctor Travers had been concerned for the petrified soldiers and had treated them with respect. To

Johnston they were simply lumps of stone. To Cowie they were injured comrades. He didn't understand the injury, but he didn't need to. These were soldiers and that was all he needed to know. The way Doctor Travers and Colonel Douglas had treated them, even when taking samples, had given the men dignity. Cowie appreciated that.

But Johnston showed no respect to the men, and when he asked questions about Travers and Douglas, Cowie's gut took against the man. Despite that he did his duty, though to the letter and no further. After escorting Johnston from the facility, Cowie thought for a long moment.

Doctor Travers left a phone number in case anything unusual happened with the statues. She also asked him to keep an eye on the areas where she had taken small samples of soft tissue. He probably should report back to her that the blood had stopped seeping an hour or so after she had left and that there were no signs of any infection. And if he happened to mention Johnston's visit... would that be betraying his duty? Not if, as Johnston insisted, he was merely following up on their visit.

'It's a release of energy that does it!' Anne exclaimed. 'Some kind of bizarre storm in Ancient Egypt, lightning in Victorian times and a huge explosion at the garage in Durnham. Every time there's a release of energy, that rock petrifies anyone in the vicinity.'

'Just thinking of it petrifies me,' Samson said.

'Well, clearly not, as you're moving right now.'

Douglas shook his head. 'Really, Miss Travers?'

'Sorry,' she said. Anne got to her feet to pace. It helped to walk and talk aloud at the same time. 'But, you're right, this is no joke. It's the best breakthrough we've had so far. We know now that it's inert until it's exposed to a large release of energy.'

'How exactly does that help us?' Bill asked.

Anne sighed with exasperation. 'Well, for one thing, it tells us what we should avoid doing with the rock, doesn't it?'

'That's a fair point,' Douglas admitted. 'Though given that we don't actually have the stone it doesn't really help.'

'It does make me wonder where the stone actually is,' Anne said, looking at him pointedly.

'That's not our part of the problem,' Douglas returned. 'We need to find out what we can about the rock and its effects.'

Anne waved away Douglas' protests. 'It would help if we had the damned thing so we could experiment on it.'

'Hang on. If energy causes the thing to be activated, is there a way to reverse the effects?' Bill wondered. 'Maybe with a different kind of energy?'

'And that's why it would be helpful to have the rock itself.' Anne smiled. 'You know, the chemical composition of the stone statues is the same as the residue from the original impact or whatever it was. Maybe we can experiment on samples of stone from the statues.'

'Will they know?' Douglas asked.

Anne paused thoughtfully. 'Yes, they will. But the real question is, will it hurt them?' And she really didn't want to think about the answer to that.

After declining Godfrey's offer, Alistair kept himself very much to himself. He was aware that he had made enemies. He was also aware that they had all seen that he was capable of taking care of himself. The daily football game was in full swing during the morning exercise period when Godfrey approached him. Nolan was, as ever now, at Godfrey's shoulder, and Alistair noted that there was no friendly smile from Nolan this time. Feigning a yawn, Alistair shifted to a more comfortable position, leaning against the wall.

'Still not ready to join in the game, Brigadier Lethbridge-Stewart?' Godfrey asked.

Alistair didn't answer. He just watched the criminal intently.

Godfrey smiled a superior kind of smile. It was the smile of a man who knew he had the upper hand. 'You're an interesting fellow,' Godfrey said.

'Am I?'

'Oh, yes.' Godfrey nodded. 'Not many get remanded into the Scrubs, and even fewer get remanded in here when they're a serving member of the military. But then, not many people are facing a trial the government would really like to hush up, at least until the election has passed.' He rubbed his chin thoughtfully. 'You know, I'm a very influential man, but I haven't been able to find exactly what you're being charged with. I own a lot of important people. All they've found out is that the government wishes you would disappear.'

Alistair didn't answer. He simply continued watching Godfrey. He knew Godfrey would have him checked out, but the speed with which the criminal obtained results surprised him.

The crook wasn't put off by Alistair's silence. 'Of course, it's not just the government that's thinking about you disappearing, is it?' He tapped the wall beside Alistair. 'Since you were sent to the Scrubs, everything you've done has been designed to get you sent here, to Maximum Security. Don't bother denying it. You picked fights with the hardest men in your wing and you put them down. That marked you as a very dangerous man, and you were sent to our little holiday camp here.' He tapped the wall again. 'And right *here* is where you want to be. We've been watching you. As soon as you got into this yard, you backed away from what everyone else was doing, didn't involve yourself. Now, some of them think it's because you're a stuck up toffee-nosed josser. I think you were after something. Something right here.' He punctuated each word by tapping his finger on the brick wall.

'Really?' Alistair asked mildly. 'And why would I do that?'

'Good question,' Godfrey answered. 'And I had to do some thinking about that. There was no doubt about it, though. Your first few times in here you were going around the walls. You were smart about it. You did it slow, like every time you moved you were just looking for a better view of the game, but you only moved that little bit at a time. Just a bit too methodical, if I might offer some advice.'

Alistair tilted his head in mock appreciation. 'Thank you.'

'And again this morning,' Godfrey picked up, 'you have come back to this point. There's something about this part of the wall that interests you.' He smiled. 'What is it?'

Alistair waited a bit before replying. He had to bait his hook well. Let the crook think he was in control... 'I have no idea what you're talking about,' he said finally.

Godfrey's tone turned hard. 'Yes, you do, and your stupid denials are rather wearing.' The voice became measured and even again. 'The fact that you needed something from this yard explains why you stopped those thugs from killing me. A fatal stabbing would stop anyone being permitted into this yard for a time, possibly weeks. That tells me you plan to be out of here very soon. I don't understand why you would think you can escape from this yard – because that is undoubtedly what you have in mind – when it's not even against one of the outer walls.' The superior expression returned. 'Of course, I could simply go and ask one of the warders.' He smiled a cold charmless smile. 'Or you can tell me.'

Alistair remained impassive. He said nothing, looking from Godfrey to Nolan and back again. He had to play this just right... 'I don't know what you're—'

Godfrey turned away. 'Come on, Nolan. Let's see what the warders say.'

'Do you think I couldn't kill you both before you get five yards?' Alistair asked in a cold, quiet voice.

Godfrey turned back to the taller man, a smile spreading on his face. 'And finally I see the man who was sent here, instead of the mask you've been wearing. That's more like it. To answer your question, I have no doubt you could easily kill us both, but if you did you would never have access to this yard again. And you know that to be true.'

'Yes,' Alistair admitted. 'I do.'

Godfrey took a step back towards Alistair. 'So tell me,' he said urgently. 'Why were you so desperate to get to this yard?'

Alistair looked between Godfrey and Nolan, apparently torn over his position. 'All right,' he conceded finally. 'You're right. I do need to be in this yard. It's my only way out of here. If I go to trial...' He paused uncomfortably. 'Well, the best I can hope for is that I spend the rest of my life in prison. That's if I'm lucky. If I'm not... There are still a few capital offences in this country.'

'Capital?' Nolan asked. 'You mean the death penalty?'

'Yes,' Alistair said bitterly. 'That's exactly what I mean.'

Godfrey chuckled. 'Oh, you *have* been a bad boy.'

'So they tell me.'

'You must tell me more.'

Alistair snorted. 'Not likely. I'm going to need that information when I get out of here.'

'And you know how you're going to get out of there?' Godfrey asked eagerly.

Alistair's shoulders slumped. 'All right. I'll tell you, but be clear. If you go to the warders or the governor, Nolan won't be able to protect you from me.'

'Spare me the threats, and tell me how you're getting out of here.'

'All right,' Alistair said. 'This prison has an interesting history. For the duration of the last war it was taken out of service as a jail.'

'I know that. It was turned into some kind of government base.' Realisation appeared in Godfrey's eyes. 'Some kind of military base, wasn't it?'

'Yes. It was one of the major headquarters for British and Allied military intelligence all through the war. They made some changes and alterations to the place, and some more were made after the war so that it could become a prison again.' This time it was Alistair who tapped the wall. 'Including this wall. On the other side of it is a passage leading to a set of iron doors with an electronic lock. A lock to which I happen to know the eight-digit code.'

Godfrey's hand involuntarily reached for the wall. 'So if you could get through this, you'd be out?'

'Yes.'

'And then what?'

Alistair frowned. 'I don't follow.'

'Once you're out,' Godfrey said. 'What then?'

'Out of the country,' Alistair replied. He tapped his forehead. 'I'm quite sure what's in here is worth enough to see me comfortably off in any number of countries.'

Godfrey barked a short laugh. 'So the gentleman soldier is just a myth. You're going to betray your country.'

'They betrayed me first!' Alistair snapped. 'All I'm doing is getting out with the chance to start again somewhere they can't find me. As soon as I'm on the Continent I'll be fine.'

'It's not that easy getting out of the country,' Godfrey said casually. 'Unless you're connected.'

'And you're connected, I suppose?'

'You suppose correctly.' Godfrey glanced back at the game of football raging behind them. 'And having recently been attacked here, I'm rather keen not to be in this prison any longer. Despite Mr Nolan's assistance, I'm concerned that the King Brothers will catch up with me.' He spread his hands wide. 'My money and influence will not help me if that happens. I hadn't expected them to move against me quite so quickly. So, you're not the only one who is eager to escape.'

'Everybody is keen to escape from this place,' Alistair snapped.

Godfrey's tone became conciliatory and friendly. 'But not everybody can help each other achieve that the way we can. I assume you have a plan for this wall?'

'It has a weak spot,' Alistair answered. 'I can be through it in a few minutes, if I'm not disturbed.'

'Not being disturbed means you're not planning this during exercise period,' Godfrey said.

'I have it planned for when we're having lunch. I just need to damage one of the locks on the way so that it doesn't close properly.' Alistair's lips quirked into a slight smile. 'Part of my training was in escaping from the enemy.'

Godfrey's laugh was genuine. 'I like the irony, but there's no need for that. I run a couple of the warders here. They'll let us out of our cells.'

'Us?' Alistair asked. 'Both of us escaping together?'

'Three,' Godfrey corrected. 'I'm not leaving Nolan behind. He'll be useful to me on the outside.'

'Thanks, Mr Godfrey,' Nolan said on cue.

'If you didn't have to do it at a lunchtime, what time would you pick?' Godfrey asked Alistair.

He answered immediately. 'Between two and four in the morning. It's when people are least responsive. It's quieter than during the day so there's a better chance of being heard, but it's an enclosed yard so the noise won't be a huge problem. The roads outside will also be quieter so there's less chance of anyone seeing us leave.'

Godfrey leaned closer. He looked eager, almost greedy at the thought of freedom. 'I can get word to my brief to come and see me this afternoon. He could arrange for a car to be waiting for us on the outside. We could go tonight.'

'No,' Alistair said firmly. 'I don't have the tools needed to get through the wall. I should be finished making a sort of chisel out of a fork I stole by next week sometime.'

'To hell with next week,' Godfrey said harshly. 'We're going out tonight, whether you're with us or not.'

'You're forgetting that eight-digit code. Without that you're going nowhere.'

'Then I suppose it's *with you*, isn't it?' Godfrey said. 'But we're going out tonight.'

Alistair didn't speak with Godfrey and Nolan again at all that day. At the evening meal and during the communal period he was alone, as he tended to be. He read a few chapters of a book and noticed a warder escorting Godfrey back, not long before they were locked into their cells for the night. Alistair could only assume that Godfrey had seen his solicitor and everything was going as he planned.

Alistair's heart thumped as he heard a key turn in the lock of his door. It was done slowly and quietly. The door half opened and a prison officer looked in. Alistair didn't recognise him at all. He indicated for Alistair to follow him onto the landing, where Godfrey and Nolan were both waiting. None of them spoke. They simply followed the warder in the near darkness down to the first of the doors leading to the corridor, which ultimately led to the exercise yard.

The warder opened each of the doors for them. Just inside the exercise yard they found a hammer and chisel waiting.

'You set all this up in an afternoon?' Alistair whispered to Godfrey.

In the near gloom, the man's grin was thoroughly evil. 'My dear fellow, in half an hour on the outside I could cost three members of the cabinet their jobs.'

'What about him?' Alistair nodded at the guard. 'He'll be suspected.'

'That's taken care of, too.' Godfrey chuckled.

That seemed to be Nolan's cue to attack the warder, punching him hard in the face. The warder went down, and Nolan was on him with punches and kicks.

'Make it look real,' was all Godfrey said to Nolan, before turning back to Alistair. 'Want to get on with the wall?'

The yard was in near total darkness. The high walls kept any ambient light from the yard and there was no moon. As they reached the wall, Alistair started running his hands over the bricks and stone.

'I can't see anything,' Nolan complained.

Godfrey cursed. 'Should have brought a torch.'

'That might have attracted attention,' Alistair said. 'I don't need it. I know this wall by touch now. I learned its shape. There.'

In the darkness they heard the sound of a chisel being dug into the mortar between bricks. There was a scraping sound as Alistair dug away at the mortar.

'Use the hammer,' Godfrey said impatiently.

'Too noisy.' Alistair kept working at the mortar and they heard dust and larger fragments falling to the ground. He worked for what seemed like an age before there was a larger, rougher sound. 'Brick's loose.' He kicked the wall, and then again. On the second kick, they heard the brick fall on the other side of the wall.

At Godfrey's instruction, Nolan took over digging. 'How did you know it was weak?' Godfrey asked Alistair.

'This was built after the war. A lot of the mortar from the immediate post-war years was inferior quality. I was in a barracks that was built at that time. It was crumbling about our ears by the late '50s.'

Godfrey nodded, then looked down at Nolan and hissed. 'Hurry it up. This is taking too long.'

A rough scraping sound and a thump told them that another brick was gone. Another followed soon after.

'You're right,' Alistair said. 'This is taking too long. Give me the hammer.'

'Here,' said Nolan.

Alistair took the tool back and a second later a loud, harsh sound echoed around the yard.

'Too loud,' Godfrey hissed. 'They'll hear us.'

'And if we don't get a move on, that warder will be missed,' Alistair said harshly. He slammed the hammer into the chisel again. A brick fell, then another as he drove the sharp metal tool through the crumbling mortar. Stepping back, he kicked at the wall again and again, dislodging a few more bricks.

Godfrey was beginning to panic. 'They're bound to have heard this.'

'Let them come,' Alistair snapped. 'This hole's big enough for us to get through now.'

'I'm first.' Godfrey pushed them aside and started squirming through the hole. He was overweight and far from being an athlete. He struggled to make much headway.

'If he gets stuck we're all for it,' Alistair said, gripping Godfrey's legs and pushing him through the small opening.

There was the sound of clothes tearing, but Godfrey eventually went through and dropped onto the bricks on the far side. Alistair followed. Nolan was last through. Godfrey didn't wait. He started along the tunnel, which sounded damp underfoot. The tunnel was in absolute darkness so that they only discovered any problems on the floor when their feet kicked against them. Alistair and Nolan took their time, ignoring the pleas of Godfrey to hurry. They only picked up their pace slightly when they heard the crook fall and yell.

'Twisted my ankle,' Godfrey said as his companions reached him. 'Might be broken.'

Alistair found the ankle in the darkness and rotated it slowly. 'Does that hurt?'

'Agony,' Godfrey replied.

'Twisted or sprained,' Alistair said in a clipped voice. 'If it had been broken it wouldn't have moved that way and we'd have been peeling you off the roof. Come on.'

Together they lifted Godfrey to his feet and helped him hobble the last few yards before they found themselves walking smack into cold metal.

'I can't even see the door,' Godfrey complained.

'Just lean against it,' Alistair instructed.

He ran his hands along the door until he felt the metal give way to the rough bricks of the wall. A few seconds later he found the metal and plastic panel with numbers. He ran his fingers across the number keys and imagined the layout. Three rows of three numbers from one to nine with the zero placed centrally below the bottom line. To the right of the zero was another key, which would open the door. He keyed in the eight digits, which made up the birth date of the Queen, and pressed for the door to open. After a second, heavy locks clicked as they were released. Alistair leaned on the door and started pushing hard.

'Give me a hand,' he demanded into the darkness and the door began moving to the side.

It screeched horribly as runners, which hadn't moved in the best part of two decades, were forced into life. The door ground to a halt at about eighteen inches open, but that was enough.

Alistair slipped through first. 'Come on.'

Godfrey squeezed and hobbled through next with Nolan just behind him.

After the absolute darkness of the tunnel, even the dull light from nearby East Acton felt as bright as searchlights, but after a moment their eyes began to acclimatise. With Nolan on one side of Godfrey and Alistair on the other, they hurried away from the prison as fast as they could manage. The expected alarms and sirens didn't follow them.

They reached the pavement, and a large dark car pulled up alongside them. For a moment Alistair thought it was a police car, but a pair of criminal heavies leaped out and carried Godfrey into the back.

'Get in,' Godfrey said quickly. 'Get in, the pair of you, or I'll leave you both where you stand.'

Alistair and Nolan did as they were told.

A moment later, the car pulled away, taking the first turn possible and was soon lost in the streets of East Acton.

The jailbreak had gone more or less exactly as planned, which meant Brigadier Lethbridge-Stewart was exactly on track.

— CHAPTER TEN —

The jailbreak dominated the BBC's news reports in the morning. The reports stated that three inmates had attacked a guard and escaped. There were very few details, and the news focused on Godfrey being involved. He was described as a 'Gangland Kingpin', an 'Underworld Boss' and his own favourite, a 'Moonlight Operator'. He thought that sounded like something Glenn Miller's Orchestra would have played.

They were in a small, cramped house near the Pembury Housing Estate. Alistair looked out of the window upstairs when he woke up; there were no cars in the street. Nobody could afford one. The houses' doors and windows needed paint. A few of them needed glass as well. There was litter on the streets. Not just paper and discarded bubble gum. There were half bricks lying around.

This was a rough part of town.

When he came downstairs he found Godfrey cackling at the news report. 'They're saying I was the one who coshed that warder.' He slapped his hands on his belly. 'Me!'

'It won't do your reputation any harm,' Alistair said dryly. He poured himself a cup of tea and took a sip. 'It actually tastes like tea,' he said with a satisfied sigh.

Godfrey chuckled. 'Better than in jail?'

Alistair couldn't resist a slight smile. 'Just a bit. I can't believe how much I missed a decent pot of tea.'

Godfrey turned to one of his men. 'Get him breakfast.'

'Anything but watery porridge,' Alistair said wryly.

'The full English,' Godfrey added. 'Bacon, egg, sausage, tomato, fried bread. The full biffter.'

'All I've wanted for the last week is marmalade on toast,' Alistair said with some feeling.

Godfrey snorted good-naturedly. 'You're in luck. We've got marmalade as well. You can have the lot. You earned it.' He sucked in a deep breath. 'Can you smell that?'

Alistair sniffed the air. 'Stale sweat, years of must and a coal fire?'

'Wrong.' Godfrey took a long swig from a mug of tea. 'You smell freedom.'

'Really? I thought freedom would smell of roses and jasmine.'

'It will,' Godfrey assured him. 'We're only holding out here for a day 'til things quiet down. They'll be turning over all of my houses and businesses today. The wife's going to go mental about that.' He sniffed. 'Can't imagine any of my girlfriends will be all that happy either. We'll be moving to another place I own tonight. If the police don't visit it today... We'll know they don't know it's mine.'

'I'll make my move when you go there,' Alistair said. 'I'll get myself out of London and then out of the country.'

Godfrey sighed. 'I thought we'd been through that. I can get you out of the country, no problem. Let's face it. I need to get myself out of here as well.'

'And leave your business behind?'

'Leave my business running London. And I'll be running my business from wherever I set myself up.' Godfrey took another sip. 'No, you stick with me. I'll get you out of the country. And all those secrets in your head you're keen to sell on... I might be able to help you with those too.'

'No, thank you.' Alistair made no effort to hide his distrust of Godfrey. 'I have my contacts. I'll be fine.'

Godfrey didn't seem overly bothered by Alistair's antipathy. 'Eat your breakfast, get yourself cleaned up. We'll have some new clothes delivered shortly.' He tugged at his prison issue shirt. 'It'll do us both good to be out of these and dressed like proper human beings again. We'll have a chat once we're fed and spruced up. There's nothing we can do in daylight anyway. They haven't mentioned you by name, but I'd be damned surprised if they haven't got your face out to every copper in England. Just relax for the day.'

One of Godfrey's men set a plate in front of Alistair. Bacon, sausage, egg, fried bread, tomatoes and black pudding stared up at him. 'Well, I don't suppose one day will make a difference.'

Godfrey smiled to himself. 'Good man.'

'What do you mean he broke out last night?' Anne asked.

Douglas just gave her a look.

'Stupid question,' Anne conceded. 'It's not exactly a statement that's open to a lot of interpretation, is it?'

Douglas consulted the notes he made while on the phone. 'Three of them went out.'

Anne looked at her colleague in confusion. 'Three?'

Douglas nodded. 'Three. Lethbridge-Stewart, Godfrey, and a low-rent thug named Nolan.'

That made Anne nervous. 'That wasn't the plan,' she said. She could tell that Douglas was as worried as she was, but he was trying not to let it show.

'I know,' he said. 'But it's got to be a tough situation in

there.'

'He was supposed to let us know when the break-out was going to happen,' Anne answered sharply. 'Sorry,' she added a moment later. 'I know you're as worried about him as I am.'

'But you never liked this whole idea,' Douglas offered. '*Unbelievably bloody stupid*, I think you called it.'

'Did I?' Anne shrugged. 'If I did I was right.' She sank back into her chair again. 'He was supposed to tell us when he was breaking out. That he didn't means he isn't in control of the situation.'

'I know,' Douglas agreed. 'We just have to trust that he'll be able to get word to us as planned.'

'And if he can't?'

'He'll find a way.' Douglas sounded confident.

Anne wondered if the confidence was for her benefit. 'Are you trying to convince me or yourself?'

'Both,' he admitted. 'Part of being an officer is showing confidence to your men and believing it yourself.'

'I'm not one of your *men*,' Anne said pointedly. 'But I understand you.'

Douglas rubbed a hand over his chin. 'Right, I suppose I should tell everyone else what has happened, assuming they haven't guessed from listening to the wireless.'

Anne caught Douglas' arm before he could leave. 'We've got trouble.'

She admired that Douglas didn't let his shoulders slump. 'Tell me,' he said.

Anne pointed at the phone. 'Just before you got your bad news phone call, I had one of my own.'

'From whom?'

'Sergeant Major Cowie. He had a visitor yesterday, asking

questions about us.'

'Who?'

'Leslie Johnston,' Anne replied sourly.

The thunderous look that crossed Douglas' face matched her own when Cowie called, and she knew why. Johnston worked for the mysterious General at the Vault, and was behind more than one of their engagements in the last few months. They both had personal reasons to dislike him, too; for Douglas it was the betrayal of their friendship and the uniform, and for Anne it was because Johnston had kidnapped her father in May. In a citadel beneath London he had slaved some Yeti to her father's mind. She promised herself, when she discovered this at the end of October, that if she came across Johnston she'd give him a very large piece of her mind. Or maybe have Bill shoot him.

'Might be for the best that he broke out last night,' Douglas said. 'If Johnston's sticking his nose in, we need to move quickly.'

'Nothing about this has moved quickly,' Anne said sourly. 'But I'm a scientist. I'm used to that.'

Douglas replied with a humourless smile. 'Patience is part of my line as well. Usually the most frustrating part.'

'So, first order of duty is to fill the others in?'

'No,' Douglas shook his head decisively. 'First thing is to let General Hamilton know that Johnston, and thus the Vault, is sniffing about, then we talk to Samson and Bishop.'

Alistair looked in the mirror with some disdain. He had to admit that he enjoyed the breakfast, and he also relished the chance to take time over washing. The clothes supplied to him were hardly to his taste, however. Everything was nylon and polyester, even the hideous paisley pattern underpants.

He had no doubt he was producing enough static electricity to power Edinburgh Castle.

'Sorry about the clothes,' Nolan said, as Alistair came down the narrow stairs. Nolan was dressed in a pair of jeans and a ghastly mustard and green jumper. 'This is a pretty rough part of the city. If we started wearing tweed and silk we'd be spotted a mile off.'

Alistair forced a smile. 'Well, at least it's better than prison uniform.'

'That's a fact.'

'What now?' Alistair asked. 'For you, I mean?'

Nolan shrugged. 'Whatever Mr Godfrey says, I suppose.'

'You're sticking with him?'

Another shrug. 'Don't have much choice now, do I?' Nolan led the way along the dingy little hall to the kitchen. He pulled a tin of Nescafé coffee granules from the cupboard and set about making coffee. 'I've got nothing here. No family, not many friends.'

'No girl?' Alistair asked. He opened the fridge and passed a bottle of milk to Nolan.

'Cheers.' Nolan took the bottle and shook it before pressing the silver foil top. 'No, no girl. I do have an ex-wife who'll be really annoyed if the filth is knocking at her door asking about me. She got lucky after me and married some bloke in an office. He's some kind of management. I didn't pay much attention when she told me about him. The important thing seemed to be that he was a better prospect than me.'

'You don't miss her much, then?' Alistair smiled.

'Not at all. Not one bit. She'll be sorry when we're set up in Spain, though. She always liked hot weather.'

Alistair latched onto the slip regarding their destination.

'Is that where Godfrey's heading?' he asked casually. 'Spain?'

It was clear that Nolan immediately knew he made a mistake and he tried to backtrack. 'Might be. He doesn't tell me things like that.'

Alistair held up a placating hand. 'Don't worry about that, old chap,' he said in a friendly tone. 'I was just feeling jealous. Where I'm heading to, with my new *tovarischy*, is going to be a good deal colder and rather less enjoyable.'

'You got a girl to take with you?' Nolan seemed keen to move the conversation away from his mistake and Alistair was happy to oblige.

'Not anymore,' he lied. An image of Sally came briefly to him, and he hated that he was not exactly lying. He forced her from his mind; their relationship was something to deal with another time. 'There was someone,' he explained, 'but it finished a short while ago.' He shrugged. 'I doubt if she'd have enjoyed crossing the Iron Curtain, so it was for the best.'

'Probably.'

Alistair opened a large, round tin on the table. 'Biscuit?' he said, offering the tin to Nolan.

'Thanks.' Nolan helped himself to a couple of pink wafers, and Alistair took a pair of Rich Tea fingers before closing the tin.

'So,' he said, snapping a biscuit in half. 'We sit around here today, waiting to hear if Godfrey's other house is clear?'

'That's the plan.' Nolan nodded. 'Probably be a bit boring but it's better than the nick.'

Alistair nodded at the back door, which led from the kitchen into a small garden. Through the frosted glass pane they could see a dark shape. Through the window they could see another of Godfrey's men standing by a garden shed. 'Those still look a lot like guards to me.'

'They're looking out for us,' Nolan answered automatically.

'And if I tried to leave?' Alistair asked quickly. 'If I tried to get back to my own plan?'

'Don't,' Nolan said softly. 'Just go with what's happening. Mr Godfrey knows what he's doing.'

Alistair glanced at the dark shape outlined against the frosted glass. 'It doesn't look like I have much choice.' He opened the biscuit tin again. 'Might as well make the most of it.' He pushed the tin towards Nolan.

As his companion again reached for the pink wafers, Alistair started making mental notes of the positions of all of Godfrey's men and wondered if there was any chance he could manage to be alone with the phone, even for a few minutes. He would need to move fast. He needed a new plan.

The pity was, he didn't have one.

By two o'clock in the afternoon, Alistair concluded that spending a day locked inside a terrace house in one of London's seedier housing estates was hardly any less boring or more liberating than a day in prison. He was able to watch the news on the black and white television before both ITV and BBC closed down for the afternoon. The radio only seemed able to pick up Radio One and Radio Two, neither of which particularly appealed to him. One was just noise while the other would send a maiden aunt to sleep.

The house still had plenty of Godfrey's men in and around it. Unfortunately, they never left him alone with the telephone and Godfrey barely left the living room other than to eat and go to the loo. When he did, at least one of his men always stayed behind in the living room.

Alistair's opportunity arrived at around half past two, and

it arrived in the shape of a short, slightly plump woman of around forty whose make up was just too thick and her hair just too blonde. She wore rings on most of her fingers but, tellingly, none on the ring finger of her left hand. If he had been asked to imagine a gangster's girlfriend, this was how he would picture her. Godfrey called her 'Roz', and they disappeared upstairs without any explanation being needed. A couple of Godfrey's men followed behind at a discrete distance. That thinned their numbers downstairs considerably.

Alistair had to create and take his opportunity while he could.

He went to the kitchen and put the kettle on to boil again. 'Not much else to do, is there?' he asked Nolan, who was sitting at the kitchen table playing patience.

'You'll turn in to a tea-pot, you will,' Nolan replied, without looking up.

'Think we should ask Godfrey if he fancies a cuppa?' Alistair asked with a laugh.

Nolan joined in the laughter. 'I think we both know what he fancies is nothing to do with tea.'

Alistair opened a drawer. 'Wrong one,' he said. 'Spoons?'

'Next one along,' Nolan said absently.

'Right you are.' Alistair pulled a tea spoon from the drawer. 'What about that lot out there?'

'They're fine,' Nolan answered. 'Working.'

'Fair enough.' He headed for the door. 'Keep an eye on the kettle, would you? Nature calls.'

'Okay,' Nolan agreed. 'But keep it quiet when you're in there. Godfrey's up there remember.'

'And I doubt if he'll be paying any attention to me.'

Alistair left the kitchen and moved along the hall then up

the stairs. One of Godfrey's thugs was standing at the head of the stairs looking sourly at Alistair, who simply pointed at the bathroom door. The goon nodded his understanding and let Alistair pass. In the bathroom, Alistair found the window slightly open. It was only six inches or so, but it was enough. He pulled an egg from his pocket. While he distracted Nolan with asking about spoons he used his other hand to slide an egg into his pocket. Distraction was a classic military tactic.

He waited a few minutes then ran the sink tap for a moment before turning back and pulling the handle to flush the toilet. As the flush sounded, he pulled back his arm and hurled the egg through the gap at the bottom of the window. He didn't wait to see if it hit the target. He was already across the small bathroom, pulling the door open. He stopped at the head of the stairs.

'Everything all right?' he asked the thug standing sentry. The thug gave a dirty laugh and Alistair joined in. 'Ask a silly question. You want tea? I'm making a pot.'

The thug thought for a moment before answering. 'Yeah, why not.'

Nolan appeared at the foot of the stairs. 'There you are.'

Alistair shrugged. 'Where else would I be.'

'Stay inside,' Nolan said.

'All right.'

The goon at the head of the stairs lost his smile and was now all business.

Alistair left him to it and went downstairs. Through the open kitchen door he could see that the back door was open. A fresh egg was oozing down the shed's door. He dipped into the living room. No one was around. He was inside for less than twenty seconds before returning to the kitchen. He waited near the table, closer to the kitchen door than the back door. He forced himself to look agitated and nervous. He picked up a vicious-looking carving knife and waited. A few minutes later Nolan and one of Godfrey's men returned. They closed the door behind them.

'What is it?' Alistair demanded.

'Nothing,' Nolan said sourly. 'Bloody kids.'

'In the garden? What if they see us?'

Nolan shook his head. 'They just chucked an egg and legged it. Little sods.'

'You're sure?'

Nolan looked to his colleague for confirmation. It came in the form of a sour nod. 'Yeah,' Nolan said. 'Used to do the same myself when I was a kiddie.'

'All right,' Alistair said warily. He pulled the carving knife from inside the sleeve where he had hidden it, and put it back on the worktop. 'That's all right.'

Nolan eyed the carving knife for a second. Alistair could see the convict considering the reaction he had seen. What had he seen? A nervous con on the run, who thought they had been found? He certainly hoped that was what Nolan saw.

'The kids just need a boot up the backside,' Nolan said. 'Not the carving knife.'

Alistair just nodded. In the corner of his eye he caught a movement in the hall. The thug from the top of the stairs looked in suspiciously.

'Something wrong down here?'

'No,' Nolan reassured him. 'Just local kids messing about. The lads outside will give them a thick ear if they come back.'

'Right,' the thug answered. He eyed the teapot optimistically.

Alistair put the kettle back onto the hob. 'I think we could use that cup of tea.'

The guard agreed and set off back for his position on the stairs.

Alistair fought hard not to look relieved. He had taken a risk, and it had worked. In the few seconds he had been alone in the living room he had phoned the number he'd memorised. It took him to an operator who was waiting for his call and only his call. He relayed the numbers typed onto the dial of the telephone and hung up. It had taken less than twenty seconds, but in that time he had given his contact all the information they needed. Getting an address for the phone number wouldn't take them long.

His back to Nolan and the guard, Alistair allowed himself a smile.

CHAPTER ELEVEN

'He's *where?*' Sally asked.

Douglas repeated the address, reading from the notebook he'd copied it into. 'Bodney Road, Hackney.'

'But that's a horrible area,' Sally said. 'Why would Godfrey go there?'

'Because nobody would look for him there,' Bishop said. 'He likes the good things in life, evidently. We wouldn't expect him to hide on a council estate. Especially one as scummy as that.'

'Exactly,' Douglas agreed. 'I don't think we, or the police, would have found them if Lethbridge-Stewart hadn't made it to the phone when he did.'

Sally nodded, taking this in. 'Now what?' She managed to sound both eager and worried at the same time.

'*Sir*. Corporal Wright, I understand this must be difficult for you, but please remember I am your superior, and in this instance, your *commanding* officer. A little bit of decorum is required.'

Sally looked at the carpet. 'Sorry, sir.'

Douglas glanced at Bishop, who offered a slight smile. Douglas rolled his eyes, then checked his watch. 'We're meeting the police at fifteen-thirty hours. It's a joint operation. We're going in with them.' He held out an arm to stop Sally from moving towards the door. 'If they see a woman on this raid they'll know something's rotten. I'm sorry, Corporal. You're staying here with Anne and Samson.'

'Samson?' Sally was confused. 'Sir, with all due respect, neither Anne nor I need to be babysat.'

'Agreed. Unfortunately, if we turn up with women and a *black* man in that kind of area… Well, it would be harder to go unnoticed.' Douglas didn't like it, especially leaving Samson out, as the man would be very useful if things went wrong, but alas, the decision wasn't his.

Sally nodded stoically, clearly not caring for the implication either. 'Yes, sir.'

Godfrey and his companion returned downstairs around four o'clock. Both looked flushed. Godfrey still slightly favoured one ankle after the previous night's fall, and Alistair heard a quietly snide aside that Roz must have done all the work. He thought it was a crass comment.

Roz left a few minutes later, going straight from the front door into a taxi that barely pulled to a stop before she was getting in the back. After she was gone, Godfrey joined his fellow escapees in the kitchen.

'Well?' he asked. 'Holding up?'

'Bored but surviving,' Alistair said.

'Sorry about that,' Godfrey said with absolutely no attempt at sincerity. He looked at Nolan. 'You any good at cooking? I'm famished.'

'Not too shabby, Mr Godfrey.'

'Good lad. There's some steak in the fridge. Fry me one with some onions and mushrooms. Boil a couple of potatoes as well.' Godfrey seemed to suddenly remember that he wasn't the only one in the room who might be hungry. 'Do some for everybody,' he added. 'No point in leaving anything here, is there? We won't be here in the morning.' He looked to his nearest subordinate for confirmation. 'We haven't heard of any trouble at the other house, have we?'

'No, Mr Godfrey,' the guard replied briskly. 'All your houses in London have been visited. Your wife's spitting feathers. Apparently they were going to arrest her for being obstructive.'

Godfrey barked out a laugh. 'That sounds like her. Where else have they looked for us?'

The goon reeled off a list he had memorised. 'The snooker clubs, the warehouses, most of the knocking shops, all of the betting shops, a couple of the dolls.'

'But they weren't watching Roz?' Godfrey asked quickly.

'No, sir. We collected her yesterday afternoon. Story is she stayed out in Reading with a friend of hers. She's got train tickets and everything to cover. The friend knows the score, too.'

'Good lad.' Godfrey moved aside to let Nolan get to the fridge, before taking a seat at the table. 'Hurry up with that, Nolan. I've got an appetite.' He turned his attention back to Alistair. 'Where would you be if I hadn't brought you here?'

Alistair glanced up at the clock on the kitchen wall. 'Hull,' he said. 'Then overnight to Norway or Holland.'

'That means you have money set aside,' Godfrey said. 'And a hooky passport?'

Alistair adopted a sly smirk. 'It's hard to travel without one.'

'Where is it stashed?'

'In an empty flat. Near Liverpool Street Station.'

Godfrey's eyes narrowed in concern. 'Your place?'

'No,' Alistair replied. 'It belonged to an ex-colleague. He died.'

161

'I'm sorry about that.'

'So am I,' Alistair answered viciously. 'And so will the ones that gave the orders that had him killed.' He took a moment, as if struggling to control himself and choose the right words. 'Nobody in government puts their life at risk,' he said. 'They make us do it. They make us put our lives on the line and take the credit when everything goes well. But when it goes wrong... Oh, when it goes wrong they throw blame at us, insult the memories of the fallen. They're not fit to lace our boots but they decide when we die.' He shook his head. 'Not anymore.'

Godfrey watched the outburst with interest. 'So this is personal as well as business?'

'It's personal, all right,' Alistair snarled. 'Revenge for fallen comrades. I'm going to hurt them,' he said quietly. 'I'm going to hurt them very badly.'

Godfrey pushed back from his seat a little. 'What can you do? What do you know? A few affairs by cabinet ministers? We all know those. We even know the cabinet ministers who are having affairs with other cabinet ministers.'

Alistair met Godfrey's gaze evenly. 'I can bring down the Government of Britain,' he said very coolly. 'I could bring down a dozen governments. All the agreements and deals to cover up lies and deaths and murders and betrayals. I have the knowledge in here.' He tapped his forehead. 'And I'm well-enough prepared to have the proof lodged with four sympathetic souls.' He stared hard at the table top. 'And don't ask who they are. I assure you, I won't tell you.'

Godfrey was quiet for a moment. Alistair knew the man was digesting his words, weighing them. 'If – and that's a big *if* – your information is as potent as you say, do you have any idea how much it's worth?'

162

'Yes,' Alistair replied. 'I do. And we both know that the people I'll be talking to have more or less unlimited funds.' He left those words to sink in. He couldn't make the next move. That had to come from Godfrey.

'They're going to call you a traitor,' Godfrey said mildly. It wasn't subtle. He was trying to poke at Alistair to see if there was any loyalty left.

'I didn't betray my comrades,' Alistair said coldly. 'I didn't send good men to their deaths on a mission they couldn't survive. I didn't send honest, decent men with families to die because it was politically expedient. If you're looking for traitors, look at the men I bring down.'

Godfrey said nothing, and Alistair was aware that both Nolan and the guard were looking at him in a very strange way.

It was fear.

They were afraid of him.

He had played his role just right.

It was up to Godfrey now.

Five streets away, in a quiet builders' yard, three army Land Rovers met with a pair of police cars and two police vans. DI William Blake was the ranking police officer. He was in discussion with Douglas and was making no attempt to hide his confusion.

'This just doesn't make sense, sir,' he said. 'I'm sorry. Call me daft but I don't understand what we're doing.'

'Don't worry,' Douglas said sympathetically. 'It'll make sense in a few days. We're playing a longer game.'

Blake sniffed and conceded. 'Well, word from on high is that you're in charge and I follow your lead, so that's what I'll do. So will my lads. I just can't promise that they won't look confused about it.'

Douglas patted the inspector on the shoulder. 'Good man.' He looked up into the dark blue sky. 'It's almost dark,' he said. 'These long nights will make it easier for us to get into position without being seen. Come on. Let's get on with this.'

Nolan did himself a disservice when describing his skills in the kitchen as 'not too shabby'. It turned out that he was a better than average chef, with a flair for cooking. His food wasn't complex, but it was just a bit different than anyone expected. He caramelised the onions and managed to find some mint to put in with the potatoes, which he cooked in their jackets, and then smeared some of the smaller potatoes in butter and roasted them to give them a crispy shell.

'You'll make somebody a lovely wife,' Godfrey said appreciatively.

Alistair cut into his steak. It was perfectly medium. *It's a shame Nolan turned to crime*, he thought. The man could have had a career in a decent kitchen.

In its own way it was a pleasant, jovial meal. Godfrey was in an ebullient mood, talking at length about the endless possibilities for the future now that he was out of prison. He would leave a trusted lieutenant in charge of business on the ground and run things himself from overseas. He was careful not to mention where that new home overseas might be and Alistair didn't let on that Nolan had already spilled the beans.

Alistair ate more slowly than Godfrey or Nolan, and when Godfrey opened a bottle of wine he declined the offer of a drink. Nolan was told to have a beer from the fridge. He wasn't important enough to merit wine. Alistair settled for water.

Godfrey helped himself to a couple of extra potatoes.

'Didn't get anything like this inside, eh?'

'Very true,' Alistair agreed. He observed Godfrey as he settled back in his chair. The man was full. He had eaten well, he had drank a couple of glasses of wine, nobody found the house they were in, and he started to relax. As far as Godfrey could see, things were working out exactly as he wanted them to. Alistair knew that wasn't going to last.

He put another forkful of steak and potato into his mouth. It was too long since he had enjoyed food quite so much.

They turned as the back door opened suddenly. One of Godfrey's men hurried in. He looked agitated. 'Something's up.'

Godfrey was instantly alert. 'What is it?'

'Street lights have gone out,' the thug answered. 'Side of the house and in the street at the front. It's pitch dark out there.'

'How widespread is it?' Alistair asked quickly.

'Can't tell, but it's as far as I can see.'

Alistair was on his feet, and peered out of the kitchen window into the darkness beyond. 'It's too much of a coincidence for this to happen while we're here.'

'I agree.' Godfrey pushed one of his men towards the door, into the hall. 'Find out what's happening out front.' The man disappeared through the door.

'How many ways out of here are there?' Alistair asked.

'Just front and back,' Godfrey said.

'What about next door?' Alistair carried on, peering into the dark.

'Old couple. I've known the family for years.'

'Any way through to their house?'

Godfrey shook his head. 'None. We thought about putting a door between the attics but it's a load-bearing wall.'

The goon Godfrey had sent out front ran back into the kitchen. 'Cars,' he said urgently.

'Police?' Godfrey demanded.

The goon nodded. 'And army. A couple of jeeps of them.'

Godfrey spun to look at Alistair. 'They're after you.'

'Of course they are!' Alistair snapped. 'Do we have any weapons?'

'A couple of sawn-off shotguns,' Godfrey said. 'And a few pistols.'

'No use,' Alistair said quickly. 'If we get into a shooting match with them we'll all wind up dead.'

'What alternative do we have?'

Alistair nodded at the window. 'They turned it dark outside so they could approach. We can use it to get out of here.'

'How?' Godfrey demanded.

Alistair indicated Godfrey's men. 'We need them to give us a distraction. Get them to the front of the house. Upstairs and downstairs. Lights on. After a minute, one of you looks out, then the lights go out and you smash a couple of windows as if you're going to fire at them.'

'Won't they fire at my lads?'

'No. They won't shoot until they have a clear target. This is a residential area. The collateral damage could be appalling. They won't take that risk.'

'And what will we be doing?'

'Going through the gardens,' Alistair answered. 'We should be able to get far enough along through the gardens that we can sneak away. If your men can keep them busy here, and if they're ready to go to prison for you.'

'They'll do what I tell them,' Godfrey snapped. 'Their families will be looked after while they're away.' He hiked

166

his thumb at the door. 'Get to it.' His men moved for the door. Nolan was with them but Godfrey caught his arm. 'Not you, Nolan. I might need a bit of muscle.'

Alistair waited a few moments after the men left before flipping the switch to turn off the lights. 'Wait,' he said softly. 'Wait...'

'What for?' Godfrey asked.

The lights in the hall went out. That was Alistair's cue. 'Now,' he said, yanking the back door open. 'Turn left, over the fences and keep going.'

After the warmth of the house, the cold air hit them hard. It sharpened Alistair's thoughts.

Godfrey and Nolan followed his instruction, clambering over the fence to the left into the next garden, and then they were on the move again towards the next fence. Alistair nimbly clambered after them and quickly overtook his companions. Vaulting a fence, he saw a shadow moving just ahead of him.

'Stop right there,' a familiar voice said.

Walter Douglas.

'Keep going,' Alistair said to his companions.

Douglas' shadow spoke desperately. 'For God's sake don't make this any worse for yourself.'

'Just go.' Alistair threw himself at Douglas. In the darkness the two shadowy figures merged into one writhing shape as the two men struggled.

Godfrey and Nolan did as they were told and kept going. Behind them, Alistair and Douglas struggled in the garden before both men went down. Alistair was first to his feet. A hard right hand sent Douglas back to the ground.

Alistair ran to catch up with Godfrey and Nolan.

'You all right?' Godfrey asked.

Alistair gasped for breath. 'I'll be fine when we're out of here.' He leaped the next fence. 'Keep up with me or I'll leave you behind.'

He led them through half a dozen gardens before they heard the thud of explosives far behind at the end of the terrace house.

'What's that?' Godfrey asked.

Alistair didn't break his stride. 'Stun grenades. They're going in.'

They went through two more gardens before reaching one with a full size gate. Alistair hurried them through the gate into the dark street beyond.

'Which way?' Godfrey hissed.

Alistair pushed past, leading them away to the left. 'This way.'

They hurried along for twenty or thirty yards before turning right into a short street, and then left into another small, narrow street. They crossed a road and hurried through a pair of gates into a park full of trees and bushes. Five yards inside the park, the street behind was hidden by the foliage.

'We're clear for now,' Alistair said, looking backwards and then scanning around the area. 'But they'll be here before long. We need to get a move on and be long gone before they get here.'

'Where to?' Godfrey asked.

Nolan spoke for the first time. 'The house you talked about, Mr Godfrey?'

'No,' Alistair said sharply, moving into the darkness.

Godfrey hurried after him and caught his arm. 'Why the hell not?'

'Because they found one of your houses,' Alistair snapped. 'We need to be sure they're not just watching your other one.

No, we'll go to the empty flat my passport and cash are in. We'll spend the night there and you can find out if your other place is under surveillance.'

'You said it's near Liverpool Street Station,' Godfrey complained. 'That's at least three miles. I can't walk all that way.'

A few hundred yards further on they reached a garage selling old used cars. Alistair found a car with a loose window in the passenger door. He drove confidently through the Hackney streets, heading in the general direction of Liverpool Street.

Godfrey promised to have one of his men dispose of the car somewhere outside London, as long as Alistair got them to the flat. His injured ankle was aching. With a show of reluctance, Alistair agreed. He let Nolan and Godfrey out and then parked a few hundred yards away before returning to them.

The flat was on the top floor of a three-storey building. It was spacious, and the only flat on that top floor. A square plastic light inside a little box was on the wall to the side of the door, just above head height. Alistair reached up and plucked a key from the top of the box. He opened the door and hurried them inside. They kicked their way through a pile of mail as they went in. Alistair quickly closed the door behind them.

'Get him through to the living room,' he said to Nolan.

'Right.'

As Nolan helped Godfrey hobble his way along the hall, Alistair scooped up the post and put it on a table in the hall before following his companions through to the comfortable, stylish living room. Godfrey was stretched out on the larger of two leather sofas, his leg resting on a cushion.

'You're sure this place is safe?' Godfrey asked as Alistair moved across to the window and pulled the curtains.

'I'm sure,' Alistair snapped harshly. 'What I want to know is how they found out about that little house of yours. We could have been caught. No,' he paused, seemingly to control his temper. 'We could have been killed.'

'I don't know,' Godfrey admitted. He sounded more frightened than Alistair had heard him before. That was exactly how he wanted the villain to feel.

'Could any of your people have betrayed you?' Alistair demanded.

Godfrey replied immediately. 'No chance. Not one of them would dare.'

'Nobody trying to get you out of the way so they can take your place?'

'They know I'd kill them if they tried.'

'Maybe they followed your woman friend,' Nolan offered.

'Might have done, I suppose,' Godfrey muttered.

Alistair's gaze burned a hole through Godfrey as he mulled the crook's words. 'All right,' he said finally. 'It's done. We got out – by the skin of our teeth, but we're out.' He pointed at the trim phone on the coffee table. 'You can use that, but only for outgoing calls. It doesn't show up on any of the telephone systems. To be on the safe side you should keep your calls under five minutes.'

'Understood,' Godfrey said.

'And don't give away our location to anyone.'

'I won't.'

Alistair nodded thoughtfully. 'Good. I'm going to get cleaned and change clothes. There's only one bedroom here, so you two will have to take the couches. I'll bring you blankets.'

Despite the cold of the early winter night, Alistair's exertions had built a sweat on him. He washed and changed into a far more comfortable set of clothes, making sure to transfer everything from his previous trouser pockets to the new trousers.

After ensuring that the bedroom door was closed, he moved a chair under the hatch leading to the loft and climbed up onto it. Just inside the hatch, covered in a thin layer of grime, was a briefcase. He pulled it down and opened it. Inside he found a British passport in the name of John Bailey and a Dutch passport for Jan Persson. Both had his photograph in them. Under the passports he found stacks of money, totalling around two thousand pounds in various European currencies. A smaller, hinged wooden box completed the briefcase's contents. Opening the small box Alistair pulled out a small pistol. Despite having become a cliché from appearing in the James Bond novels and films, many branches of the British services really did favour the Walther PPK pistol. It was small, reliable, with excellent stopping power. Alistair slipped the pistol into the waistband of his trousers at the small of his back. The spare clips went into his trouser pocket. Arranging his sweater so that the pistol was out of view, he returned to the living room with his passports and the stacks of cash.

'You weren't joking about being ready, were you?' Godfrey said. Some of his confidence seemed to have returned.

'No,' Alistair said. 'I wasn't.' It was time to push a few things home to Godfrey. 'Listen,' he said. 'They're going to be looking for three men tomorrow. I think in the morning we should go our own ways. Your men can take you two wherever you're going and I'll make my own way out of the country.'

Godfrey was immediately suspicious. 'You trying to ditch us?'

'I'm trying to make sure I don't get caught,' Alistair answered. 'After tonight they're going to shoot on sight. They won't risk me getting away again. No,' he amended himself carefully, 'they won't let any of us get away again. They can't know what I've told you or how involved we are. You need to be careful. They won't try to take prisoners.'

'You're sure you can get out of the country?' Godfrey demanded.

'Of course.'

'Will you be safe where you're going?'

Alistair smirked. 'Russia is a very big country hidden behind a very big iron curtain, and it will be in their interest to keep me safe when I'm there.'

'And if we came with you?' Godfrey said eagerly. 'Would they protect us?'

'I doubt it,' Alistair answered. 'You're no use to them. All you have to offer is two mouths they need to feed.'

Painfully, Godfrey swung his injured leg down from the couch. 'What if I did have something?' he asked. 'What if I had a weapon you wouldn't believe?'

Alistair snorted. 'A weapon? You're a gangster, Godfrey. A crook. You're out of your league with governments.'

'Maybe, maybe not.' A hint of the old swagger was in Godfrey's voice. 'I've got something they'll be interested in for sure. I'll take you to it tomorrow.'

Alistair looked unconvinced. 'Better we go our own ways.'

'Wait,' Godfrey said quickly. 'Please.'

That was it. Godfrey had said *please*. He had pleaded with him for his future. The gangster had conceded position to him.

'All right,' Alistair said eventually. 'I'll see what you have. If you can improve my hand when I get over there, I'll take you. If not, we go our own ways.'

'You'll like it,' Godfrey said, trying hard to hide his relief. 'You'll like it.'

Douglas and Bishop returned to the safe house not long before midnight. The rest of their group immediately had questions, all of which stopped when they saw the livid bruise on the side of Douglas' face.

'Who on earth did that to you?' Anne demanded.

'Who do you think?'

'How is he?' Sally asked.

'I'm fine, thanks,' Douglas muttered. 'He's fine as well. Everything went as planned.'

Anne pointed at his face. 'Including that?'

'He had to make it look real,' Douglas said. He touched his cheek and winced. 'Feels real as well.'

'So is the shiner you'll have in the morning,' Anne said. 'That's going to look very nasty.'

'Worth it.' Douglas shrugged off his jacket.

'You got it to him?'

Douglas nodded. 'In the fight when we both went down. It was simple enough.'

'Good.'

'So,' Douglas said. 'Where is he?'

Alistair stretched out in a comfortable double bed. He was beginning to doze but he would sleep only lightly. His door was locked but wouldn't resist an attack by a determined man. He was convinced that the two men asleep on the couches didn't suspect him. On the other hand, one couldn't be too careful.

He looked at the metal disc in his hand. It was around an inch across with a ridged surface. As long as he carried that, his team would be able to track him.

He slipped his hand under the pillow and released the disc. He would pick it up in the morning before leaving.

Before fully drifting into a sleep he moved his hand under the pillow and wrapped his fingers around the butt of the Walther PPK.

CHAPTER TWELVE

The report on the attack became the lead story on TV and radio news broadcasts. Or, at least, a largely fictional version of it. The official story was that an armed gang had been planning a series of raids. The presence of guns and explosives led to the police co-operating with the army. The news reports all stated that the operation went without a hitch and half a dozen armed men had surrendered to the authorities without a shot being fired. No mention was made of any link to the recent jailbreak from Wormwood Scrubs, the story which had been demoted to second item on the news.

Leslie Johnston mused that a cynical man might have thought that the positive story was being pushed hard to make up for the bad press the jailbreak had brought.

It was an interesting little aside but he had bigger issues to think about, and he was about to move on when he saw two words in a brief report by the police inspector.

Colonel Douglas.

What in the hell was Dougie doing participating in a bit of gangland shenanigans? Even if the army were to be involved, surely it would be the regulars rather than Douglas' mob?

The affair was now a good deal more interesting. Johnston read the records of the men who had been arrested. It wasn't mentioned in the arrest documents but their records all said the same thing. The men were known to be employed by Hugh Godfrey, the gangster who had escaped with Lethbridge-Stewart.

Were they involved simply because of Lethbridge-Stewart's escape? That would make sense. At least it would have made sense if Douglas and his mob hadn't been hanging around London in secret, investigating some ancient stone statues, and visiting similar statues of a more recent vintage.

'They were turned to stone,' he murmured, thinking of the statue he'd visited. 'And that cargo was stolen by gangland thugs.'

The connection was obvious. Leslie Johnston knew he had to find Hugh Godfrey.

Alistair woke early. It was pitch-dark outside and the rest of the flat was still silent. He washed and dressed without rousing his companions, and made sure that he had his tracking device in his pocket, disguised among spare change. The Walther PPK was again in place at the small of his back, hidden by a heavy sweater, and the spare clips in his trouser pocket.

As soon as he was dressed, Alistair went to the kitchen and made himself a cup of coffee. He had to make do with powdered milk, which tasted nothing at all like milk, but a few teaspoons of sugar made the coffee palatable. There was no bread or fresh food in the house, but there were tins in the cupboard along with a box of Scott's Porridge Oats. He didn't fancy tinned meat and potatoes for breakfast so he set about preparing a pot of porridge, making enough for all three of them. He flipped the wooden spoon so that he held it by the bowl and stirred the porridge with the handle as if it was a traditional Scottish spurtle.

The porridge had just started to bubble and spit when Nolan came into the small kitchen. He looked into the pot.

'Not porridge?' he said.

Alistair lifted out a thick dollop of porridge. 'None of that watery nonsense we had in prison,' he promised.

Nolan made himself a coffee. As an afterthought he made another cup, picking the nicest mug in the cupboard. 'Mr Godfrey's in the bathroom,' he said.

Alistair sniffed. 'Has he spoken to his people?'

'Not yet. He was pretty groggy when he woke up.'

Alistair chuckled. 'It was quite a busy night.'

'Yeah,' Nolan agreed quietly. 'Are you really a traitor?'

Alistair pushed a salt seller in front of Nolan. 'Eat up.'

Nolan ate his breakfast in silence. Alistair turned on the transistor radio to pick up the news. 'Unfortunately it only gets Radio One. Not my cup of tea at all, but at least they carry the news.'

'I like Radio One,' Nolan commented through a mouthful of porridge. 'My kind of music.'

Alistair harrumphed. David Bowie's *Space Oddity* took them into the latest news broadcast. The raid on the house was still the top news story, followed by the jailbreak.

'Wonder if anybody's been both the top stories on the news before?' Nolan asked. 'Good to know we haven't been caught anyway.'

'As long as it stays that way.'

They both looked up as Godfrey entered. What hair he had was wet and he was still hobbling slightly. He looked disdainfully at the porridge on the stove. 'Not exactly last night's steak, is it?' he grumbled.

Alistair noted that hint of grumbling self-pity with

satisfaction. He still had the upper hand. 'It'll do for now,' he said. 'If I had known I'd be using the place, I'd have tried to get a few supplies in. Still, we'll be gone in a few hours.'

'Get it for me,' Godfrey said, and Nolan quickly moved to do as he was told. 'How were you planning to get to Hull?' Godfrey asked Alistair.

'Train,' he answered quickly, using the backstory he had rehearsed so many times in the last two weeks. 'There's a cargo train that does a south to north run every morning. It picks up goods from Hull docks. Takes them there too. It always stops at a siding just outside Euston for ten minutes after it leaves the station heading north. It's occasionally been used to carry military gear north. Getting on board that would be easy enough.'

'Could all three of us get on board if we had to?'

'If we had to. Given up on your own men?'

'No,' Godfrey replied quickly. His response was so immediate that it could only seem hollow.

Alistair didn't want Godfrey to crumble completely. He needed the criminal to retain some of his arrogance and confidence. Just enough for him to stay useful. 'Good. You're only valuable to me if you have something worth trading when we get where we're going. Whatever it is, get it and we can leave this country.'

'All right.' Godfrey nodded. 'All right.'

'Do you have any kind of transport that can get us out of here?' Alistair asked.

'I've been thinking about that. I have my hands in a lot of businesses. There's a painter and decorator's van that will do the trick. We can be in the back with the paint and the sheets. They've never stopped the van before, though. It's a local business and nobody knows it's mine. I've used it to get people out of town a few times.'

'Good. How quickly can you get it here?'

'Half an hour.'

'Perfect,' Alistair said. 'There'll be plenty of traffic. Even if there are roadblocks, the police won't hold up every car and van once the horns start sounding. The army would but the police won't. They'll want to keep the traffic moving.'

Nolan set a bowl of porridge in front of Godfrey, and Godfrey aimed a thumb at the door 'Get yourself cleaned up.' He turned to Alistair. 'I'll make the call now.'

'Good.'

'They're on the move,' Anne said.

She was seated in the back of a transit van belonging to the newly-established Post Office Telecommunications, all white on the outside with a picture of their ubiquitous mascot, Buzby, the star of the popular BBC3 kids' cartoon. The equipment around her was modern but had nothing to do with delivering the latest telephones to homes. In front of her was a round, glowing scope which showed a map of London with a shining green light in the middle. The scope was attached to a small bank of computers and the aerial on top of the van.

Douglas leaned over her shoulder to peer at the scope. 'To where?'

Anne pointed at the street on the scope. 'Here.'

Douglas considered for a moment. 'They'll be slow in traffic.'

'But it's heavy traffic,' Anne added.

'They'll get through,' Douglas said confidently. 'He's got his tracker device so we can know where he is and call off any roadblocks in their way.'

That seemed fair to Anne. 'And we know what vehicle he's in, so it should be all right.'

'As long as everybody plays their part.'

Friday morning traffic in London was always insanely busy. Adding roadblocks to that only made it worse. Car horns blasted regularly and drivers cursed as they waited and slowly edged forward, waiting for their turn to go through the inspection.

Five from the front of a queue in a north London street, a Bedford van, its side panels spattered with paint, idled as it waited. Two bored-looking men in well-used overalls sat in the cab of the pug-nosed van, puffing on their cigarettes. The vehicles ahead were cleared quickly enough. A young policeman approached the driver's side of the van as it pulled to a stop.

'Hello, boys,' he said.

The driver gave a weary-looking nod of greeting. 'All right.'

'How many of you are there?'

The driver pointed at his passenger. 'Just the two of us.'

'Should be three of us at least,' the passenger grumbled. 'It's a three-man job, at least.'

'Just me and Happy Harry,' the driver confirmed.

The policeman pointed at the back of the van. 'What have you got in here?'

'Would it surprise you if I said paint?'

The young policeman laughed. 'Stupid question, sorry.'

'Don't worry about it, son,' the driver said. He opened his door. 'Come on, I'll show you the back.'

He led the way to the back of the van and pulled the doors open. It was a mess inside, piled halfway up the interior. Ladders and planks of wood lay on the floor and leaned against the sides, with huge tins of paint and carelessly discarded sheets covering most of the contents.

'Bloody hell,' the policeman said.

The driver shook his head sourly. 'Useless idiot up front didn't secure everything properly. Want to get up in there for a proper look?'

The policeman shook his head. 'No need. It's fine.' He pulled at one of the doors and stepped aside to let the driver close up the van. 'But if I was you I'd get your mate to empty it out when you get to your job.'

'You're damn right, and he will,' the driver said. 'Need anything else?'

'No.' The young policeman led the driver back to the cab and went back to his position as the driver climbed in. Just after he heard the door slam shut he turned and waved the van on. 'You can go through.'

The driver waved and released the clutch, quickly changing up into second gear. Once the checkpoint was out of sight, he shouted back through a grille into the back of the van. 'We're clear.'

In the back, the metal floor panel nearest the driver's cab flipped up. Alistair, Godfrey and Nolan sat up and started squeezing themselves out of the hidden floor space.

Godfrey patted the metal panel appreciatively. 'Nobody ever notices a fake floor if it's covered with junk.' He dusted himself down. 'Wish one of my boys had cleaned it up before we went in there.'

Alistair flexed his back. 'It wasn't meant for someone of my height, that's for sure.'

'Or my girth,' Godfrey chuckled, patting his belly. 'But it got the job done again.' He braced himself against the side as the van hit a pothole. 'Careful where you're driving. It's hard enough to stay on our feet back here.'

A muffled voice came from the front. 'Sorry, Mr Godfrey, sir.'

Nolan pulled a larger paint tin closer. 'Sit on this, Mr Godfrey.'

'All right.' Godfrey sat and spread his feet wide to brace himself. 'I suppose I can take this for an hour.'

'An hour?' Alistair asked. 'Where are we going?'

'You'll find out when we get there,' Godfrey said cagily. 'You'll find out when we get there.'

Alistair shrugged. 'As long as you don't slow us down or get us caught, I don't care where it is.'

'You'll find out soon enough.'

'Keep your distance,' Douglas called through the grille to the front of the POT van.

Bishop's voice returned quickly, 'Right, sir.'

'What's the range on this set-up?' Douglas asked Anne.

'Just over a mile.'

Douglas returned to the grille. 'Give them half a mile. We'll keep you updated with directions.'

'They just turned left,' Anne said. 'About three hundred yards ahead.'

'Turn left three hundred yards ahead,' Douglas relayed. He turned to the other seat in the back of the van where Sally sat holding an RT set. 'Pass that on to the troops. Tell them to stay a mile or so behind us.'

'Yes, sir.'

Godfrey was fairly accurate with his estimate of how long the journey would take. An hour and ten minutes after passing through the roadblock, the van pulled into the drive of a delightful old house on the edge of the village of Cradle End. It was a solid, square building, made of sturdy grey stone, and had once been a farmhouse. Now its grounds consisted of no more than a spacious garden of around half an acre. The drive was in need of repair but it put some distance between the house and the road. Trees and bushes finished the job of supplying the privacy Godfrey craved.

'Splendid house,' Alistair said appreciatively as he walked back and forth, trying to get the feeling back into his legs.

'Thanks,' Godfrey said. 'It's where I was planning on moving to when it looked like Ronnie and Reggie were going to take over London totally.'

Alistair froze in horror. 'You own this place? They're bound to have it under surveillance.'

'Calm down, General,' Godfrey said with a hint of his old arrogance. 'I wasn't stupid enough to buy it myself. I put the money through several people to get the house. Nobody knows it belongs to me.'

The front door opened and a tall thin man with sandy hair looked out. He had the look of a guard dog about him. 'Mr Godfrey,' he said.

Godfrey went into the house. 'Everything all right?' he asked.

His subordinate nodded and dropped into step at Godfrey's shoulder. 'Exactly as you asked, sir. We've got food in for you, plenty of the lads around.'

'Nobody was followed? We had enough of that yesterday.'

'We were careful,' the tall man assured him. 'Nobody knows we're here.'

'Let's keep it like that.'

'Right, Mr Godfrey.'

The house was spacious and surprisingly tastefully decorated. The front door led into an expansive hall with a reception room on either side, and a number of doors discreetly positioned along the walls. A large, polished wooden staircase dominated the centre of the hall. Alistair noted with interest that the furnishings were expensive and high quality. Either Godfrey or his wife had a tasteful eye, not to mention a deep pocket. He assumed it was Godfrey's wife. She came from a wealthy family who had fallen on hard times. The marriage was reported to have given financial security to her family while opening doors in business and society to Godfrey that he would otherwise never have dreamed of. Whether it was a marriage of any affection, Alistair had no idea, but it had been a good business deal for everyone involved.

'This way.' Godfrey led them through to the reception room on the left, which was clearly a part of the house he considered solely his. An antique desk sat to one side facing into the room. Behind the chair was a bookshelf which was only partly filled. The books were new, hardback and leather-bound editions of the classics. None of them had ever been opened. The rest of the room also had book cases, though none of them bore any books on their shelves. At the centre of the room, covered by a dust-sheet, was a snooker table with a large light suspended over it. A number of comfortable-looking couches were set around the large room. The positioning of the desk was a clear message, though. The person sitting at that desk oversaw the room like a king from his throne.

'Splendid house,' Alistair said admiringly.

'Thank you,' Godfrey replied. He turned to his tall subordinate. 'Right, Hansen, who knows about this place?'

'The boys who are here only saw the place for the first time today,' Hansen answered. 'Only the people you told know about it, unless anybody blabbed.'

'If they did, they'll be sorry,' Godfrey promised. 'The wife doesn't know I'm here, does she?'

'No. She thinks you're in Brighton.'

'Good, let's keep it that way. She'll have my guts for garters when she hears I'm selling this place.' Godfrey took a seat behind his desk. Alistair could see the man's confidence grow as he took a position of power. That confirmed him as a fragile sort who needed to be constantly reminded that he was in charge and that he wasn't going to be challenged. He didn't want his men to know he was no longer in charge of his plans. It confirmed what Alistair already suspected about the man.

'Selling?' Hansen asked.

'Yeah, selling,' Godfrey snarled. 'I can't come back to this country, can I? No, best to have the money. For business,' he added quickly. 'We can use it in the business.'

'Understood,' Hansen nodded. 'The boys in Plymouth are ready to get you across to Spain. The plan is to take you in through Portugal. Land in Lisbon and take you from there.'

'Change of plan,' Godfrey said dismissively. He pointed at Alistair. 'I'll be leaving the country with him.'

Hansen looked uncomfortable about the change. 'Sir?'

'You heard,' Godfrey answered. 'He's got a buyer for a piece of merchandise I picked up a while ago.' He leaned forward, beckoning Hansen closer. 'It's a solid deal, son. Best we've ever made. It's worth a few days' delay in putting my feet up in sunny Spain.' He winked. 'A lot of money.'

The greed in his employer's voice put Hansen at ease and he visibly relaxed. 'Anything you say, sir.'

Godfrey nodded at the door. 'Go and rustle up a decent breakfast for us, would you. Anything but porridge.'

Hansen left to carry out Godfrey's instructions.

'Anything I can do, Mr Godfrey?' Nolan asked.

Godfrey thought for a moment. 'Yes, you're pretty handy in the kitchen. Go and help Hansen. Tell him I sent you.'

'Yes, Mr Godfrey.'

Alistair waited until Nolan had gone before speaking. 'I'll be going north in the morning. There's still time for you to go back to your original plan. Plymouth then Lisbon doesn't sound too bad.'

Godfrey cut him off. 'If I'm tarred by escaping with you I've got no option except to go with you. Besides, I'm pretty sure I can bargain my way into a good deal with your new *comrades*.'

'That depends what you have to offer,' Alistair said calmly.

'I'll show you.'

Godfrey pushed himself out of his comfortable leather swivel chair and started pulling books from the shelves behind him. A metallic rectangle was embedded in the wall behind the shelves. As he approached, Alistair could see that the wall was concrete rather than plaster.

'That's a solid-looking safe,' he said.

Godfrey nodded. 'One of the benefits of my line of work is that I know a good deal about safes. How to keep them locked as well as how to open them.' He spun the dial quickly, reversing its direction twice, before twisting the handle downwards and pulling the door open. 'And the one thing I learned about them was that there's always a clever sod able to open a safe. That's why I play it cagey.' He plucked a sheet of paper from the safe and moved to the snooker table.

On the wall by the table was a snooker hall style

scoreboard with two brass markers running up to '20', with two more runners to the side marking increments of twenty. He released a catch at the side of the board and swung it outwards. Behind it sat another safe, this time with three dials.

'This is a good deal more complex. It has a clock inside run by a battery. The dials match numbers as codes to the time, the date and the day of the week. That sheet of paper had the information I needed to decode it.' He tapped his forehead. 'But half of the info is stored up here, so nobody but me can open this.'

'Very impressive,' Alistair admitted. He genuinely admired the workmanship, if not the reasons for its existence. 'What happens if the battery runs flat?'

'Three back-ups,' Godfrey answered. 'And if needs be, it can leech off the mains.'

'You're not taking any chances.'

'Not likely.' Godfrey reached inside the safe and produced a wooden box around six inches deep, six inches wide and nine or ten inches long. He returned to his desk and set the box down.

'What is it?' Alistair asked.

Godfrey flipped the box open. Sitting on a red velvet inlay was a dark grey rock just smaller than a fist.

'A stone?' Alistair hissed icily. 'You think they'll take us in with open arms when you offer them a piece of stone? Are you trying to get us killed?'

Godfrey carefully picked up the stone. 'This isn't an ordinary stone,' he said, tapping the side of his nose knowingly.

'Really?' Alistair made himself sound as if he didn't believe a word Godfrey was saying.

Godfrey was obviously eager to show he had an advantage over Alistair. 'You remember that incident in August last year? Parachute Regiment had their cargo stolen?'

Alistair pretended to think before answering. 'In a village somewhere?' he said thoughtfully. He nodded, as though memories were returning. 'A pitched battle, wasn't there? Some soldiers were killed in an explosion?'

'That wasn't our intention,' Godfrey said quickly. 'We went out of our way not to hurt anybody. We used tear gas to make sure nobody got hurt.' He grimaced in a near apology. 'They came after my boys and started the shooting while they were just hiding out in a garage. One of your lads shot a petrol pump and it went up.'

Alistair carefully avoided giving any comment on Godfrey's telling of events. 'Which doesn't explain that stone you have there.'

Godfrey continued eagerly. 'After the explosion, your boys were turned to stone. Petrified or something.'

'Turned to stone?' Alistair sounded incredulous. 'Utter poppycock. It's not possible.'

'I know,' Godfrey replied eagerly. 'It's impossible but it happened. If you don't believe me, it won't be hard for you to find out about it.'

Alistair took a step closer to the desk and peered down at the stone. 'But how?' he asked. 'How can a simple stone do that?'

Godfrey spread his hands wide. 'I haven't got a clue, but do you think your *tovarischy* would be interested in it?'

Alistair reached for the stone, then pulled his hand away. 'If that could be turned into a weapon, it would be devastating.'

'So,' Godfrey smiled, 'do you think they'll be interested?'

'I'm sure they already know part of it, but to get their

hands on the rock itself...' Alistair nodded absently. 'Oh, yes. They'll want it all right.' He looked away from the stone and caught Godfrey's gaze. 'I'm not surprised the government wants you dead.'

'That puts us in the same boat, doesn't it? So, are you sure you can get us out of the country?'

'Yes,' Alistair confirmed. 'I'll have to phone my contact.'

'Why?' Godfrey was immediately suspicious.

'So that he knows when I want to go and how many people he has to sneak onto the train and onto the ship.' Alistair glanced at the door, to make sure they were alone. 'Is it three or just the two of us?'

Godfrey thought about the question for a long moment. It was obvious that loyalty to Nolan wasn't motivating him. 'Yes,' he said finally. 'Three. A bit of extra protection won't go amiss.'

'Good,' Alistair said. 'Nolan helped me when I was inside. It feels like I owe him.'

'But you'd have left him behind if I'd said it was just the two of us.'

'Of course,' Alistair replied blandly.

'Fair enough.' Godfrey picked up the stone again and turned it over in his hand, examining it. 'So, this contact of yours. Who is it?'

'Matt Randall. Formerly Captain Matthew Randall.'

'Ex-soldier?' Godfrey sounded dubious. 'Is he likely to help an escaped con get out of the country? What about his duty?'

'Matt gave up on his duty a long time ago. He'd say it was more accurate that his duty gave up on him. He was a good officer. They treated him badly.'

'You trust him?' Godfrey pressed. 'With your life?'

'He trusted me with his,' Alistair answered. 'So, I need to call him to make arrangements for tomorrow morning. I assume you can have false passports ready for you and Nolan by then.'

'I could have passports ready for us before breakfast is ready,' Godfrey boasted.

'I won't use the phone here. I doubt if there's any chance of a problem, but there's no point in taking risks. I saw a phone box about half a mile outside the village. If one of your chaps could drive me there we can do this quickly and, of course, he can keep an eye on me to make sure everything is above board.'

'Do I need to keep an eye on you to make sure everything is legit?'

'No, but you're going to do it anyway, so this way at least we just get it out in the open and don't play games about it.'

'Fair enough.' Godfrey laughed. 'I'll get Hansen to drive you there after we've eaten; unless a bowl of porridge was enough for you.'

Alistair made a face and snorted. 'I've had enough porridge for a dozen lifetimes.'

'Right,' Godfrey said, 'let's see what they've got for us.'

Half a mile from Godfrey's house, a wooded hill overlooked the village. On a farm track cutting through the trees, a rather incongruous POT van pulled to a stop. An army Bedford lorry was labouring along the track a hundred yards behind.

Douglas didn't wait for his men to arrive. He leaped down to the ground before turning to offer Sally assistance. She didn't need help and dealt with the drop easily on her own. He felt Anne's withering glance from inside the van, but was relieved there was no verbal dressing down. Bad enough having a female NCO out in the field like this, but to bring with them a civilian... Douglas wasn't best pleased, but he chose to make the best of it. Still, at least Anne was staying inside the van to monitor her equipment.

'This way,' he said, leading the way off the road into the trees. He looked back at the soldiers disembarking from the Bedford. 'Get the surveillance equipment over here,' he called out to Samson, who was getting the troops into shape. 'Be quick about it, and be quiet about it as well.'

'Sir.' Without hesitation Samson began ordering his men into position.

The soldiers ran to obey, bringing high powered binoculars and cameras with telephoto lenses. Three soldiers took their positions, scrutinising the house. One would scan the upstairs windows, one the downstairs, and the third would watch the house's grounds.

Douglas took a set of binoculars offered by Bishop. 'Thank you, Lieutenant.'

'Sir.'

'Everybody stay out of sight,' Douglas commanded. 'And watch out for light hitting your lenses. That'll give our position away quicker than anything.'

'You heard the colonel. Snap to it!' Samson ordered.

The soldiers settled into their positions. Douglas swung his binoculars across the scene below. He could see movement behind several of the windows, and a couple of men patrolled the garden. Both were clearly armed with short barrelled shotguns.

'Anybody got sight of him?' Douglas asked.

The answer came from Sally. 'There. In the car.' She was pointing to a car which had come out from behind the cover of a bush and was heading onto the drive. The moustached face in the passenger seat was unmistakable. 'Is he making a break for it?'

'At that speed?' Douglas asked, watching the car trundle along the drive. 'No, he's up to something, though.'

'The tracker is still working,' Anne called, peering out of the back of the van. 'I can see he's on the move.'

Douglas scratched his chin thoughtfully. 'I wonder where he's going?'

The dial-tone purred three times in Lethbridge-Stewart's ear before he heard the receiver at the other end being picked up. He pushed the first of his coins into the slot.

'Hello?' a cautious voice said.

Lethbridge-Stewart spoke in a friendly and cheerful tone. 'My dear fellow, how are you? Listen, your wife's not listening there, is she?'

'Relax,' the voice came back. 'I'm off the network. Nobody's listening in.'

'I'm glad to hear it,' Lethbridge-Stewart returned briskly, all business again. 'I'm looking to be on my way in the morning.'

'Sounds fine.'

'Yes,' Lethbridge-Stewart said dryly. 'Thing is, I won't be travelling alone. There'll be three of us.'

'Three?' The man on the other end sounded angry. 'That wasn't the deal.'

'It is now, Randall,' Lethbridge-Stewart said with a challenging edge in his voice. 'If you don't like it, I'll make other arrangements.'

'No, no. I can do it,' Matt Randall's voice came back in a more conciliatory tone. 'But it'll cost you, and I'm going to need pictures of the other two who are travelling.'

'What for?'

'Documentation doesn't just happen by accident, you know that. I'll need pictures. Ideally with them bearded up.'

'Beards?' Lethbridge-Stewart asked.

'I can sneak one through. Three of you...? There'll need to be disguises.'

'It's not my decision on the other two,' Lethbridge-Stewart said. He beckoned to Hansen. 'He needs to talk to you about Godfrey and Nolan.'

Hansen took the phone and spoke briefly with Randall. Lethbridge-Stewart heard only Hansen' side of the conversation, though he knew exactly what Randall would be saying on the other end. He had been in the briefings about that.

'What do you need?' Hansen asked first. More short answers followed. 'What for? Why can't he use the one we got done for him? I don't know if he will. I can't say. Because I can't say; he's the boss and I ain't. Of course he does. I can't say yeah or no to that. That's fair enough. I get it. I understand. Get the train to Bishop's Stortford. We'll meet you there, or we won't. Depends what Mr Go... the boss says.' He listened for a few moments before handing the phone over to Lethbridge-Stewart. 'He doesn't like the idea of coming here.'

Lethbridge-Stewart put the phone to his ear. 'It's me again, Randall.'

'The other fella gone?'

'He's not far away.'

Randall picked up on the cue. 'Right. Do you want me to come there?'

'If it's the only way to get what you need. Just make sure you're not followed.'

Randall snorted on the other end. He sounded insulted. 'You ever met anyone who can follow me?'

'Get there as quick as you can. Somebody will be waiting for you.'

'Right.'

Alistair hung up. 'He's cautious.'

'That's one word for it,' Hansen answered.

Alistair smiled wryly. 'He's damn rude, too, but he's the best I know at getting anything you need.'

'Fixer, eh?'

'Something like that,' Alistair agreed. 'Shall we go back?' He looked around. 'I'm rather nervous being quite so exposed.'

'Yeah. Come on.'

Hansen slid behind the wheel and started the engine, setting them on their way back to the house.

No matter how careful Matt Randall or the army engineers were, Leslie Johnston found someone just a little bit smarter. Randall's line was one of many under surveillance, not for any threat to the UK, but for an opportunity for Johnston to push his own agenda. As soon as Lethbridge-Stewart's instantly recognisable voice appeared on the line, the operative listening started recording and set about tracing Lethbridge-Stewart's location. Twenty minutes later a sheet of A4 paper appeared in front of Johnston.

He looked up at Laurence Bowen. 'Urgent, I take it?'

'You could say that.'

Johnston trusted Bowen's sense of priorities. He put aside what he was doing and read the new piece of paper. It was a transcript of the telephone conversation between Randall and Lethbridge-Stewart. The additional lines at the top and bottom had Johnston on his feet.

Bowen hadn't moved from the other side of the table. 'What do you think?'

'We're moving in fifteen minutes,' Johnston said. 'Get everybody ready.'

— CHAPTER THIRTEEN —

Hugh Godfrey had never been a great snooker player. However, he thought the full-size snooker table added a touch of class to his study. Like the books, it was for show. On this day, however, he was enjoying himself just knocking the balls around the table. After so long in prison, this was something he could *choose* to do. On a whim he even turned the light above the table on. Adopting a gravelly, slow tone like the commentator on *Pot Black*, he spoke as he circled the table.

'And Ray Reardon, always thinking six shots ahead, dazzling his opponents with his careful planning and precise moves, settles down for his next shot.'

He brought the cue through, sending the white ball the length of the table where it struck the yellow, sending the coloured ball towards the pocket. The yellow rattled in the jaws of the pocket before bouncing clear.

'Bugger.' He was sure he had that one. Maybe it was the light that had put him off the shot.

Godfrey strode across to the door and turned on the main lights in the room. It didn't matter that it was mid-afternoon. The sun was low at that time of year and the clouds made the room dull. The lights came on, immediately making the room much brighter.

'That's better,' Godfrey muttered and went back to the

snooker table. He got down on a shot and potted a long red. 'Much better.' Moving around to line up the black, Godfrey reached into his pocket for the cue chalk. Instead his hand found the rock. He was surprised to find it still in his pocket. Why hadn't he put it back in the box? It was priceless to him. It needed to be kept safe.

He didn't remove the stone from his pocket.

No, surely the safest place was with him. He would keep it close to hand.

He withdrew his hand from the pocket, leaving the stone where it was. A TV sat in the study, opposite one of the couches. It was a new, colour set. He turned it on. Snow stared at him. It was afternoon so the channels would all have shut down. He turned away from the TV without switching it off and turned on the radio instead. He turned the dial away from the awful racket of Radio One until he found the reassuring tones of Dean Martin on Radio Two.

'Everybody loves somebody, Dino?' he chuckled. 'You're right, and I love *me*.'

He settled down on his shot, sending the black cleanly into the corner pocket.

'There he is,' Anne said.

She emerged from the van after tracking Lethbridge-Stewart's movements on the scope. Initially, Douglas had been ready to move the entire unit in pursuit, but when Anne placed Lethbridge-Stewart at a public call box he surmised that his old friend had decided it was time to phone Matt Randall. A message over the shortwave radio a few minutes later confirmed the idea. From there it was obvious that Lethbridge-Stewart would soon be heading back to the house. It was also obvious that they were coming to the end of this mission and they would be moving into action soon.

He called Samson over and explained the situation. With a salute, Samson returned to the rest of the men.

'All right, lads,' he said. 'We'll be on the move soon enough. Keep your eyes sharp for the Brig's signal.'

Watching the beautiful old house, Douglas felt his shoulders rise and forced himself to relax. This could be a long wait. 'Relax,' he murmured to himself. 'Relax.'

The first thing Alistair noted when he entered the house was how loud the music was being played in Godfrey's study. It was a light orchestral piece, not really suited to the volume.

'Godfrey? Godfrey?'

The older man didn't respond until Alistair called his name a second time. He was entertaining himself by smashing snooker balls around the baize.

'It's you,' he said, looking up from the table. 'Everything set?'

'Getting that way,' Alistair replied.

'What?' Godfrey cocked his ear, unable to hear the reply properly. He turned down the radio and looked at the snowy-screened TV in confusion for a second before turning it off. 'Right,' he said. 'What were you saying?'

'I said, we've got things moving. But we need you to do a few things before we can go.'

'Such as?'

Alistair turned to Hansen. 'Why don't you tell him?'

'All right.' Hansen relayed his conversation with Randall to Godfrey. He seemed uncertain as to how his employer would react to the revelation that Randall was on his way. Instead, Godfrey looked to Alistair.

'Do you trust him?'

'I trust that he'll get me out of the country because the price is right,' Alistair said, 'and I trust his fondness for getting the right price for what he does.'

Godfrey pondered for a moment before nodding. 'I know where I stand with a man who has a price. Bring him and we'll get this over with.'

'Right, sir,' Hansen said. 'I'll go and get him. I'll take one of the lads with me.'

'You'll need a description of him before you go,' Alistair said.

'Don't you want to go and meet him yourself?' Godfrey asked.

'And risk being seen by the police? Not a chance.'

Godfrey's mouth quirked into a slight grimace. 'Fair enough. Give Hansen the description and he'll pick up your mate.'

'I'll do you a cuppa and you can tell me over that,' Hansen said, heading for the door.

Alistair agreed and followed. As he left, he heard Godfrey turn the music up again. Frank Sinatra singing about something that happened in Monterrey. Again the music was too loud. While he had no objection to Sinatra, he did wonder why the music had to be so blessed loud. He was glad to be getting into the kitchen away from it.

Johnston was not a man who enjoyed getting his hands dirty, which is why he was the right hand man to the General. He had operatives who did the work for him. In this instance, however, he was intrigued by the situation with Lethbridge-Stewart and the petrification of soldiers.

The General had cautioned him on getting too caught up in Lethbridge-Stewart's latest little adventure, but Johnston reasoned if anybody should understand why Lethbridge-Stewart needed to be monitored it was the General.

'Monitored is one thing, Leslie. Getting close is another. Don't underestimate Alistair. The old man should be kept at arms-length until I'm ready.'

It was good advice, so Johnston ignored it anyway.

The Bishop's Stortford Railway Station was remarkably bland and typical of a small town train station, with Victorian brickwork being the dominant feature of the place. It had three or four platforms but Johnston only cared about the platform bringing the train from London.

He positioned six of his men along the station but cut that number to four, sending two to sit outside in the vehicles. The platform was simply too small for so many men to be anything but a warning to anyone experienced in subterfuge.

Johnston showed photographs of Lethbridge-Stewart, Godfrey and Matt Randall to his men so that they would know who to look out for. He didn't expect all three to be present but he liked to cover all eventualities.

Johnston himself took up a seat in a café, seated well away from the door so that any eyes that strayed through the window would dismiss him as a nondescript background figure reading a newspaper.

The train pulled into the station just a few minutes behind schedule, which seemed to be regarded by the waiting passengers as something somewhere between a triumph and a miracle. Through the shuffling mass of passengers getting off the train and those waiting to replace them on the next leg of its journey, Johnston spotted a familiar face.

Matt Randall had clearly glanced around the platform as he waited for the old woman ahead of him to get off the train. Having stepped down onto the platform, he became very difficult to spot. Despite his height, he managed to blend into the crowd, and Johnston lost him twice, only spotting him again by watching the eye-line of two of his own men and working out Randall's position from those.

Johnston left the café, walking in a relaxed manner, following the direction Randall had taken. He was aware of his men following. He gave a slight gesture to Bowen to hang back. He didn't want to risk being spotted.

Just outside the main entrance, Johnston saw Randall being stopped by a tall, rugged, sandy-haired man in a tan leather jacket. The fellow looked like a rough sort who was trying to appear more civilised.

An ape in a suit is still an ape, Johnston thought. Obviously someone who worked for Godfrey. Of Godfrey himself there was no sign. Lethbridge-Stewart was nowhere to be seen either. Johnston gave the prearranged signal for his men to do nothing and to blend into the background.

Randall and the ape talked quietly and quickly, with Randall tapping his satchel. He also quickly pointed under his left arm to where a very slight bulge gave away the presence of a shoulder holster. The ape nodded and led the way to a green Vauxhall. Once they were seated, Johnston saw Randall quickly reach under his arm and hand something across to the ape. Obviously his pistol.

Johnston's men returned to the cars, and Johnston made his way back to his as the green Vauxhall pulled away. He slipped into the passenger seat. 'Follow at a distance,' he told Bowen.

'Yes, sir.'

The engine revved and the car eased out after the Vauxhall. 'Give him some space,' Johnston said. 'If they realise they're being followed they'll make a run for it. Drop back.'

Bowen slowed and let the Vauxhall pull ahead before he increased speed again and kept the Vauxhall just in sight.

'Better,' Johnston nodded his approval. 'Better.'

It was Bishop who spotted the returning Vauxhall. 'It's coming back,' he said without moving the binoculars from his eyes. 'He's got a passenger with him.'

Douglas had been watching the house. He took his binoculars back along the drive and recognised a familiar face in the passenger seat. 'It's Randall.'

'Do you move in now?' Anne asked. She was holding out a mug of hot, army tea to Douglas. He took the mug.

'Maybe,' he answered. 'But not until we get a signal from inside.'

'How long do you think that will take?'

Douglas shrugged. 'Honestly? I have no idea. Why? You getting bored of our company?'

Anne jerked her head towards the van. 'I wasn't thinking about me.'

'Ah.' Douglas understood exactly what Anne meant. 'How is Corporal Wright?'

'Busy,' Anne answered. 'I left her in charge of the scope.'

'Keeping her distracted?'

'Keeping her busy,' Anne corrected. 'I think she'll feel more connected if she can see where he is on the scope.'

'Makes sense,' Douglas agreed. 'You weren't an officer in a previous life were you?'

Anne scowled in a good-natured, playful way. 'You know, I'm not sure if that's a compliment or an insult.'

'It's one of those,' Douglas answered with a smile. 'Or neither. I'm not sure.' All through the little piece of banter his eyes never shifted from the house below.

'He'll be all right,' Anne said. 'He's good at what he does and he's too stubborn to let anything go wrong.'

'I know.'

'And he's too scared of Sally to let himself get hurt.'

Douglas half smiled. Clearly Anne didn't know as much about *that* relationship as she thought. Still, not his place to educate her. 'I know that, too. It's just… This has been an odd mission. I'm keen for it to be completed so we can get back to a hint of normal.'

'When do we ever get normal?' Anne said softly.

'You know what I mean.'

She nodded. 'I do. I'd like some normal back, too. I haven't spent enough time with my father these past weeks.'

Douglas glanced at her. 'How is he?'

'Bad tempered, irascible, forgetful.'

'That sounds like him,' Douglas said.

A cloud passed over Anne's face. 'Yes, but sometimes *he* doesn't sound like him anymore.'

'We all get older,' Douglas said softly, keeping the conversation for their ears only. 'We know it's has to happen.' He sighed. 'But we're never quite prepared for the people in our lives to get older. Still, his little adventure on the Orkney Islands must have been good for him?'

'For a while, yes, but that was almost six weeks ago.'

'As long as that?' Douglas shook his head. 'Doesn't seem that long ago I came up against the Bandrils.'

Anne joined him in staring at the house. 'I wish it was just that…' Now she sighed, and shook her head. 'Those people who were turned to stone. Do you think they would rather have grown old?'

'I can't speak for them, but I know that if I had to choose

between getting old and going through what they have...? Yes, I'd want to grow old, see my son become a man, see the girl that wins his heart.'

Anne smiled softly. 'Exactly, I *know* they would rather have grown old, too. They'd have aged with their families around them.' She visibly shook herself. 'Go down and tell him to get a move on, would you? I'd like to get back to Edinburgh to see my father.'

Alistair was summoned to the study as soon as the car was spotted in the drive and was already waiting there when Matt Randall was escorted in. Alistair had to ask Godfrey to turn down both the music and the heating. Both were overpowering. Alistair was relieved to see Randall was unharmed. Logic told him that Godfrey needed the documents and skills Randall was bringing. Experience and sense told him that a villain like Godfrey was unpredictable. Randall was led into Godfrey's office by Hansen.

As he was brought in, Randall greeted Alistair with a cheeky smile. 'Hello. Sorry.' He paused for effect. 'Should that be "hello, *sir*"?'

'You know damn well it shouldn't,' Alistair replied. 'It's good to see you.'

'You mean it's good to see me because I'm your passage out of dear old Blighty.' Randall didn't sound offended.

Godfrey cut through the banter. 'Was he armed?'

Hansen pulled Randall's pistol from his pocket and handed it across to Godfrey. 'Handed it over as soon as we got in the car, Mr Godfrey.'

'No objection?'

Hansen shook his head. 'He didn't like it but he didn't cause a fuss.'

'It wasn't worth jeopardising business,' Randall said straight to Godfrey. 'I'm here to do a job and make some money. I can't do that if I'm standing on a platform waiting for a train back to the Smoke, and that was what your boy here told me would happen if I didn't hand it over.'

'He was right,' Godfrey said. 'So, let's get to business. You can get me and my boy Nolan passports overnight?'

'Yep,' Randall replied. 'But at short notice, it won't be cheap.

'How much?'

Randall puffed his cheeks out and appeared to give the matter some thought. 'Well, I charged the brigadier here two and a half grand for the full escape package.' He stared accusingly at Alistair. 'Though that included being in a car outside the Scrubs waiting for him when he escaped. I was a little surprised to hear he got out without letting me know first.'

'It was a last minute change of plan,' Alistair said impassively.

'Like dropping an extra two men on me with less than a day's notice?'

'How much?' Godfrey repeated.

Randall flicked a hand in Alistair's direction. 'He was two and a half, so that would be five thousand for the two extras, but I'll need to pay someone on top of my usual crew to get this done in time, so that's a bit extra. Six grand for the pair of you. That gets you both from here, past customs and immigration, across to Europe where Mr Moustache has had me get a car waiting. I'm told it's not a bad little motor.'

'Six grand?' Godfrey said angrily. 'Six grand? That's twice what the average man makes in a year.'

'True.' Randall smiled. 'But if I was an average man I

couldn't get you out of the country at a day's notice, could I?'

'You're a crook,' Godfrey snapped.

'Is there anybody in this house who isn't?' Randall asked reasonably.

Godfrey looked Randall up and down for a moment before he replied. 'All right. It's bloody extortion but I'll pay the six grand.'

'Cash works for me,' Randall said cheerfully. 'I've never liked cheques. Banks give me the heebie-jeebies. People keep robbing them.'

'Cash,' Godfrey agreed. 'After you do whatever needs doing.'

Randall flipped his satchel open and pulled out a brown paper bag. From inside he withdrew a greying beard. 'You're the one they've been putting on telly. You're the one they'll be looking for most. So, you need to turn into a disgusting old Norwegian sailor nobody will look at twice.'

'I don't talk Norwegian.'

'Neither does the bloke who's going to wave you through. Act drunk. You'll be fine.' Randall pulled a small plastic container from his satchel. 'Coloured contacts, a beard and the wig I've got for you, your wife wouldn't recognise you.'

'Suits me,' Godfrey said. 'Right. Let's get on with it.'

After Randall had been delivered to the house, the troops from the Fifth's 2nd Battalion focused their attention on the house and its grounds, preparing for whatever action would be necessary. It wasn't until at least half an hour after Randall arrived that they spotted the cars that were parked out of view of the house; out of view but clearly watching the entry to the drive. Both cars were in the shade of whatever bushes were

206

still wearing their leaves. They were on opposite sides of the entrance and a good way back. Whenever a vehicle came out of Godfrey's house they would be in position to see it and follow it.

As soon as Samson alerted Douglas about the cars he sent a couple of men to have a closer look with their binoculars – and with stern orders to stay out of sight – but both returned empty handed. They couldn't make out much. The cars were in shade and the only light came from the occasional spark of a match as someone lit a cigarette.

'They know how to hide,' Douglas said to Anne, as they all gathered around the POT van. 'They're professionals.'

'Another gang?' Anne asked.

'I think we can take a better guess than that. Johnston's men, and they've thrown a spanner in the works.'

Nods of agreement from Samson and Bishop.

'What are we going to do?' Anne pressed. 'Can you capture them?'

'Not without letting Godfrey know we're here.'

'So? What do we do?'

Douglas thought hard for a long moment, chewing on his bottom lip as he did so. 'Nothing,' he said finally.

'Nothing?'

'Sir?' Samson stepped forward, but Douglas held up a hand.

'Nothing,' he repeated. 'One of the first lessons we're taught at Sandhurst is to avoid knee-jerk reactions. No,' he continued thoughtfully, 'we have the advantage. Godfrey doesn't know anyone is watching him, and our friends in those cars don't know we're watching them. Let's see what they do and take it from there.'

*

'First one of you who laughs gets a hiding, got it?'

Godfrey stared at his reflection in the mirror. The dirty grey beard and wig completely changed the look and shape of his face. The coloured lenses also changed things considerably.

'Told you that you wouldn't recognise yourself,' Randall said. He sounded pleased with himself. 'If I'd had time I could have got you a nice alchy's red nose and some rotten teeth, but we'll make do.'

'Just get on with it,' Godfrey complained. 'These lenses are killing my eyes.'

'Won't be long,' Randall promised. He turned to the spectacled man with a thick mop of shaggy hair. 'Right, Woodstock, let's get your picture taken.'

Nolan, under the heavy disguise, did as he was told. He stood with his back against a blank featureless wall while Randall took his picture with the camera. The camera flashed once. 'And another,' Randall said. Nolan stayed still and the camera flashed again. 'Right, that's you done.' He turned to Godfrey. 'Your turn.'

The crook did as he was asked, taking Nolan's place against the wall. 'Here?'

'Perfect.' Randall nodded. 'You know the drill. Keep your face neutral. No expression. Nothing to draw attention to you.'

'You think this bloody hair won't do that?'

The bulb flashed bright.

'Another one,' Randall said.

The bulb flashed again.

'Right, that's us done,' Randall said.

'Do another,' Godfrey demanded.

Randall shook his head absently. 'No need. These'll be

fine.'

Godfrey took a step forward and slapped Randall hard. 'I said take another one.'

The room stopped. Everyone stared at Godfrey in silent shock. The violence came completely out of the blue. The oddest thing was that through his rage, even Godfrey seemed surprised.

Alistair started to move forward but Randall held up his hand. 'No,' he said. 'If you want another picture taken, I'll do it.'

Godfrey regained his usual composure. 'Right you will,' he said, resuming his place against the wall.

Randall peered into the camera, and a moment later the bulb flashed.

'Another one,' Godfrey said. He sounded greedy, almost desperate.

'All right,' Randall said, 'but this is the last one I can take. The flash is dead after this one.' He clicked the camera and the flash flared. 'That's it,' he said. He clicked the camera again. There was no flash.

Godfrey didn't answer immediately. Randall's words seemed to take a little time to register with him. 'Right,' he said eventually. 'Okay. What else?'

Randall pulled hand-written sheets of lined paper from his satchel and handed half of them to Godfrey. The other half went to Nolan. 'Your cover stories,' he said. 'You won't be stopped and questioned but it's better to have all the angles covered. If anybody asks you where you're from, stick to what's on these sheets and you'll be fine.'

'If we get asked anything we'll be sunk,' Godfrey answered. 'It'll mean somebody's onto us.'

Randall shook his head. 'People get bored on boats. They

start conversations with strangers to pass the time. If they talk to you, they'll just be trying to kill some time.'

'If they talk to me, maybe I'll just kill them.'

'Or if you don't want to attract attention and wind up getting all three of your thrown back into jail,' Randall said sarcastically, 'you could just pretend to be drunk and asleep.'

Godfrey looked at Randall with distaste. 'You've got a mouth on you.'

'And a brain as well.'

'And we're paying for those,' Alistair interrupted. 'We're all stuck in this together.' He passed between Godfrey and Randall, forcing them both to take a step backwards so that he could get through. 'We need Randall to get us out of the country and he needs us to pay him for that. Everybody's on edge because we're getting to the sharp end of this business. Let's keep our heads and we'll all get out of this in one piece with a decent profit in our pockets.'

'Fair enough,' Randall agreed.

Even Godfrey conceded. 'All right. Let's just get on with it.' He took the papers Randall had given him, and went back to his desk. 'Get him back to London and we'll get this done.'

Hansen hurried out into the hallway. 'Yes, sir.'

'Well, Randall,' Alistair said, gently easing Randall towards the door. 'You're absolutely certain everything is in hand?'

'Absolutely, your brigadiership,' Randall replied.

'Good.' Alistair nodded. 'Just don't leave anything to chance.'

Randall looked pained and insulted. 'Have some faith.'

They almost reached the door when Hansen ran in. He looked agitated.

'What is it?' Alistair demanded.

'Cars at the front,' Hansen said.

Godfrey was on his feet immediately. 'What do you mean?'

'Two cars,' Hansen said. 'One on either side.'

'Police?' Godfrey demanded.

'No markings. We can't see who's inside.'

Godfrey swung angrily to face Randall. 'You sold us out.'

'Don't be stupid,' Randall protested. 'If you get caught, I don't get paid.'

'Unless you're already filth.'

'What do you mean?' Alistair demanded. 'What are you saying?'

'I'm asking if your mate here is working for the coppers.'

'Of course he isn't,' Alistair said angrily.

Godfrey turned to him suspiciously. 'And what makes you so sure?'

'Whoever they are,' Randall said desperately, 'straight up, they're not with me. Straight up.'

'Shut him up,' Godfrey snapped. Immediately, Nolan slammed a forearm into Randall's kidneys and the ex-army man's knees buckled.

Godfrey turned back to Alistair. 'I'll ask you again. How come you're sure he's not working for the police?'

'Because it would mean he had betrayed *me*,' Alistair said. 'He wouldn't do that.' Whoever was outside, he knew they weren't with Randall. 'Straight up' was a simple piece of code. When repeated it meant that what was being said really was genuine.

Godfrey eyed Randall suspiciously. The former soldier was still on the ground, Nolan's hand on his shoulder, keeping him down. 'You don't think he'd sell you out?' he said to Alistair.

'No.'

'Why not?'

'Because he knows what would happen if he did.'

'I didn't,' Randall said desperately. 'I don't know who they are, and I'm in it as deep as you.'

'You're in it deeper,' Godfrey said.

'What do you mean?' Alistair demanded.

Godfrey ignored him. 'Find out if he's telling the truth,' he said to Nolan.

'Now wait a minute,' Alistair protested.

He was too late. Nolan was already slamming his fist down into Randall's face. Randall's head jerked violently sideways under the impact. Stunned, he straightened in time for another thundering punch to slam into his face.

'Enough!' Alistair barked. 'He wouldn't betray me. There's nothing in it for him.'

Hansen grabbed Randall by the hair and pulled him upright. Blood was already flowing from Randall's mouth. It sprayed as Hansen slammed his fist hard into the ex-soldier's gut. Randall took a step towards Hansen but Nolan caught his arms, pinning them behind his back. Two more hard shots slammed into Randall's stomach. His knees dipped but he refused to go down.

'Who are they?' Godfrey asked.

'I don't know.'

Godfrey nodded.

Hansen drove his fist into Randall's jaw. Blood sprayed across the carpet.

'Who are they?' Godfrey repeated.

'He doesn't know!' Alistair shouted angrily. 'He already told you.'

'You believe him. I don't.' Godfrey turned to Nolan. 'Next time our friend here speaks, break Randall's neck.'

'Yes, Mr Godfrey.'

'Who are they?' Godfrey said again.

'I don't know,' Randall repeated.

Godfrey nodded. 'Again.'

Another body shot.

'Again.'

The fist slammed into Randall again.

'Again.'

Another punch.

'Again.'

The fist jerked Randall's head to the side.

'Again.'

The room heard Randall's nose break.

'Another?' Hansen asked.

Godfrey shook his head. 'You'll just knock him out cold.' A vicious smile appeared on his face. 'And we don't want him cold. Burn him instead.'

It was obviously an order Hansen had heard before. 'All of him or...?'

Again Godfrey shook his head. 'Metal toasting fork in the kitchen. Heat it on the gas ring. Use it on his feet. He'll talk quick enough.'

'Yes, sir.'

Alistair risked speaking again. With Hansen a step away he was sure he could stop Nolan before he permanently injured Randall. 'And what if he has nothing to tell?'

'Then he'll use some of the money I pay him for plastic surgery.' Godfrey's head tilted towards the door. 'Hurry it up, Hansen. We need him to talk quick.'

As an instinct, Nolan also switched his gaze to the door. Randall took his chance at the lapse in concentration, elbowing Nolan hard in the stomach and jerking his head backwards, slamming it into Nolan's face, breaking his nose. He pushed Nolan into Alistair, and Alistair made sure they both went down heavily. Randall turned to run for the window.

Godfrey was in his way. His punch hit Randall's jaw square on. The jaw broke and Randall dropped to the floor unconscious.

'That's how it's done.' Godfrey turned to Alistair and Nolan, who were struggling to their feet. Hansen stood in the door. None of them were looking at the unconscious Randall. Every one of them was staring at Godfrey. 'What? Have you never seen a proper punch before?'

It was Hansen who spoke. 'Your hand.'

Godfrey looked at his underling in confusion and then lifted his hand, and the smug expression faded from his face.

His hand was dark grey and calcified. It had turned to stone.

— CHAPTER FOURTEEN —

Godfrey stared at his hand in shock. Everyone else in the room was doing the same.

'Bleedin' hell!' Nolan breathed.

'What the hell's happened to your hand?' That came from Hansen in the doorway.

Godfrey was still staring at his hand. His mouth opened but he seemed unable to form words. He was silenced, shocked by the dull grey stone in the shape of his hand.

'Some sort of glove?' Nolan asked.

Alistair took a step towards Godfrey. 'Let me see that.' He reached for Godfrey's hand but the smaller man flinched away.

'Don't touch me.'

'Don't be an idiot, man,' Alistair snapped. 'You can see what's happening to you. You need to see a doctor.'

Godfrey didn't answer. He just kept staring at his hand.

'Godfrey,' Alistair said loudly. 'Can you hear me?'

'Mr Godfrey?' Hansen spoke from the doorway. 'Mr Godfrey, what do you want us to do?'

'Do?'

'The cars outside,' Hansen continued. 'We have to get away from here.'

'Yes,' Godfrey finally agreed. He was having difficulty forming words. 'We have to get away. We have to go...' He stopped, apparently trying to focus on where he should make for now. '*I* have to go...'

'We can't go anywhere,' Alistair snapped. 'You just beat our only escape unconscious.'

'Escape.' The word seemed to resonate with Godfrey. 'I will escape.'

'We all will,' Alistair said firmly. 'But you have to see that something is wrong with you.'

Godfrey didn't answer.

'Look at your hand, man. Look at what's happening.'

'It looks like stone,' Nolan said.

'That's exactly what it looks like,' Alistair agreed. 'And he has to see a doctor about that.'

Godfrey snapped his head towards Alistair. 'No doctor.'

'Look at what's happened to your hand, man!' Alistair roared. 'You could be dying.'

'No,' Godfrey said dreamily. 'I'm coming back to life.'

Alistair gripped the stone wrist. 'For God's sake, man, look at your hand.' He tore at Godfrey's sleeve. The rough grey patina ran up the crook's forearm. A lighter mottling near the elbow showed where the transformation was still in progress. 'That stone you have is doing this to you. You have to get rid of it.'

A single apparently nonchalant flick of his arm sent Alistair flying. He landed hard on the snooker table and was carried over the far side by the momentum of the blow. He landed hard and felt a sharp pain in his arm. He hadn't heard anything break and hoped the arm was still in one piece. It ached as he pushed himself up, but it took his weight.

Nothing broken.

Nolan and Hansen shared the same shocked expressions. Neither could believe what they had seen.

'Is that natural?' Alistair demanded. He pointed at the grey stone hand. 'Is that?'

Neither man answered, but both stared at the hand.

'You work for me,' Godfrey said. 'Remember that.' He glanced first at Hansen. 'You're going to get me out of here.' He looked at Nolan and pointed at Alistair with his flesh and bone hand. 'If he tries to follow, kill him.'

'Mr Godfrey?'

'You heard,' Godfrey snapped.

'I thought we were all going...'

'Do as you're told!' Godfrey roared.

Alistair could see that the shouting had cowed Nolan, and the criminal moved to block the path to the door.

'Come on,' Godfrey said to Hansen. 'You're getting me out of here.'

'Don't do it, Hansen!' Alistair shouted. 'He's not thinking clearly.'

Hansen looked quickly at Alistair. There was uncertainty in the man's eyes. Alistair pushed home the doubts Hansen must undoubtedly be feeling. 'Look at what's happening to him. It's not natural.'

Hansen looked at Alistair a second longer, then turned and followed Godfrey from the room.

'Damn it, man!' Alistair roared and came around the snooker table, heading for the door.

Nolan moved to block his path. 'You heard what he said. I have to stop you.'

Alistair took a step to the side. Nolan covered the move. 'Don't be a fool, man. You saw what was happening to him.'

'I don't know what I saw.'

'He has a hand of stone!' Alistair shouted. 'It's spreading up his arm.'

217

'No.' Nolan shook his head. 'That's impossible.'

'It's possible,' Alistair snapped. 'And you saw it. Are you too stupid to accept the evidence of your own eyes?'

That touched a nerve. 'I'm not stupid.'

'There are men outside – probably police or worse – and Godfrey's left you behind to take care of me while he escapes.' Alistair stared hard at the convict. 'You're going back to prison, Nolan. That's your best bet. If those men out there come in shooting, you're going to the undertaker. Are you willing to face that?'

A doubt flickered across Nolan's face, but he stood firm. 'I work for Mr Godfrey,' he said. 'I don't want to hurt you, and I won't if you don't try to follow him.'

'You think I want to be here when that lot come crashing in?' Alistair demanded.

From outside came the roar of a powerful engine starting. Nolan again blocked Alistair's path. 'Let him go, Alistair. Just let him go and we can escape out of the country wherever, just like we planned.'

'No.' Alistair shook his head sadly. 'There is no escape out of the country, Nolan.'

'What?'

Alistair was taking a risk, but he was also running out of time. Nolan needed to get out of his way. Hopefully the truth would shock him into stepping aside. 'There were never any charges against me,' Alistair said. 'I was infiltrated into the prison to make contact with Godfrey and to help him escape. You were a complication I hadn't expected.'

'I don't believe you.'

'Believe it!' Alistair snapped in his most military tone. 'I was in prison undercover, on a mission to make Godfrey reveal the location of that stone he values so highly. If everything had gone to plan, the train tomorrow would have been stopped a few miles outside London and we'd have recovered the stone and Godfrey. Things didn't go to plan. You saw what it's doing to him. Something about it did the same to four good soldiers last year when Godfrey stole it. We want it back.'

Nolan struggled to take in Alistair's story. 'You're a copper?'

'No.' Alistair shook his head firmly. 'Army.' He barked as though on the parade ground, 'Now step aside before Godfrey gets away!'

Nolan ignored the order. 'So you lied to us? You lied to me?'

'Yes. I took no pleasure from it, but I had to do my duty.'

'You played us like idiots,' Nolan shouted. 'I helped you out when you got into a fight. Was that part of your plan?'

'Your involvement was never part of any plan.' Alistair could see the rage rising in Nolan.

'You let me make a mug of myself. You let me break out and throw my life away – after I helped you.'

'You made the decision to escape. I didn't force you,' Alistair snapped sharply. 'Now get out of my way before Godfrey causes Lord knows how much damage.'

'Not on your bloody life,' Nolan hissed.

The convict threw himself at Alistair with a vicious roar. Alistair managed to block Nolan's punch but the man's impetus knocked them both flat. He scrambled to his feet in time to see Nolan lurching towards him. In his hand Nolan swung a vicious iron poker. Alistair leaped back just in time. The poker missed him by inches and he swept up a snooker cue from the table. Holding it like a quarterstaff, he blocked the poker's swing and, in the same movement, rammed the

219

heavier end of the cue into Nolan's gut.

The thief staggered back and dropped to a knee before pushing himself back up and throwing himself at Alistair, driving his shoulder into the soldier's stomach, forcing him back to the floor. He immediately swung a punch at Alistair's head but the soldier knew it was coming. He deflected the blow to the side and jack-knifed forwards, slamming his forehead into Nolan's face. He saw that Nolan was dazed and quickly hooked an arm over the back of Nolan's neck, pulling down until he could reach under to lock his hands together. He squeezed hard, cutting off the flow of blood and air to Nolan's head.

Nolan thrashed around, trying to free himself, but Alistair's grip limited the movement in Nolan's arms. He tightened his grip, pushing Nolan's head down further until the man's struggles weakened and he slumped, becoming a dead weight. Alistair kept the grip in place a few seconds longer, making sure that Nolan wasn't playing possum. When he was sure the man was out, he released the grip and pushed Nolan aside. The man sprawled with a heavy thud and Alistair scrambled to his feet.

On his way to the door, Alistair stopped to check on Randall. His colleague was still breathing but it was laboured and painful. His jaw was smashed and the wet sound of his breathing told of internal injuries.

Alistair was torn. Randall needed help but he could hear Godfrey's car moving away along the drive. It sounded as if the car was ready to turn onto the road.

He couldn't lose Godfrey now.

He ran for the door. One of Godfrey's goons appeared at the door just as Alistair reached it. The thug didn't see the punch to the stomach coming and wasn't prepared for it. He buckled forward and Alistair pushed past him into the hall. Before he reached the door he heard the thump of an impact and the screech of metal against metal. A second later, as he pulled the door open, the gunfire started.

A quarter of a mile away, the sudden burst of activity at the house sent Douglas into immediate action.

'Move now!' he bellowed. 'Everybody back to your vehicles.'

The troops ran back to the Bedford and, as he threw himself into the passenger seat of the Land Rover, he found Anne already in the wide seat between himself and the driver.

'Don't dawdle,' she said sharply, 'and don't blame Bill either. I told him I was coming and I'm telling you the same, so get in.'

'Damn it,' Douglas muttered, pulling the door closed behind him. 'You're both on a charge when this is over.'

'If you say so.' Anne turned to Bishop. 'Drive.'

Bishop released the clutch and the Land Rover started forward.

'Forget the road,' Douglas ordered. 'It'll take too long. Straight across.'

'Yes, sir.' Bishop turned the wheel, taking the Land Rover down a steep incline towards the flat open grass below.

The Land Rover bumped and jostled over roots and fallen branches, picking up speed as it rattled downhill. It hit the flat ground with a hard bump and bounced forward. Bishop accelerated, moving up into third.

Looking behind them, Douglas saw the huge shape of the Bedford careening down the slope behind them, bouncing almost out of control. He was astonished that it was still in one piece when it reached the bottom of the slope and he heard the big engine pick up speed.

'I'm amazed it didn't snap an axel,' he muttered.

Anne gripped the Spartan dashboard tightly. 'I'm amazed this thing hasn't done my back a mischief,' she protested. 'Doesn't the army bother with suspension and shock absorbers?'

'You wanted to come, remember?' Douglas laughed.

Anne just glared at him.

'Hedge ahead, sir,' Bishop said tersely. 'What do you want me to do?'

Going around was safer... but Douglas was in no mind to delay. 'Looks flimsy enough, Lieutenant. Straight through.'

'Yes, sir.'

Bishop's boot pressed hard on the accelerator and the Land Rover shot into the hedge.

At the front of the house, Brigadier Lethbridge-Stewart took cover behind a low stone wall bordering a section of lawn. Ahead, three of Godfrey's men were engaged in a shooting war with a group of men on the far side of the hedge. Lethbridge-Stewart spotted a couple of the faces through the shrubbery but didn't recognise them.

That meant they weren't his men.

Godfrey's men were outgunned but they held better defensive positions. A house provided far better protection than a hedge. Unsure of who these men were, Lethbridge-Stewart chose not to intervene. He needed to get after Godfrey. The painter's van still sat in the drive. He would have to use that.

He barely reached the van when a thud from the rear of the house, followed by the rough roar of an engine, stopped him. An army Land Rover crashed through the previously perfect hedge and bounced towards him, screeching to a halt a few yards away, ripping up the beautiful turf. A welcome face peered out of the passenger door.

'Thought you might need a hand, sir,' Douglas said.

'I need a lift more than a hand,' Lethbridge-Stewart thundered. 'Don't get out. Godfrey's making a break for it.' He ran around to the driver's side of the vehicle. He yanked the driver's door open. 'Lieutenant Bishop, join Samson in that.' He pointed at the Bedford, which had just flattened the remainder of the hedge at the back of the house. 'Take command. I want you and Samson to capture both sides in the battle taking place over there. Understood?'

Bishop leaped out and saluted. 'Understood. Sir.'

'Get on with it.' Lethbridge-Stewart jumped into the driver's seat and slammed the door shut.

He was surprised to see Miss Travers seated in the middle of the Land Rover. 'How did you know Samson was in the Bedford?' she asked.

'I know my men,' Lethbridge-Stewart replied, wondering why she was even here.

'Do you know where Godfrey's going?' Douglas asked.

'Not a clue,' Lethbridge-Stewart answered, 'but it'll have to be somewhere close.'

The assertion puzzled Miss Travers. 'Why?'

Lethbridge-Stewart lifted the clutch and was looking for second gear almost instantly. 'Because his hand has turned to stone,' he said, 'and it's spreading.'

They reached the end of the drive. The car to the left was only just in view. To the right, the other car tilted into a ditch and showed signs of damage from another car's impact.

'He went that way,' Lethbridge-Stewart said. 'I heard the crash.'

223

The Land Rover moved off, Lethbridge-Stewart easing quickly up through the gears. It protested at taking country roads at the required speed but he managed to keep it on the tarmac.

'What did you mean when you said his hand had turned to stone?' Miss Travers asked.

'It was that blasted rock; he touched it.' Lethbridge-Stewart glanced away from the road to scowl at Miss Travers. 'His hand is turning to stone. He broke Randall's jaw with it.'

Randall. He had forgotten Randall.

'Do you have an MO with you?' he asked Douglas. 'Randall needs one.'

'Where is he?' Douglas asked, reaching for his radio.

'In the study. There's another man there as well. He should still be unconscious. That's Nolan.'

'The one you escaped with?'

Lethbridge-Stewart grunted. 'I had to apply a choke hold. Make sure he gets medical assistance as well. He saved my neck in prison.'

'Doesn't sound like he was saving your neck in that house,' Miss Travers said.

'That's as maybe, but I want him treated as a patient first and a prisoner second.' Lethbridge-Stewart flicked his mind from the house behind to the escaping man somewhere ahead. 'Miss Travers, have you found out anything about the stone?'

'Have you seen it?'

'Yes,' Lethbridge-Stewart answered, keeping his eyes fixed on the road. He took a turn too fast, causing all of the passengers to lurch sideways, before he straightened the Land Rover and pushed down harder on the accelerator. 'Godfrey

224

had it in his pocket. He's kept it on him since we arrived.'

'And it's turning him to stone?' Miss Travers asked.

Lethbridge-Stewart nodded. 'Almost to the elbow so far.'

'That's different than before. The change has always been instant.'

'Not this time.' Lethbridge-Stewart gave a sharp blast on the horn and over took a tractor pulling a trailer.

Miss Travers rubbed her chin thoughtfully. 'In the past there was always a sudden source of energy – the explosion, lightning, whatever it was when the stone crashed here... A sudden, violent release of energy. There's been nothing like that this time?'

'Nothing,' Lethbridge-Stewart affirmed. His mind thought back to the house, to the stifling heat, the electrical equipment all playing... 'But he did have every bit of electrical gear in the house working, even if he wasn't using it, and he had the heating up full. He was even blasting music.'

'It's all energy,' Miss Travers said, an expression of focused fascination on her face. 'It's absorbing energy at a lower level and working more slowly.'

Douglas stowed his radio. 'He must be having kittens at the thought of turning to stone.'

Lethbridge-Stewart frowned. 'Oddly enough, no. He stared at it. He was shocked but it passed. He seemed remarkably calm about it. He was the only one who was calm, I assure you.'

'I don't understand his reaction,' Douglas said.

Miss Travers snapped her fingers. 'He had the stone on him?'

Lethbridge-Stewart nodded. 'Yes.'

'And it was after he started carrying the stone that he turned all the electrics and heating on?'

'Yes.'

'And then his hand started transforming?'

'Yes.'

Miss Travers looked at her companions expectantly. 'It's obvious, isn't it?' she said. 'His personality changed when he had the stone, as well as his body. Remember what we told you about people suffering some kind of mania when they were in contact with the stone?'

'Oh, yes,' Douglas agreed. 'So, that's happening here?'

Miss Travers nodded thoughtfully. 'Godfrey turned the electrics on. Why would he do that? How would he know to do that? Unless the stone influenced him to do it?'

Douglas looked at her with a confused scowl on his face. 'How can a stone do that?'

'I don't know, but you read the report from Santorini. It's not so far-fetched that somehow that piece of rock can influence a mind in some way, is it? It's the only thing that makes sense. The stone affected him to feed its power and then it started...'

'...To take control of him?' Lethbridge-Stewart finished for her.

'Exactly.'

Lethbridge-Stewart slowed the Land Rover. There was a junction in the road ahead. 'Three options,' he said. 'They could have taken any of them.'

'I can call up a couple of choppers,' Douglas suggested.

'Do it,' Lethbridge-Stewart ordered. He turned his gaze to Miss Travers. 'Where will he go?' he asked. 'If his personality is changing, if this thing is controlling him, what is it likely to do? Will he try to get out of the country?'

Miss Travers' brow furrowed. 'Possibly. Or...'

'Or?' Lethbridge-Stewart leaped on the thoughtful tone in

226

her voice. He knew the subtleties of his colleague's tics well enough to know that this one meant that she had an idea.

'It wanted power,' Miss Travers said. 'Energy. Maybe it'll try to get more power.'

'That makes sense. But where? Every house has electricity.'

'And a lot of them have a phone. Besides, it's used to huge releases of electricity. It'll want something bigger.'

Lethbridge-Stewart grabbed an Ordnance Survey Map from the open glove compartment. He unfolded it easily and quickly tracked their location. 'We're here,' he said, pointing. His finger traced the printed line of road, following its path straight ahead. 'Leads to a motorway,' he said. He followed the turn right, but Miss Travers yelped and stabbed her finger at the map. She followed the other turn and pointed at a small marking.

'There,' she said certainly. 'That's where he's going.'

'What's there?' Lethbridge-Stewart demanded.

'A new power station,' Miss Travers answered. 'The locals hate it being so close to them. They wrote petitions, orchestrated marches and even voted out their MP as a protest, but it's gone ahead anyway.'

Lethbridge Stewart considered for a moment. If they took the wrong turn, Godfrey would get away and the whole mission would be a failure. The idea of failing Pemberton burned. When Hamilton briefed him on the particulars of Old Spence's mission last year, Lethbridge-Stewart jumped upon the chance to finish the mission his old friend began. And maybe return a few lumps along the way. After all, Old Spence wasn't around to do so himself. 'What do you think?' he asked Douglas.

'I think I'm out of my depth,' Douglas answered honestly. 'But if Anne is sure, that's good enough for me.'

'And for me,' Lethbridge-Stewart agreed.

The Land Rover shot off, taking the corner in second. Lethbridge-Stewart was already accelerating before the tyres stopped squealing in complaint.

'How far is it?' he demanded.

Miss Travers squinted at the map. 'A couple of inches on this.'

Lethbridge-Stewart scowled and Miss Travers handed the map to Douglas.

'I'll let Walter tell you. He likes maps. By the way,' she said, turning back to Lethbridge-Stewart. 'It's good to see you again.'

Johnston felt the rough bark of a huge tree against his back and breathed a sigh of relief that it was there.

The gun battle started suddenly. He had to assume that his cars weren't as well hidden as he had ordered. There would be hell to pay about that. He would skin someone for it.

He saw the first car pull out of the drive. It turned right and accelerated hard, hitting Johnston's other car a hard glancing blow on the side, sending it into a ditch.

He only caught a glimpse of the man in the passenger seat, but it was undoubtedly Godfrey. The driver was taller and more powerfully built but he couldn't see the man's face. He guessed it was Lethbridge-Stewart.

Johnston had to get back to his car and follow. He and his men had abandoned the car when the shooting started. The battle moved to the side of the house. It was enough for him to risk running back to the car.

By the time he turned the key in the ignition, Johnston knew he had been wrong about the driver's identity.

An army Land Rover followed Godfrey's car out of the drive and away along the lane. Behind the wheel was the unmistakable figure of Lethbridge-Stewart.

Where the hell had the army Land Rover come from?

Another burst of gunfire came from the far side of the house's grounds. Through the hedges, Johnston could see army troops spilling from a large lorry and engaging with both his men and Godfrey's. They wore the unmistakable Stewart Tartan on their glengarries. The Fifth Operational Corps – Lethbridge-Stewart's toy soldiers. Johnston called to the nearest man to disengage. He got a nodded reply but his men were pinned down, unable to move.

He put his foot down and drove the short distance to the second car. He threw the passenger door open. 'Get in.'

The three closest men made it to the other car. Before the last could join them, Johnston ordered the doors closed. 'You get that car moving and get the others out of here,' he shouted.

He didn't wait for a response, and he didn't look back. He knew his men would do as they were ordered.

It was good luck that the road ahead had no turn-offs for several miles. He caught sight of the Land Rover ahead fairly quickly. He knew that reliable as Land Rovers were, they weren't the fastest vehicles available. He dropped speed to keep a distance between them and when Lethbridge-Stewart pulled to the side, Johnston dipped into a slight opening where there was a gate to the field by the road. He hugged the verge, watching for a few minutes as the Land Rover sat still. He wondered what was happening. Lethbridge-Stewart was obviously following Godfrey. So why stop? The only answer was to follow.

The Land Rover took off again and Johnston followed at

a distance. Up ahead, he saw the lights on the ugly square back of the car indicate a left turn at an intersection. He'd looked at maps of the basic area before coming. If his memory was correct, this was farming country. It produced crops and livestock. All except for…

The power station.

Johnston increased speed.

As soon as the Land Rover entered the car park, Lethbridge-Stewart knew Miss Travers' guess had been correct.

A security guard lay on the ground, apparently unconscious, blood seeping from a vicious wound in his temple, and from both his nose and mouth. That was usually a sign that he had fallen forward, probably unconscious when he hit the floor and unable to protect himself at all.

Miss Travers was quickly at the fallen man's side, checking his pulse. 'He needs an ambulance,' she called.

They were thirty yards from the glass doors leading into the power station. They could see movement through the glass. A moment later terrified staff started streaming out, running to get away from the place.

'I'd say that tells us where Godfrey is,' Douglas said.

Lethbridge-Stewart nodded. He was already running for the door. 'Come on.'

They reached the doors just after the power plant's employees started pouring out. Getting through the mass of clearly terrified people made progress slow.

'Where are they?' Lethbridge-Stewart yelled. 'Where did they go?'

A few of the fleeing people pointed behind them but nobody spoke. They were just too scared.

Lethbridge-Stewart pushed his way through the crowd,

with Douglas close behind. An open hall led to a set of double doors. The workers were coming through those.

'Must be this way,' Lethbridge-Stewart called.

The crowd started to thin out as they moved through the doors into a long wide corridor.

Lethbridge-Stewart caught the arm of an older technician in a lab coat. 'Where are they?' he demanded.

'Back there.' The technician pointed. 'The Control Room.' He broke free and hurried away.

Lethbridge-Stewart started up a wide set of stairs two at a time. He was aware of Douglas at his shoulder.

'Everybody must be out now,' Douglas said. 'There's nobody left coming our way.'

'That's something,' Lethbridge-Stewart said.

They made it to the top of the stairs. Douglas reached for the handle of the double doors ahead but Lethbridge-Stewart caught his wrist. 'Carefully.'

Douglas nodded his understanding. 'Yes, sir.'

Lethbridge-Stewart gripped the door handle and yanked hard. He pushed himself backwards against the wall, to the side of the door. No gunfire came. At his nod, Douglas dropped to a crouch and looked around the door.

'Clear.'

The two men went through and looked along the corridor stretching in front of them. Six feet wide, with concrete walls painted white. Ten yards along on the right, a pair of heavy doors obviously led somewhere important. Both men moved to the doors without a word being spoken. They took positions on either side. Lethbridge-Stewart was covered by the left door, while the wall protected Douglas. Lethbridge-Stewart mouthed a count up to three. On three he pushed the heavy door open and quickly ducked back. Bullets smacked into the doors and the wall but didn't penetrate.

'One pistol,' Douglas said. 'A thirty-eight at least.'

'Hansen.' Lethbridge-Stewart nodded. 'He fired three. That should mean he has three shots left.'

'Unless he reloaded.'

Lethbridge-Stewart smiled grimly. 'Always looking on the bright side, eh?'

Douglas checked his sidearm quickly. 'How do you want to do this? We only have one weapon, too.'

Lethbridge-Stewart reached to the small of his back and produced the Walther he had retrieved at the safe house. 'Not quite. I didn't think I could fight my way out alone, so I didn't try it.' He placed the sole of his boot on the door. 'On the third kick. I'll go in first, you come in right after me. When we're inside, you take Hansen and I'll see to Godfrey.'

'Right, sir.'

Lethbridge-Stewart pushed hard with his foot, swinging the door open. Another shot hit the far side of the door.

'Two.'

Lethbridge-Stewart pushed again. The door swung in and was hit by another shot. He glanced quickly at Douglas then pushed the door a third time.

Another bullet cracked into the door. Both Lethbridge-Stewart and Douglas were already on the move. Lethbridge-Stewart was first through the door. He saw a desk five yards inside the room and threw himself behind it. Before he hit the floor he heard a metallic *click* as the pistol fell on an empty chamber. He had his pistol raised to offer cover but Douglas was already inside the control room, his revolver aimed at Hansen who was fumbling to reload. Hansen obviously realised that he was out of time and threw the weapon at Douglas. The pistol hit him on the arm. The blow caused little damage but did deflect Douglas' aim enough for Hansen to launch himself towards Douglas. The two collided hard and went down in a flailing heap of punches.

Lethbridge-Stewart could trust Douglas to deal with Hansen.

While Hansen and Douglas grappled, with both men landing heavy blows, Lethbridge-Stewart sprinted for the door marked *Caution: Danger*. Throwing it open, he hurried through to a large room, the far wall of which was filled with a banks of computers. Desks and control panels were positioned all around the room. At the far end, a door opened to the outside. It moved softly in the breeze. There was no sign of Godfrey within the room, so Lethbridge-Stewart sprinted for the open door. Pulling it wide open, he saw that it opened onto a metal staircase on the side of the building, which led down to some kind of power room with a huge transformer of some kind outside it. Running towards it, his arm a solid unmoving lump at his side, was Godfrey.

Lethbridge-Stewart started running down the stairs.

Douglas had no idea who this man was, but he was as tough as old boots. Wherever he had learned to fight, he had been a good student. They grappled violently, each trying to gain the upper hand. Douglas broke free and landed a right hand that should have put down a horse. Hansen simply threw another punch. It thudded high in Douglas' chest. Douglas staggered back under the weight of the blow but was relieved it had hit his chest rather than his chin. It was when the next blow also landed near the same area he realised Hansen wasn't aiming for his chin.

The thug was trying to punch him in the throat.

Douglas had seen the damage a heavy blow to the neck

could do. He had seen men die painful and terrified deaths from crushed windpipes. Hansen's right hand was swinging towards him again. Douglas dipped his shoulder and allowed the big man's momentum to bring him forward. Straightening up quickly, he flipped Hansen over his shoulder. The big criminal landed hard and Douglas turned, readying himself to kick Hansen hard, but the big man was still alert.

He grabbed Douglas' raised foot and twisted, sending Douglas sprawling. Hansen was on him in an instant, driving his thumbs at the soldier's throat.

By the time Lethbridge-Stewart reached the bottom of the ladder, Godfrey had reached the door to the power room. The older man was struggling to run and Lethbridge-Stewart's long strides covered the gap to the door in no time, but not before Godfrey closed the door behind him.

Lethbridge-Stewart yanked it open. Years of training saved his life. He saw the stone fist swinging towards him out of the corner of his eye and managed to duck enough to avoid a worse fate than Randall. The fist hit his shoulder hard and deflected up onto the side of Lethbridge-Stewart's head behind his ear. The initial impact on his shoulder took most of the force out of the blow but it was still enough power to send him reeling backwards and start a ringing in his ear. He ignored it and charged forward again.

This time, Godfrey wasn't waiting inside the door. He'd already reached a panel marked *Danger*. He pulled it open. A loud buzzing sound filled the room. Lethbridge-Stewart immediately recognised the sound as electricity.

'Come away from there before it kills you, Godfrey.'

The small man didn't react to Lethbridge-Stewart's voice. He reached out his hands towards the panel. The crackling grew louder, and the smile on Godfrey's face grew wider. A rapt smile of achievement and relief rather than one of pleasure.

'For God's sake don't touch it,' Lethbridge-Stewart bellowed. 'It'll turn you to ash.'

Godfrey slowly turned to look at Lethbridge-Stewart, an expression of real contempt on his face. 'I don't need to touch it.'

His voice was rough and sounded as if he was choking. As he got closer, Lethbridge-Stewart could see the dark grey of the stone now engulfed Godfrey's entire arm and was affecting his neck. The arm now moved with an agonising slowness, the hand closed into a permanent fist.

'Just step away and we'll talk about it.' Lethbridge-Stewart moved closer.

Godfrey didn't budge an inch.

Lethbridge-Stewart carried on. 'Godfrey, just move away.'

'Godfrey?' The older man sounded confused. 'What is Godfrey?'

'What sort of damn fool question is that? *You're* Godfrey.'

'Godfrey?' the man repeated the word as if he had never heard it before. 'No, I am not Godfrey. I am...'

Lethbridge-Stewart was closer. 'Yes? Who are you?'

'I am... far from home.'

'Home?'

'A different place than this. A different world. A different reality. Through the empty nothing.' The words came with difficulty. 'I am Rakis, and I must return to Glastra.' Godfrey choked as the act of forming the word caught in his mutating throat.

Lethbridge-Stewart leaped on the opportunity. He threw himself at Godfrey, driving his shoulder hard into the man.

It felt like he had tackled a stone pillar. Part of Godfrey's side must also have been transformed, but the little gangster's human legs were still unaffected and they staggered under the impact. Lethbridge-Stewart ignored the pain in his shoulder and swung a huge right hand into Godfrey's jaw. It should have dropped him. Instead he only staggered back a pace, before raising the mutated grey arm and resumed lurching at Lethbridge-Stewart.

Douglas lashed out with his fists and kicked hard with all his might. He made a vicious contact with the man's groin and the pressure on his throat eased for an instant. But only an instant. The fingers tightened again. Douglas fought, flailing at his bigger opponent. The edge of his vision was turning black. He knew he was close to passing out. He had to fight. Had to stay awake. Had to...

The pressure stopped. Distantly, as though through a tunnel, he heard a man grunt. There was another noise. A solid impact.

Douglas forced his eyes open. Over Hansen's shoulder he could see Anne Travers holding a fire extinguisher. She was swinging it at Hansen, but he blocked it with his arm.

Balling his fist, Douglas pushed the first knuckle of his middle finger outwards so that when the hand clenched that finger was slightly elevated from the fist. He swung it hard, aiming for Hansen's eye.

He hit his target and Hansen screamed in pain, giving Douglas the chance to roll away from the criminal. Douglas lurched to his feet, preparing himself to meet Hansen's charge, but when Hansen erupted to his feet, his pistol was back in his hand.

Douglas forced himself forwards.

A single gunshot stopped him.

Hansen looked at the gun in his hand.

And then at the hole in his leg.

Screaming in pain, Hansen dropped to the floor.

Looking round, Douglas saw Anne Travers holding his revolver. Shock was clear on her face. She stared at the man on the ground. Douglas took the gun from her. 'I'll secure him. You go and phone for an ambulance.'

Anne stared for a moment longer, then pulled herself together and made for the nearest phone. Douglas wondered if he would have to tell her later that the pistol the crook had been aiming was empty. Probably. But she did the right thing. It was just going to hurt her for a while.

Keeping the revolver aimed at Hansen, Douglas kneeled beside the criminal. He was bleeding at a steady rate, but Anne had missed vital arteries. He thought it would probably be best to slow the flow of blood to that area though.

'Right you. Take your belt off and use it as a tourniquet on that leg.'

Energy.

Miss Travers had mentioned that the rock required energy. It was feeding on the power plant. Lethbridge-Stewart shot out an arm to close the hatch Rakis (the man was no longer Godfrey, Lethbridge-Stewart realised) had opened. He was too slow. Rakis' arm clubbed him aside. The blow took Lethbridge-Stewart on the top of his arm. Had he been more lightly muscled he was sure the arm would have been broken. Even though he was sure it was still in one piece, the blow deadened the arm and he struggled to make it move as he tried to defend himself from another attack from Rakis.

The little man expected him to move backwards or to the

side. Instead Lethbridge-Stewart met him head on, slamming his good fist into Rakis' jaw. Again he staggered back without falling. Like a boxer getting into a clinch, Lethbridge-Stewart tried to pin Rakis' discoloured arm to his side. If that was out of the equation, he was sure he could deal with the possessed crook. He put every ounce of energy he had into pinning the arm tight to Rakis' side.

It was no use. The arm swung him away with ease, sending him sprawling across the floor.

As Lethbridge-Stewart picked himself up, he saw Rakis return to the open hatch. The electricity crackled as he stood close. The mottled grey on the man's throat grew visibly as he fed on the energy.

'What is that stone?' Lethbridge-Stewart shouted.

Rakis produced the stone. He looked at it with reverence. 'My consciousness,' the rough voice gasped out. 'My thoughts, my essence. Part of my brain, sent here when my body was destroyed.' He held it up triumphantly. 'In this I survived death, I survived being expelled from my own reality.'

'Reality?' Something itched the back of Lethbridge-Stewart's mind, something to do with his stay at Deepdene back in April. *A different reality*, Rakis had said. A different...

Rakis lifted his hands and looked from one to the other. From the grey stone hand to the pink fleshy one. 'This body will be mine. It will change. Become the most advanced life on this world.'

Lethbridge-Stewart pulled himself to his feet. 'I've heard that before.'

Rakis was still holding the stone in his left hand. 'You have seen nothing. This primitive world knows nothing. I will be like a god here.'

'I've heard that before, too,' Lethbridge-Stewart answered

viciously. 'Usually by someone as sad and inadequate as you.'

The taunt, though a blatant lie, worked. Rakis lurched away from the open hatch, swinging his arm at Lethbridge-Stewart again. This time Lethbridge-Stewart was ready and he dodged backwards to avoid the blow. He dodged the next blow as well, and kicked out, taking Rakis' knee from under him. Lethbridge-Stewart grabbed at Rakis' flesh and bone hand, trying to prise the fingers apart to make him drop the rock. The fingers felt rough and cold. Looking at the hand gripping the stone, Lethbridge-Stewart saw with horror that the fingers were blackening, hard and unyielding to the touch. Gripping the rock was turning the other hand to stone.

Rakis' arm crashed into Lethbridge-Stewart's side. He felt a rib break under the impact and a moment later the force of the blow sent him crashing into a large metal panel. He tried to stand but his legs wouldn't obey him.

Rakis turned away and returned to the open hatch. He reached out both hands, turning the hand holding the stone palm upwards. Lethbridge-Stewart could see the grey mottling moving up the hand. Like ink seeping into blotting paper it crept up to the wrist and beyond. It was moving up the neck as well, crawling over the chin towards the mouth. A dull orange glow started to appear within the stone.

Rapture returned to Rakis' face as the stone grew brighter. The brighter the stone glowed, the faster the mottling spread across Rakis' arm and face.

Lethbridge-Stewart forced himself to move. He had no idea how powerful this Rakis would become, but he knew that it was a malignant force. He pulled his Walther from the belt of his trousers.

'Step away from the panel or I'll shoot.' Lethbridge-Stewart aimed his revolver at the small man.

Rakis looked confused for a moment then laughed. A dismissive laugh. Lethbridge-Stewart was insignificant to him.

The stone stretched further onto Rakis' face.

Lethbridge-Stewart squeezed the trigger on his revolver. Three shots hit Rakis square in the chest. All three ricocheted away.

Rakis laughed louder.

Lethbridge-Stewart stared at the scene desperately. He had to stop this before Rakis was entirely transformed. He had no idea how to stop the flow of power and he couldn't force Rakis away from the hatch.

A hatch Rakis could easily move closer to, but looked like he would go no closer than a foot or two to it. Why not? Surely if he was feeding on the energy he would be better directly absorbing it?

Unless he couldn't.

Unless it was too dangerous to him?

It was a gamble. A guess based on the few facts at his disposal, but it was all Lethbridge-Stewart had.

Summoning all the energy he possessed, Lethbridge-Stewart charged at Rakis. He slammed into the smaller man, driving his shoulder into Rakis' stomach. He ignored the pain of ramming his shoulder against hard unyielding stone and drove harder with his legs. Rakis staggered and Lethbridge-Stewart gave everything to a final shove, pushing Rakis back into the hatch.

Electricity crackled viciously and Rakis screamed as tens of thousands of volts tore through his body. The stone glowed and Lethbridge-Stewart threw himself as far across the room as he could.

The stone in Rakis' hand glowed brighter.

An instant later, an explosion rocked the room.

Douglas had
only just finished handing Hansen on to the plant's security
when the sound of a distant explosion echoed through the
station.

All the lights went out.

Lethbridge-Stewart's ears were ringing. Bright colours flashed
and swirled in front of his eyes. Slowly the kaleidoscope faded
and the bells in his ears began to fade. He made it back to his
feet unsteadily. It took a few moments for him to realise that
the lights in the station were off and the only light came from
two windows high in the wall behind him.

He staggered towards Rakis.

The man was completely blackened. At first he thought
the man had been burned. Looking closer he saw that Rakis
had been entirely transformed to stone. So had the hatch, the
wall around it, the equipment beyond and the floor of the
room, out to within a few feet of the place Lethbridge-Stewart
had landed.

If he hadn't made those few extra feet... He didn't want
to contemplate that. He put his hand close to Rakis. Heat
poured from the stone man. Precariously gripped in one hand,
Rakis still held the stone, the glow now receded to only a few
cracks and fissures which looked more like veins than
anything stone.

Lethbridge-Stewart held his revolver by the barrel and
used the handle like a hammer, tapping the stone until it
dropped from Rakis' grip to the floor. Whatever damage it
had done, the stone seemed inert for the moment.

'I'll take that,' a voice said from the doorway. A slim man
emerged. Lethbridge-Stewart was surprised to see it was

Leslie Johnston.

'Will you?' Lethbridge-Stewart tried to sound indifferent, tried to sound as if every inch of him didn't ache. Johnston's presence didn't help to explain anything, although at least now Lethbridge-Stewart understood who had attacked Godfrey's house. The Vault, after the alien rock.

'Yes.'

'And why should I hand it over to you? Things have changed since we last met, Lieutenant. We don't need the Vault to safeguard things, thank you.'

Johnston aimed a gun at Lethbridge-Stewart. 'I have a gun,' he said.

'Yes, and so do I.'

'True but you're holding it by the barrel. The best you can do with it like that is use it as a hammer.'

Lethbridge-Stewart glanced at his revolver. 'You may have a point.'

'So, bring the stone over to me.'

'And if I say no?'

'That would be very unwise.'

Lethbridge-Stewart looked down at the rock. He could still see the little veins glowing. He heard a quiet crack from it as the stone settled from its exposure to energy. 'All right,' he said. 'I'll kick it across.'

'All right.'

Lethbridge-Stewart pulled his foot back and then drove it down on the stone. There was a harsh crunching as Lethbridge-Stewart felt the stone crumble under his heel. 'Sorry,' he said nonchalantly. 'Football was never my game. Always more of a rugger man myself.'

Johnston glared at him. 'What have you done? How does that help you?'

242

Lethbridge-Stewart took advantage of his opponent's shock to flip the revolver in his hand so that he held it in the regular fashion. Now both men were aiming revolvers at each other. 'Ensured that this didn't fall into your General's hands.'

'He won't thank you for this.'

Lethbridge-Stewart glanced at Godfrey's remains. 'In the circumstances, Johnny, I'm not sure I actually care.' Sirens wailed in the distance. 'I'd imagine that's the police. I'm sure they'll want to talk to everyone involved. You included.'

'I'm sure they would. Another time, Alistair.' Johnston stepped smartly backwards, pulling the door after him.

Lethbridge-Stewart ran to the door. He pulled at it but Johnston had jammed it somehow. Lethbridge-Stewart kicked the door twice, three times. On the forth kick there was the sound of something happening to the lock and the door swung open. Douglas was on the outside with Miss Travers at his shoulder.

Lethbridge-Stewart brushed past them into the open, looking all around. 'Where is he?' he demanded. 'Did you see him?'

Miss Travers looked confused. 'See who?'

Lethbridge-Stewart was still looking around. 'Leslie Johnston. He tried to take the stone...' There was no sign of anyone. Lethbridge-Stewart carefully returned his revolver to his waistband. 'Never mind,' he muttered. 'It's done now.'

'Where's the stone?' Miss Travers asked.

Lethbridge-Stewart nodded at the open door he had recently come through. 'The stone's in there, crushed to dust, and Godfrey... Well, he's not going anywhere in a hurry.'

Miss Travers looked through the doorway. 'A shame, but at least the Vault don't have it in their possession.'

'Small consolation.' A wave of exhaustion and dizziness

hit Lethbridge-Stewart. He realised that the adrenalin that had kept him going must have been fading. Every ache and pain returned in full force.

He summoned what felt like the last of his energy and headed for the stairs leading back into the control building. 'If somebody can get me a coffee I'll explain what happened.'

'You'll be lucky,' Miss Travers snorted. 'Some idiot knocked the power out.'

The Convoy - Epilogue

As a colonel in the Parachute Regiment, Pemberton was not used to being summoned to Strategic Command at Fugglestone. But here he was, in the office of Major General Oliver Hamilton. He'd heard much about Hamilton, mostly from his old friend, Lethbridge-Stewart, who had been sponsored by Hamilton ever since Sandhurst, but this was the first time they'd met. And he still wasn't entirely sure what any of it had to do with Hamilton. Pemberton had already been debriefed, and didn't appreciate having to go over the events of last month again.

He thought he'd put that disaster to bed, but then again Pemberton knew, things were rarely that simple.

Hamilton had finished, so now it was time for Pemberton to ask a question. 'And what of the men, sir? I've asked, but nobody seems to know where they've been taken.'

'Need to know, Colonel, and I'm afraid you do not need to know. Officially they were killed in action, and...'

'But, sir, that's not—'

Hamilton cut him off. 'It's what the official record will say, and what the families will be told. Or do you have something better to tell them?'

Pemberton didn't. This was way beyond anything he had ever encountered before. 'Captain Knight and I will inform the families, sir, if that's okay.'

'I thought you might want to take that responsibility.'

Pemberton stood and saluted. 'Sir.'

'I'm sorry, Colonel,' Hamilton said, returning the salute.

'What of the cargo?' Pemberton asked, before leaving the general's office.

'Lost for now. But, I assure you, we will track it down. And when we do, those responsible for... Well, they will be brought to account.' Hamilton picked up a manila folder and handed it over to Pemberton. 'New orders for 1 Para.'

Pemberton accepted the folder and looked at the orders inside. 'Training?'

'Yes, we're working with the RAF and Royal Marines to create a Special Forces Support Group. Things are changing out there, Colonel, more than people realise. And the British Military need to prepare for the worst of it. 1 Para will be a key part of the Special Forces Support Group.'

Pemberton saluted. Orders were orders. But he couldn't help wonder just what his superiors were about to put his men through.

— CHAPTER FIFTEEN —

L ethbridge-Stewart looked at his reflection in the mirror. His uniform felt wrong. After not wearing it for so long it felt restricting. Strangely it also felt loose. He had lost some weight since being sent to prison. Well, he could start regaining that soon enough, and part of that was going to be a meal with Sally. Dougie kept her out of Lethbridge-Stewart's path while he was at the hospital getting a once-over. Lethbridge-Stewart appreciated Dougie's tact. The reunion was emotional and far from professional. It was best done in private without any soldiers to witness it.

He hadn't slept well. His broken rib and countless bruises and injuries made lying in bed uncomfortable. Every time he moved there was another sharp stab of pain. He was in for a few days of that. He had strong painkillers and instructions to take them regularly at four-hour intervals, but they were liable to make him drowsy so he halved the dosage, taking one every eight hours.

He was due to meet with General Hamilton for a debrief early in the afternoon, but Lethbridge-Stewart had some business he wanted to deal with first, and so he ignored Sally's strong suggestion that he sleep late.

Emerging from his bedroom in the Richmond safe house, Lethbridge-Stewart ignored the pains and locked a smile on his face. It just didn't do for an officer to show discomfort.

His colleagues were eating breakfast in the kitchen. Samson had been assigned Mess duties, and insisted on cooking a breakfast of bacon, sausages, eggs and mushrooms. It looked like too much for any man to eat but Lethbridge-Stewart demolished the lot and still had room for a couple of slices of toast with chunky marmalade.

'Good work, Samson,' he said, patting the man's shoulder. 'You might get a promotion if you carry on feeding the CO like that.'

Samson laughed. 'Thanks, but warrant officer will do me fine.'

'Bishop,' Lethbridge-Stewart said easily, 'get the car ready. I want you to drive me somewhere.'

'Very good, sir.' Bishop scurried away to get the car started.

'Anything I can help you with, Al?' Dougie asked.

'No,' Lethbridge-Stewart replied, but then thought for a moment. 'Actually, just to be on the safe side you better come with me.'

Governor Clemence was incandescent. 'You came into my prison undercover?' he spluttered.

'And broke out of it undercover,' Lethbridge-Stewart replied.

'And I wasn't informed? I shall be contacting the minister about this. I should have been told.'

'Really?'

'Yes. This prison is my responsibility.'

Lethbridge-Stewart rose from his seat and glanced at Douglas. His friend was poker-faced. That meant he had taken a dislike to Clemence. In situations like this Douglas usually wore a politician's smile. 'Of course,' Lethbridge-Stewart said pleasantly. 'I was sent here under orders from

248

Cabinet level, but if you wish to complain then you must do as you see fit. Just as I fully intend to.'

Clemence leaned forward. 'And what does that mean?' He was stopped by a knock at the office door. 'Come in,' he snapped irritably.

The door opened and Prison Officer Fulton entered smartly. He stopped short, surprised by the presence of two army officers in the room, one of whom had his back turned.

'You sent for me, sir?'

'Actually, *I* did,' Lethbridge-Stewart said, turning.

Fulton's eyes widened. 'You?'

Lethbridge-Stewart smiled tightly. 'That's right. Don't I merit a salute from an old soldier now I'm back in uniform?'

Fulton turned to Clemence. 'I don't understand, sir.'

'Neither do I, Mr Fulton. Not fully. However, it seems that Brigadier Lethbridge-Stewart infiltrated our prison undercover to gain the confidence of Godfrey for some reason he won't explain.'

'*Can't* explain,' Lethbridge-Stewart corrected crisply. 'National Security. I'm sure you understand. Broadly, it all went to plan.' He paused, fixing Fulton with a cold glare. 'Of course, the beating that put me in hospital slowed things down somewhat.'

Fulton shifted uncomfortably.

'Scotland Yard will be talking with you about that, Fulton. I've already given a full statement detailing your complicity in the attack. In fact, I believe Inspector Turner is waiting outside to speak with you.'

'Governor?' Fulton looked desperately to his superior for help, but Clemence couldn't meet his gaze.

'I'm sure you'll be fine,' was all he could find as a reply.

At a nod from Lethbridge-Stewart, Douglas yanked the

office door open. 'Outside,' he said to Fulton.

The warder squared his shoulders and marched out with Douglas following.

'The inquiry won't go well for you,' Lethbridge-Stewart said in a neutral tone.

Clemence just nodded. 'Ignorance is no defence, is it?'

'No, it isn't. You know, it might go better for you if you resigned. If you co-operate you might escape with your pension intact.'

'Yes,' Governor Clemence agreed dully. 'It might be better if I just resigned.'

Johnston was itching to get on, but the man on the other end of the phone was not as eager.

'And you're sure that's what you overheard?' the General asked.

'Yes. Godfrey, possessed or whatever he was, said the rock, this bit of an alien brain, came from a different reality.'

The General was silent for a moment. When he spoke again, his tone turned chipper. 'That's excellent, thank you, Johnny. I expect you back at the Vault in the morning.'

Johnston said thanks and hung up. The General had an odd fascination in the idea of other realities, and so Johnston made a point of telling him. A distraction, to keep the General occupied while Johnston tied up a loose end of his own.

Stanley ambled back to his cell. He was hurried along by the warders but he moved just a little slower than they wanted. It was a small win but he would take it. He didn't push it, though. The screws were all on edge. He heard a rumour from one of the trustees working in the offices that Fulton had been taken away by the police. The thought brought a smile to his round face.

He found a surprise sitting in the cell's solitary chair.

'Alistair.' Stanley shook his head sadly. 'Caught you, did they? Well, they'll throw the book at you for this. Extra ten years at least.' He looked at the crisp military uniform his cell mate wore. 'What are you doing in that get-up?'

Alistair smiled and rose from the chair. 'There are no charges against me, Stanley.'

'Insufficient evidence?'

'There were never any charges against me,' Alistair said. 'I was sent in here to find Hugh Godfrey, befriend him, resolve the problem.'

Stanley frowned as he assimilated the information. 'You was never on remand?'

'Not really, no.'

'So you was always with them on the outside.'

'No,' Alistair replied. 'Not in the way you mean at least. The governor and the warders had no idea about why I was here. Fulton would never have had a part in my beating if he had known.'

'Fulton?' Stanley reached into his pocket for a strip of chewing gum. He tore it in half, putting one half in his mouth and the other back in his pocket. 'I just heard rumours about Fulton.'

'That he's been arrested?' Alistair smirked. 'I heard those too. He's currently answering questions in response to a statement I gave.'

'He's up the creek, then.'

'Probably,' Alistair agreed.

'Listen,' Stanley said nervously. 'I suppose you've told the governor all the stuff I told you when you was in here.'

'Not everything. I'm not here to… grass you up, as it were.'

Stanley gazed at him suspiciously. 'Then why *are* you here?'

'To thank you,' Alistair said simply. 'You were kind and helpful to me while I was here and you had no need to be.'

'Well, I thought it was *us* and *them*,' Stanley answered. 'I just didn't realise you was *them*.'

'Nevertheless, I appreciate your kindness,' Alistair said, rising, 'and I wanted to say thank you.'

'Oh, right.'

Alistair pointed at Stanley's bed. 'And I brought you a few things you might find useful.'

'Oh?' Stanley pulled a plastic bag from his bed. He weighed it for a moment then tipped it out onto the table. Several large bars of chocolate, tubes of sweets, ten packets of twenty cigarettes and a stack of magazines and paperbacks scattered across the table. Stanley looked at the stash then back at Alistair. 'Think this buys off the guilt for lying to me.'

Alistair shrugged slightly. 'I don't have any guilt at doing my duty, Stan. This is just a thank you.'

Stanley picked up a magazine and flipped through. 'And so's this – thank you.' He dropped the magazine and smiled. 'And this lot more than buys you out of trouble anyway. Don't mind if I trade some of this, do you? I could probably own the wing with this much snout.'

'Snout? Ah, yes.' Alistair remembered the slang for tobacco. 'Well, try not to become a gangster in here.'

Stanley chuckled. 'I'm not really built for it.'

'When you get out,' Alistair said, 'give me a call. I've left a contact number with the office here. I'm sure I can help find you a job that'll keep you out of mischief.'

'A job? Proper hard work?' Stanley sounded horrified. 'What are you trying to do? Kill me?'

Alistair smiled. 'Call, or I'll come looking for you.'

'All right.' Stanley sucked his lip for a moment. 'So this thing Godfrey was involved in... How bad was it?'

'I can't give you any details.'

'But it was bad?'

'Very.' Alistair nodded. 'Bad enough to be a risk to the entire country.'

Stanley thought for a moment. 'Just as well you did something about it, then.' A look of concern appeared on the convict's face. 'He's not coming back here, is he?'

'No,' Alistair reassured him. 'Godfrey won't be coming back. He won't be causing anyone trouble anymore.'

Stanley looked uncomfortable at the reply. 'Should I ask what happened to him?'

'No. Best not to.'

Stanley just nodded. 'Well... just as well if he was a wrong 'un. So,' he said, obviously keen to change the subject. 'Back on duty, are you?'

'I was never off duty,' Alistair reminded him. 'But I am back in uniform.'

'So, pint tonight, is it?'

'Dinner with the girl you told me to forget about.'

'You're seeing your girl tonight and you're wasting your time here?' Stanley pointed to the door. 'On your bike. Naff off and be happy.'

Alistair stopped at the door. 'Thanks again, Stanley.'

Stanley picked up a bar of Cadbury's Dairy Milk chocolate. 'On your bike, posh boy, I've got chocolate to eat.'

RSM Sandy Cowie was again in the room with the statues, and again he was in the company of Anne Travers and Colonel Douglas. He hoped they might be able to bring some hope for the poor lads who were turned to stone. Instead, all they had to offer was another statue in the shape of an old man and the possibility that they could end the suffering of the lads permanently. They thought that if the soldiers were exposed to a strong enough electric charge it would complete the transformation and finally end their lives.

Cowie wasn't sure how he felt about that. Killing his own lads just seemed wrong and something that could never be right. And yet they were suffering and there was no way to save them. He was glad it was a decision somebody much further up the chain would have to make.

As for the new statue, Doctor Travers said he was different. He had been transformed in a different way to the others.

To Cowie, it looked even worse than the soldiers.

Whatever it was, and whatever happened to the man, whether he was friend or enemy, it was no way to end up. Cowie started reading bits of the newspaper to the statues. Once a day he would come in and read a few pages of sport or news. He would read to this new one, too, at least until they decided what to do with him.

Thousands of miles away in Egypt, Mr Shehab looked at the small section of a secluded garden where he placed the statues of the Egyptian soldiers. Anne Travers told him how the soldiers' suffering could be ended. Until he could decide how he would make that happen – if he could bring himself to do it – these men would see the sunlight again and feel rain on their faces. The garden surrounded an old family house which was now empty and only ever used when guests came visiting.

'You are my guests now,' he said quietly.

He walked away and left the statues – the men – to face

the setting sun.

In his small London office, Johnston seethed. He was not used to losing.

He looked up from his contemplation at the man standing in front of his desk.

Another who failed to best Lethbridge-Stewart. Johnston smiled. He still had some clout. 'Are you quite clear on what I need done?'

'I understand,' the man replied in a thick London accent. 'I'll deal with him. In fact, it'll be my pleasure. I owe him.'

'Yes, I know. I didn't pull strings to get you out of there for the fun of it.' Johnston sized the man up. The General wouldn't be happy, but that was of little concern to Johnston now. He always knew this day would come. 'Just get it done.'

The last train of the day pulled in to Edinburgh's famous Waverly Station five minutes early. Anne Travers was first to disembark with Douglas, Samson and Bishop a few paces behind.

Private Atkins was waiting at the end of the platform, his Land Rover parked nearby. 'Welcome back, ma'am,' he said, saluting Anne.

'You don't have to salute me, Private. I'm still not in the army.'

'CO would have my guts for garters if I didn't though, wouldn't he?' Atkins said nervously. 'And I like my guts just as they are.'

'I'm sure you do.'

Without another word, Anne slipped into the passenger's seat. She was keen to see her father and to discuss with him what Godfrey could have meant by 'another reality'.

Atkins snapped out another salute. 'Sir.'

Douglas acknowledged the salute with a brief salute in return.

'Brigadier not with you?' Atkins asked.

'Following us up on the sleeper,' Douglas answered. 'He had a few meetings to attend before he could leave.'

The Caledonian Sleeper left Euston on time at nine o'clock. Lethbridge-Stewart and Sally Wright arrived with ten minutes to spare after an early meal at an Italian restaurant. By the time the train pulled out of the station they stored their luggage in their berths and retreated to the Club Car. It was the first time they had spent alone since the end of the mission. It had been Douglas' suggestion that Sally remain behind to act as Lethbridge-Stewart's aide for his last few hours in London. Nobody was fooled, but it gave a professional veneer to them spending some time alone.

Lethbridge-Stewart and Sally were the last to leave the Club Car, just after one, having spent hours talking, catching up, and simply spending time together. Talk of Christmas soon came up, with Sally wondering what they were going to do for the festive season. Lethbridge-Stewart wasn't too sure, but he figured it was time he introduced Sally to his mother properly, and so it was decided that they'd have Christmas Day at his flat in London, and if they could get hold of Owain they'd invite him too. They only left the Club Car after catching sight of the chief steward stifling a yawn for the second time.

'I suppose it is rather late,' Lethbridge-Stewart said as they carefully made their way along the corridor. The train jostled as they went, forcing them to brace themselves against the walls.

They took their time over saying goodnight before retreating to their respective berths. Their rooms were adjacent with a connecting door. It was locked but neither minded. They were tired and had an early start ahead of them. Nevertheless, Lethbridge-Stewart smiled as he heard the sounds from the other side of the thin metal wall as Sally prepared for bed.

He was relaxed by her company and by the excellent whisky the Club Car had provided. He changed into his pyjamas and, after setting the alarm, was soon drifting into peaceful sleep, rocked by the gentle swaying of the train.

Lethbridge-Stewart's eyes opened. There was a noise. It wasn't the usual sounds of the train. This was something different. A metallic click. He reached for the light switch, but before he made it a bright light shone in his eyes.

'Don't move.'

The voice stopped him dead. He recognised it immediately. 'Nolan.'

The small light by the bed flicked on. Nolan was standing by the bed, a small torch in one hand, a pistol in the other. 'Surprised to see me?'

'Very much,' Lethbridge-Stewart said. 'I rather expected you to be back behind bars.'

Nolan shrugged. 'I didn't expect you to be some copper either.'

'Army, not police.'

'Same difference,' Nolan answered angrily.

Lethbridge-Stewart didn't look around the room, but tried to remember where he had placed each piece of luggage. Unfortunately, the case containing his gun was behind Nolan, as far from the door as Lethbridge-Stewart had been able to place it. If he moved, he was sure Nolan would have no qualms in shooting him where he lay. However, there was no way he could launch himself at the man.

'I assume you woke me up so that I would know who killed me?' Lethbridge-Stewart said calmly. 'To prove yourself the better man, or something like that?'

Nolan snorted. 'I won't shoot you unless I have to. Don't worry, though, you are going to have a fatal accident.'

'How unfortunate for me.'

'I'd be happy to shoot you where you are, but that's not what I was told to do.'

'Orders?' Lethbridge-Stewart asked. 'From whom? Not Godfrey, he's beyond giving orders to anyone.'

Nolan snorted. 'Not Godfrey. You're not so smart, are you? Not really.'

Lethbridge-Stewart considered. It had to be Johnston. A bold move for him. One the mysterious General couldn't have sanctioned. 'Leslie Johnston,' Lethbridge-Stewart said calmly. 'He must have rubbed a few palms to pull you from custody.'

Nolan tensed. Lethbridge-Stewart heard it. The man knew he had said too much again. 'Get dressed.' Nolan flicked the nose of the gun towards Lethbridge-Stewart's clothes. 'But if you try anything...'

'I understand.'

Lethbridge-Stewart eased himself out of bed very slowly. Carefully he removed his pyjamas and donned his clothes again. 'Tell me,' he said finally, 'what kind of accident will I have?'

'A fatal one.'

A humourless laugh came from Lethbridge-Stewart. 'Other than fatal.'

'You're going to have an accident as the train crosses a bridge a few miles ahead. I was going to use the Forth Bridge...'

'Until you found out that the Forth is north of Edinburgh and I get off before it.' Lethbridge-Stewart shook his head sadly. 'You should have paid more attention in school, Nolan. Or less attention to the Thirty-Nine Steps.'

'And you should have paid more attention to keeping your berth secure. You didn't even hear me come in.'

'True.' The train shook as it took a corner. Nolan grasped a cupboard handle while Lethbridge-Stewart pushed a hand against a wall to steady himself.

That gave him his one chance to get out of the situation alive. Six inches from his hand, inset into the wall was a chain. Without thinking he gripped the chain and yanked hard.

The effect was immediate. The train braked hard, throwing everything and everyone forward out of control. Lethbridge-Stewart had a second to prepare himself. Nolan hadn't and was thrown over the bed. His hand slammed into the metal wall hard. Lethbridge-Stewart was on it instantly, gripping the wrist of Nolan's gun hand and slamming it into the wall over and over until Nolan dropped the gun. Lethbridge-Stewart swatted it away out of reach.

Nolan jerked his elbow back, catching Lethbridge-Stewart on the chin and the soldier toppled backwards. He rolled aside in time to avoid Nolan's boot, which slammed into the wall where Lethbridge-Stewart's head had been a second earlier. A vicious right hand rocked Nolan's head but he kept fighting, landing two hard right hand shots on Lethbridge-Stewart's jaw. The soldier shook them off and dug a hard left into Nolan's ribs, followed quickly by a right that opened a gash on the crook's cheek.

The door behind Lethbridge-Stewart opened unexpectedly. 'Alistair?'

Sally's intrusion was the distraction Nolan needed. He charged at Lethbridge-Stewart, forcing him backwards into Sally. All three toppled out into the corridor.

Lethbridge-Stewart's first thought was to protect Sally. 'Get clear.'

Nolan seized the opportunity and punched him hard in the side, his fist slamming into already injured ribs.

Sally pulled herself clear and Lethbridge-Stewart lashed out with a foot, kicking Nolan's leg out from under him. He kicked out again, this time catching Nolan on the temple. Lethbridge-Stewart looked around for the revolvers, but both were lost somewhere in the shadows in the sleeper car.

Nolan was already on the move. He kicked Lethbridge-Stewart hard in the side.

The agony in his broken ribs brought a groan of pain from the soldier. He tried to ignore it and swung a punch at Nolan's jaw. It missed by a fraction, its momentum pulling Lethbridge-Stewart off balance.

Nolan moved quickly, his arm crooking around Lethbridge-Stewart's neck. He squeezed tightly.

Instantly, Lethbridge-Stewart was struggling to breathe. He tried to gasp in air but Nolan tightened his grip. Lethbridge-Stewart felt the muscles in Nolan's arm tighten as he increased the hold. He didn't have much time.

The edge of his vision was darkening.

Random flashes of colour.

His strength was fading.

Fading.

Not long.

No. It wouldn't end like that.

Lethbridge-Stewart jerked his head back into Nolan's face. He heard a scream of pain.

Good.

He slammed his head back again.

The grip loosened.

He stabbed his elbow hard into Nolan's stomach and heard the wind forced from the crook's body.

Keep fighting, Lethbridge-Stewart thought. *Don't stop.*

He grabbed Nolan by the hair and slammed the man's head hard against the wall opposite.

The carriage lurched.

He slammed Nolan against the opposite wall again. This time the convict's head hit the window. A loud cracking sound filled the corridor and a web of cracks appeared across the glass.

The train lurched again and Nolan staggered against the window. His weight shattered the glass and cold, night air whipped through the corridor. Nolan grabbed a long shard of glass and pulled hard. He didn't seem to notice it cutting his hand as he stabbed it towards Lethbridge-Stewart's gut.

Lethbridge-Stewart stepped aside just in time. Before Nolan could recover his arm to strike again, Lethbridge-Stewart threw himself forward, putting all his weight into slamming Nolan against the wall.

Nolan's body tilted backwards at the waist and he screamed as his momentum took him through the shattered window. The scream lasted several long seconds before a distant splash told of Nolan's fate.

Gasping for breath, Lethbridge-Stewart looked out of the shattered window. The train was on a bridge of some sort. It looked modern and damned high.

'This must have been where he was going to kill me,' Lethbridge-Stewart said quietly.

'Alistair? Are you all right?' Sally returned to her feet and caught him under the arm as he slumped. 'Alistair?'

As the adrenalin faded, every ache and pain and bruise came back to haunt Lethbridge-Stewart, and he allowed Sally to take some of his weight.

A middle aged attendant rounded the end of the corridor and hurried towards them, looking flushed and angry. 'What daft gowk stopped the train?' he demanded in a broad Scottish accent. 'There'll be hell tae pay. I'll throw him aff the bloody train.'

'Too late,' Lethbridge-Stewart said wearily. 'I already did that.' He pointed a finger downwards. 'You'll find him about a hundred feet in that direction.'

'You did what?'

Lethbridge-Stewart ignored the question. 'How long till we get to Edinburgh?' he asked.

'An hour and a half,' the attendant replied. 'Mebbe a bit longer now we've had this stop.'

'Fine,' Lethbridge-Stewart said. 'Call ahead and have the police meet us at Waverly.' He flashed his ID pass. 'Get to it, man,' he added in his most official voice. 'Then cover that window and clear up the broken glass.'

'Right, sir,' the attendant replied automatically.

As the attendant hurried away, Sally pushed her door open. 'Your berth is a mess. You can use mine.'

Lethbridge-Stewart was too weary to care what the attendant might think about that. Or anybody else come to that. He slumped onto Sally's bed.

Johnston. Damn the man. Of course with Nolan dead Lethbridge-Stewart had no evidence. He shook his head. 'I need to put in a call to Peter Grant.'

'The Corps man at the MOD?'

'Yes. See if he knows anything about this General who runs the Vault.'

Sally looked at him, confused. She didn't need to ask. 'You'll find out,' she said. 'Just not right now. Try to relax. It'll be busy when we get to Waverly.'

'You're right,' Lethbridge-Stewart agreed. 'Guns,' he said. 'Two of them in my berth. Can't leave them lying about.'

Sally went to fetch the weapons. She returned a minute later, a revolver in either hand. By then, Lethbridge-Stewart was already fast asleep.

Sally leaned against the wall, checked the safety catch on one pistol and put the other down. She listened intently and prepared to stand watch until they reached Waverly.

Over two weeks had passed and it was Christmas Eve, and once more the General was in his office at the Vault. It wasn't ideal, but he had no one to spend Christmas with, so he didn't mind. If nothing else, the Vault was unusually quiet, which gave the General a chance to tie up a few loose ends of his own.

One such loose end was the photo in his hand. Its showed Owain Vine, Alistair's nephew. 'I just received your picture,' he said into the phone. 'What's he doing in Japan?'

'Settled in a meditation centre in Kyoto,' said the young male voice on the other end.

The General nodded, and considered. The attempt to kidnap Owain on Santorini last month had proven a disaster. Another tact was needed. 'Get close to him. It's almost time.'

He put the phone down and stood up. He walked across his office and looked down at Leslie Johnston. The man, his face bruised and bloody, glanced up through swollen eyes.

'You went too far. I told you. Alistair Lethbridge-Stewart is my problem, not yours.'

Johnston went to speak, and coughed out blood. 'But… why? You've never explained.'

The General crouched down. 'I've never needed to. But, since you're going to be dead within an hour, I may as well tell you.'

'Dead?' Johnston coughed again. 'You don't think all this is enough? Two weeks in the deep freeze? The beating?'

'I warned you, Johnny. But you didn't listen. Worse, you put out a hit on Alistair.' The General tutted and leaned forward to whisper in Johnston's ear. 'Alistair's family, and although he may be on the opposite side to me right now, he's still my brother.'

Abruptly he lashed out, his solid fist knocking Johnston unconscious.

General James Gore stood up and smiled. He needed to move his plan up a step or two. Before Alistair came knocking at the Vault's door.

Exclusive look at
Night of the Intelligence
Andy Frankham-Allen

Unfortunately, for Owain, despite three weeks in Shimogyo-ku, Kyoto, peace was proving a difficult thing to keep hold of. Every time he thought he was close, it seemed to slip out of his fingers. He closed his eyes again, and repeated the *nembutsu* chant. '*Namu amida butsu, namu amida butsu…*'

In his mind he heard the instructions of Guru Mizutani Kenzaburō. 'Visualise Amida Buddha. Have no thought but one thought, and that is Amida Buddha. Merge your consciousness with all of creation; this in itself is both no thought and all thought.'

Again, Owain's breathing wavered and the whispering voice of the Great Intelligence entered his mind. 'I am waiting for you. You cannot escape me, James-that-was. You will be me, always.'

'*Namu amida butsu, namu amida butsu,*' Owain chanted, focusing his mind on his breathing. *Inhale, see the air move through your nose, down your throat, fill up your diaphragm. And exhale.*

'Be mindful of your body,' Guru Mizutani said. 'Consider how you sit, feel gravity pulling you down. Feel the stresses in your muscles, and will them to relax. Feel the calmness come over you, and breathe normally. In and out. Out and in. Notice the sounds around you, take them in, notice the scents, the aromas. Notice the taste in your mouth, and once again notice your breathing. Feel it rise and fall, like a wave on an ocean.'

Owain let out a breath of air and opened his eyes. He looked at the people sitting either side of him, all in a straight line, all with their eyes closed facing the guru, who led them in chanting the *nembutsu*. Guru Mizutani opened one eye, but his chanting continued. He nodded slowly at Owain, silently excusing him. Careful not to disturb his fellow students, Owain removed himself from the *seiza* position, unfolding his legs from beneath him and stood up. His bare feet moved quietly across the wooden floor and he exited the meditation hall.

He'd barely managed to put on his socks and trainers when someone called his name. He looked up from tying his laces to see Jipps approaching him.

Jody Phillips was a fellow seeker, also from the UK, visiting Japan to study the Jodo Shinshu Buddhist tradition. They'd been talking for a couple of weeks, after she had accidentally taken his favourite spot in the common room of the meditation centre. A quick and easy friendship had sparked up, and she'd insisted on being called Jipps. And here she was, dressed in her usual flared jeans and dyed t-shirt, beads worn around her neck and wrists, her long brown hair in several pony-tails, all ending in green.

'Oh, hi,' Owain said, standing up. 'Aren't you supposed to be in there?' He pointed to the hall he'd just left.

'I am, but running a bit late. Discipline is really not my thing.' She smiled hugely at him, and Owain laughed. 'Not sure if Jodo Shinshu is for me.'

There were a lot of disciplines to master, Owain had to admit. For his own part he hadn't decided whether the Shin tradition was right for him, either, but he did ascribe to the basic Buddhist Dharma of going out there to discover what was right for you. To experience everything, to find your place. And after October and November he really did need to find out what worked for him, what would give him the peace and understanding he needed.

He spent a lot of time travelling after he'd managed to track down Kara's parents and told them about her death, spoke to many practitioners of several Buddhist traditions, including some Theravadan monks in Thailand. He'd also spoken to some Taoists, which in turn led him to Shinto. It was looking into that oldest of Japanese religions which brought him to Kyoto and the meditation centre in the heart of Shimogyo-ku.

'Well, what it is the Dalai Lama said? *If you find my teachings suit you, apply them to your life as much as you can. If they don't suit you, just leave them be.*'

'You read too much.'

If only Bill was here to hear that, Owain thought. But Jipps was right. Owain had read a lot in the last few months.

Jipps shrugged. 'Thing is, though, if I left who'd you talk to?'

Nobody, Owain wanted to answer. He could still hear Anne in his head telling him that isolation wasn't the answer, but she had been wrong. Yes, he'd met a lot of people since leaving Santorini in November, but he'd essentially kept himself to himself, just him and the Buddhist and Taoist texts, and when he didn't feel like studying, he would meditate, let his mind wander while he played his guitar.

'I'll get by,' he said.

'You have to let someone in at some point you know,' Jipps said softly, and sat down on the bench. She patted the space beside her. With a good-natured sigh Owain sat. 'What is it you're really after here?'

It was a loaded question. Jipps wanted to know, both as a friend who wanted to help him for altruistic reasons, and because he had told nobody else. Not really. But Owain wasn't sure where to start. He thought he'd been on the right path after he left Bledoe at the end of March, but then in October he'd gone on holiday to America with his uncle and

269

had come up against the Great Intelligence again. That confrontation had brought it all back. The loss of his twin brother, the pain that still sat within him like a deep hole of nothing, and what was to come. How could he possibly hope to explain all this to Jipps?

She was nice, intelligent even, but she didn't really believe in *karma*, the idea of many lives, that your experiences carried over to the next life. Owain wouldn't have believed it true, if he hadn't discovered how very real it all was. He had seen the ultimate realisation of *karma*, the final product of all the experiences of *his* thousands of lives embodied in the bodiless entity that had once called itself Mahasamatman. Thousands of lives yet to come. He knew, for an absolute fact, that he had lived one life previous to the one he was living now. From 1926 to 1938 he had been a boy called James, a boy corrupted and destroyed by the Great Intelligence, Owain's own ultimate destiny.

While in Thailand he heard a Buddhist tale called *Sitting in the Shade of the Bodhi Tree*, which told of the journey of Siddhartha, the man who would become the Buddha Shakyamuni, and how Mara the Tempter, the embodiment of evil, was terrified by the prospect of a man achieving enlightenment. Mara knew that should Siddhartha attain enlightenment then the power it held over the world, delusion, would be threatened. It was a story that held great meaning to Owain, for he felt like Siddhartha, trying to gain enlightenment to defeat the Intelligence's hold on his soul.

Jipps shrugged again. 'Okay, you don't have to tell me. But, you should look at the Four Noble Truths, especially the—' She stopped abruptly, and gently punched him on the arm. 'Hey, don't look at me like that. I do listen to some of the lessons.'

'Sorry,' Owain said, playfully rubbing his arm. 'You hit like a girl.'

'I know. Strange that.' Her smiled faded. 'Seriously, though, the Second Truth might be just what you need to look into.'

Owain knew the Four Noble Truths well enough. He'd studied them a lot over the last few months, and understood all about the Truth of Suffering's Cause. *Duhkha*, dissatisfaction; the feeling you got when things were not as you wanted them to be. From birth to death, *duhkha* was in everything. *All suffering, without exception, comes from desirous attachment or craving.* The Buddhists had a word to describe the complete removal of *duhkha*, and that was *nirvana*. The complete eradication of greed, hatred and delusion. And he tried so hard to remove all those things, to ensure that he would never be open to the Intelligence again. But then New York happened, and worse, the events on Santorini.

He lowered his head. 'I've tried, Jipps, really I have. That's why I'm here, to find the right path. To step away from the world for a bit.'

Jipps smiled and stood. 'In that case there is someone I want you to meet. He arrived last week, and I reckon you'll get on really well with him.' She grabbed Owain's hand and pulled him up. 'He totally gets all this stuff about peeling away the veils of misconception. He's been through a lot. You two may have a few things in common.'

Deep beneath the Cheviot Hills in Northumberland sat a facility that, on paper at least, was owned by the Ministry of Technology. But underneath that guise of cultural and industrial advancement was a darker truth. An organisation that tracked down and used, or more often *mis*used, alien technology. From its conception it had been run by a mysterious man known only as 'the General'. A man whose reputation suggested dubious origins, and even more dubious morality. But by those directly beneath him, he was known simply as General Gore.

He spoke with very measured tones, his accent obscuring the truth of his birth. Most people guessed him to be in his late forties, although he was closer to his mid-fifties, and yet he had been born in 1926. How could such an incongruity exist? Because he was a time traveller.

General Gore had been born in a small English village called Bledoe. But not the same village being visited by Alistair Lethbridge-Stewart; his Bledoe was a very long way away. For he wasn't just a time traveller; he came from another Earth, in a parallel universe. And on that world he had been known as First Major James Lethbridge-Stewart.

If there was one thing he hated, even more than disloyalty, it was bureaucracy. He had been promised a free hand by Mr Benn himself, but as with all politicians the reality of his promises did not match the intent, and so once again Gore was stuck behind his desk reading budget reports, a most tedious exercise. What he really wanted was a distraction.

A knock at his door.

Gore looked up from the papers before him and smiled. Whatever it was, it would do nicely. 'Enter!' he snapped.

The door opened and one of his underlings entered. Gore supposed he should really know the man's name, but very few made it at the Vault, and Gore had better things to do with his time than remember the names of people who he'd most likely never see more than twice.

'Sir, the report you've been waiting for,' the underling said with a nervous stutter.

Gore clicked his fingers and pointed at the desk. 'Give it to me, then.'

'Um, yes. Yes, sir, sorry.'

Gore waited while the man scurried forward and carefully placed the manila file on the desk, and then rushed out of the office as quick as his legs could take him. Once the door was closed, Gore smiled. He wasn't as bad as his reputation suggested, but better fear than be surrounded by idiots.

He opened the file and started reading the report. He hadn't got very far when the phone on his desk rang. He picked it up. 'What is it?'

'General,' said the voice of Mrs Anderson, 'you asked me to inform you when the body had been discovered.'

Gore smiled. That was good news; another part of the plan falling into place. 'Good to hear. Tell me, have the police made contact yet?'

'No, sir. A group of ramblers came across the body. No doubt the police will be informed soon.'

'Excellent. Let me know when there's further developments.'

'Yes, sir.' Mrs Anderson hung up.

Gore lowered the receiver gently and rubbed his greying beard. It was only a matter of time now before his brother found out, and then...

He returned to the file, but once again the phone rang. He snatched up the receiver. 'Now what?' he snapped.

'Sorry, sir,' Mrs Anderson said. 'Just had a call in from the main gate. Mister Townsend has arrived.'

'Who?'

'From the Ministry, sir.'

Damn it. An inspection. Now. Keeping his voice as calm as possible, Gore said, 'When he arrives keep him out there.

I'll let you know when he can enter.'

'But, sir…'

'Let Mr Townsend stew for a while. I will not be subjected to the whims of the Ministry of Technology.'

'Yes, sir. Of course, sir.'

Bureaucracy, how he hated it.

Determined to not be disturbed again, Gore left the phone off the hook and returned to his agent's report.

After weeks of observation his agent had finally started making moves to engage with the target. Gore smiled. It had been almost ten months in the planning, ever since news of Owain Vine had first crossed Gore's desk. It was, indirectly, Anne Travers fault, back when she had worked at the Vault. She had mentioned Alistair's nephew, whom she had met in Bledoe, and if there was one thing Gore knew a lot about, it was the Lethbridge-Stewart family tree. The Vines had no link to that tree, but after looking further into things, Gore had discovered what had transpired in Bledoe last March. The connection between Mr Vine and Alistair, and, more importantly, the link between Mr Vine and the James Lethbridge-Stewart of this world.

And so, after months of trying to track Mr Vine down, Gore sent an agent to make contact with him in New York, to find out if Gore's research was actually true.

It was.

And now, after three weeks in Japan, and one engaging with people close to Mr Vine, his agent was ready to make direct contact with him once again.

Gore could just picture it now. Mr Vine wouldn't see it coming.

Also available from Candy Jar Books

LETHBRIDGE-STEWART: THE GRANDFATHER INFESTATION
by John Peel

The late 1960s and pirate radio is at its height.

Something stirs in the depths of the North Sea, and for Radio Crossbones that means bad news.

Lethbridge-Stewart and his newly assembled Fifth Operational Corps are called in to investigate after the pirate radio station is mysteriously taken off the air, and a nuclear submarine is lost with all hands.

ISBN: 978-0-9935192-3-9

Also available from Candy Jar Books

LETHBRIDGE-STEWART: TIMES SQUARED
by Rick Cross

When Brigadier Lethbridge-Stewart, his fiancee Sally Wright and nephew Owain Vine embark on a much-needed holiday in New York City, the last thing they expect to find is a puzzling mystery involving coma patients, a stranger from a distant land and a dark menace lurking in the bowels of the city's labyrinthine subway system.

Before long, they're battling an ancient evil pursuing a deadly campaign of terror that could bring Manhattan under its control... and the world to its knees.

ISBN: 978-0-99351-92-9-1